BELL OF THE NIGHT

ALLISON WELLS

Enjoy the journey!

Allison Wells

MONSTER IVY PUBLISHING

*Hi Heather! *hugs**
*Hi Madison! *air kiss**

CHAPTER 1

"You go in that room, and you do whatever it is you do that makes you so popular." Madam Knight wagged a chubby finger while her other hand rested on the soft pillow of hip that jutted out to the left. The bracelets she wore on her wrist pinched her skin, and the charms jingled as her finger shook. Madam stank of cigarette smoke and roses. The neckline of her black dress plunged deep, revealing her large chest – an asset she insisted on showing off at all times. Even the apron worn by the madam seemed designed to aid her gaudy display.

She wondered if she would end up like Madam Knight in her old age. The thought disgusted her, and she absently ran her hand down the curve of her slim body.

"Do you hear me?"

Attention returned to the woman who controlled her every move. "Yes, ma'am." She kept her eyes low, her voice soft and submissive.

She knew how to play the game. She had learned at an early age. Girls who didn't obey went hungry and were worked harder. It wasn't a position she wanted to return to.

Girls who did as they were told were favored, they were treated and fed well and had nice beds to sleep in.

Madam Knight raised an eyebrow and pressed past, her ample rear swishing down the hallway. She disappeared into the parlor of the spa, her shrill voice greeting another client who patiently waited his turn.

New Orleans, Storyville, to be exact, wasn't the place for proper young women. But she had not been proper since setting foot in Madam's brothel years earlier. She had learned quickly and become a master at what she did, paying the price when she didn't do as she was expected.

She turned toward the closed door before her – the room was called The Parisian, mainly for its lavish gold walls and deep red furnishings. A little statue of what Madam called the Eiffel Tower was inside. With a deep breath, she heaved the door open. It wasn't heavy, but the weight of her life was, and it forced her to push harder. Her step was cautious, her eyes kept low. Some girls entered a room with gusto. She had learned that being demure, shy even, was the way to act with most. The customer always wanted to be in charge.

This was a new client – a first-timer. She had been with several boys for their first experience in the brothel. A few of them were unable to go through with it, but most did. The majority were nice, very few treated her poorly. Out of this one, however, she expected the latter.

Madam had said his name was Jimmy Arnold, the heir to the Arnold Hotel dynasty. Like many others, his father had brought him to the spa for his grand entrance into manhood. Madam had recommended her for this particular client because of her gentle nature. She wondered why one of the other more pliable girls hadn't been sent to this room, as they were meek. She wasn't meek, she only acted that way.

She entered the room and gave a cautious glance toward the hotel heir through her lowered lashes. From about five feet away, she guessed he stood more than a head above her with short hair the color of corn silk. He looked neither nervous nor aggressive. In fact, he almost looked bored. Perhaps this was not his first time, and his father had no clue. That would make things easier, but he was hard to read. She gave a small curtsy and stood in the center of the room, awaiting his first move.

He took a step toward her, his soft heel soundless on the carpet. He reached a hand to her chin and lifted her face with a single finger. She met his gaze but did not smile. Smiling was saved for saying thank you or for her regular clients who often gave her cash personally so she could hide it away. His stormy blue eyes examined her while his other hand rubbed the fabric of her dress between his fingers.

The dress was the color of the sky, made of silk. Despite her social status, she was always well clothed. Madam made sure every one of her dresses was blue, the color chosen for her. It was a good color for her, the coolness playing off the warmth of her dark curls. Her hair, almost black in color, wound in tight ringlets down her back, though she usually wore her hair pinned to the top of her head to keep it under control. Her eyes were also nearly black in color, but her skin was as pale and smooth as milk. She had overheard Madam once saying she was the most beautiful of all her girls, but she figured all the girls were told that if they brought in enough money every night.

The young Mr. Arnold released her chin and stepped back. "How does this work?" he asked. "Do you do as I tell you?" Disdain was in his voice, but he was curious. That she could tell.

"Yes, sir," she replied, her voice low and soft. "Or I can help … things … if you desire."

"I think I know what I would like." The hotel heir pulled his shirt off over his head, revealing a well-toned chest. She used to flinch and look away when men would expose their chest, but it no longer held any emotion for her.

He went around to her back and quietly undid her dress. She closed her eyes and prayed to a God she wasn't sure existed for someone to rescue her – but nobody ever came. It was ritual for her now; the clothes came off, and she prayed for a miracle that never happened. Then she did her job for the few pennies Madam allowed her to keep.

When it was over, she helped Jimmy Arnold dress, as it was her personal custom. She always helped her clients look just as sharp going out as they did coming in, as if they had not just used her body for pleasure. She spoke as little as possible, especially to clients who turned out like Mr. Arnold. Even though she could tell he was inexperienced, that hadn't stopped him from treating her like dirt. Worse than dirt.

Dressed, the hotel heir tossed a penny to her. "I suppose I should tip you for making sure I look respectable leaving this place. I might just come back to see you again."

The girl did not want to look desperate for the coin, but she had precious few to call her own. She tucked the penny into a hidden pocket along her collar and followed him out of the room. Once they were in the parlor, the younger Mr. Arnold was met by his father, who promptly slapped him on the back and handed him a lit cigar.

"Happy sixteenth birthday, my boy," he bellowed. The boy looked at her and nodded his head. His father's gaze followed. "Ain't she a ripe one? I may have to come see you myself, darlin'! Just don't tell your mother, Jimmy."

She stared ahead. When Madam shot her a sideways glance, she curtsied a little and batted her eyelashes the way Madam liked. To not flirt back with clients was to risk losing dinner for the night, and they received so little as it was.

Madam showed the men out the door with a wave and a smile, her chest leading the way.

"Well done, my pet, well done!" Madam exclaimed as she came back into the parlor. "Mr. Arnold paid a small fortune for his son's sixteenth birthday. And the young Mr. Arnold surely wasn't bad to be with, was he? Quite a handsome boy. I trust you showed him the ropes."

"He didn't seem to need much showing, Madam. I did as expected, though," she replied, her voice still as timid as she could make it.

Madam snickered. "Good girl. Now, he didn't give you any extra money, did he?"

Madam made sure there were no pockets on any girl's dress so they could not keep money on them. She regularly checked in their underclothes drawers or rifled through their things for hidden coins or bills they might hide from her.

"No, Madam," she lied.

She hated lying, but it was the only way she would be able to save some money for when she was kicked out on her twenty-first birthday for being too old for Madam's clients. She had stitched tiny pockets into the collar for coins, completely undetectable from Madam's random searches. She had made a larger space along her hemline for bills, though those were fewer and farther between.

"Of course not," Madam cooed, pinching her cheek until it hurt. "You are one of my best girls, aren't you? Now, if you don't mind, a Mister Smith is waiting for you in The Magnolia Room. He asked specifically for you and didn't mind waiting when I told him you had … ah … run on an errand for me. We do want our clients to feel like they are the most important one, you know."

"Yes, Madam." She curtsied and turned to the mirror.

Taking extra care, she straightened her hair and adjusted a few pins. A fresh coat of lipstick ran smoothly across her lips. She didn't care what color it was, just that it went over her lips and protected them from the onslaught they experienced nightly. Fluffing a few wrinkles from her dress, she was ready for the next one. She knew several Mr. Smiths and wasn't sure which one was waiting for her.

She walked down a different hallway and knocked on the third door on the left. All the doors were worn, the handles smooth from use. Glancing down the dimly lit hall, she could hear laughter come from one of the other rooms. There was no gaiety for her once the sun went down.

When a deep voice bade her to enter, she did. It had not been ten minutes since she had left the company of Mr. Arnold, and when Mr. Smith – the one with the mustache and body odor – practically ripped her dress off, she knew it would be a long night.

~

New Orleans was exactly as Teddy Sullivan expected. Brightly colored and jubilant on the outside – teeming with depressed sinners and the downtrodden on the inside. He had just moved to the Southern port city from rural Maryland on his journey to save the wicked souls of the world. His home parish was full of those already saved, boring folks whose worst sins were gossip and gluttony. Christ had called his followers to reach the ends of the earth, and by golly, this was it.

Colors popped out at him everywhere he looked. Some buildings were bright yellow, others green or blue. He even passed a pink house. Never in his life had he seen a pink house. Teddy was lured into the opulence he saw. But that opulence had been bought with the devil's money, he knew. And he was determined to change the city for the better. He would paint New Orleans for the Lord instead of the enemy.

His mentor, Billy Sunday, would be so proud of him, Teddy thought. Once he got a church up and running, he would write to Reverend Sunday, the so-called "baseball evangelist," and let him know all about his success. There was no room for failure in Teddy's mind. New Orleans would be a city won for Christ.

Teddy turned around, suitcase in hand, and surveyed the damage the devil had caused. He knew he could save lives here if he could get a foothold. His first order of business was to find a room to sleep in. His second order of business was to find a place to preach.

As he strolled along Basin Street, he came to the Night and Day Spa for Men. It was a cheery yellow house, three stories tall with feminine lace curtains in all the windows. Deciding it looked clean, Teddy entered in hopes that they could direct him toward a cheap place to rest his weary head.

A large woman with too much cleavage protruding forth to be in good taste greeted him warmly as he stepped into a plush parlor.

"Hello, Sir! Welcome to the Spa. How may I assist you this evening?"

"Hi, yes, ma'am. I'm sorry to bother you. I'm new in town and am looking for a cheap room to rent. I figure as you probably see a lot of new arrivals you could recommend a place?"

The heavyset woman frowned, probably upset that he wasn't giving her business, but perhaps once he had settled in, he could come in to witness to her employees and customers. Plus, Teddy had heard all about spas and their healing qualities before and thought some time in a steam room sounded good.

"Well, I happen to know Mr. Arnold of Arnold's Hotels. He has several across New Orleans. Will you be here long, Mr. –?"

"Sullivan," he answered with a smile. "And yes, I'm moving to the area, but I don't mind holing up in a hotel for a bit so I can get settled."

Teddy looked around the room a little more. The furniture was near opulent – the most luxurious he had ever seen. Everything decorated in rich reds, greens, and golds. From the corner of his eye, he saw two young girls enter the room. The abundant hostess took up most of his view, but Teddy could almost swear that the taller of the girls, the one with red hair, was wearing a nightgown. The other girl, smaller with dark curly hair, wore a blue dress with a neckline that sunk nearly as low as that of the woman before him, though her chest wasn't nearly as abundant. Teddy hoped his eyes were simply playing tricks on him in the low lighting. He knew maids could hike up their hems for tips, but this was outrageous. What kind of spa was being run in by this grotesque woman? The sin in this city was worse than he thought.

The smaller girl looked up and met his gaze briefly. She lowered her lashes in a move Teddy might have thought was flirtatious, but the pain he saw behind her eyes outweighed the allure of a pretty face. She wasn't playing coy with him; she was hiding the windows to her soul.

"Wonderful, Mr. Sullivan," the woman said, drawing his attention back to her and her ample bosom. "We love new residents here at the spa. Go down this road here three blocks and make a left onto Canal. The Arnold Arms will be on your right. You can't miss it, and Mr. Arnold welcomes people who want to stay long term. Just tell him Victoria Knight sent you."

She gave a hearty chuckle, though Teddy didn't know what the joke had been. The woman ran her hands down her sides and swayed her hips a little. Teddy did his best to look anywhere but at her.

"Thank you, Mrs. Knight. I appreciate your kindness," he said, trying to block the girls from his mind and remember the directions.

"Any time, Mr. Sullivan. Next time you come in, remind me, and we'll give you the newcomer's discount."

"Thank you," Teddy said as he slipped out the door.

He surveyed the windows again and noticed what a large spa Mrs. Knight ran. He wondered at the services they offered. As far as he knew, spas offered steam rooms, hot baths, and other aquatic therapies. This spa's offerings must be vast to use such a large building, he mused.

As he tried to make sense of the directions given to him, Teddy's mind was drawn back to the curly-haired girl with the pain in her eyes. Despite the poor lighting and the near blackness of her eyes, he could still see the hurt that lingered there. He would definitely have to return to that spa and gauge their receptiveness to attending church services.

The Arnold Arms Hotel soon sprawled out before him a good eight stories high, its grandeur and presence foreboding. The building had at one time been white, but the paint was now yellowed with age and salty air. However, that didn't diminish the majesty of the place. Teddy wasn't sure he had the cash to afford a room in such a locale, but he walked through the front door to see. Maybe they would take pity on a poor minister from the North.

"Excuse me, sir. I am in need of a room for at least a week, if not several weeks," he said to the suited lad behind the counter. "But I'm not entirely sure I can afford such a swanky place."

The boy gave a lazy smile in return. "I'm sure we can work something out, sir. I'm the owner's son, so I can help you with anything you need. What brings you to our fine city?"

"I'm a minister, come to find a flock for the Lord here in

New Orleans," Teddy exclaimed with a smile, his enthusiasm shining through.

The blond-headed teen did not return his smile. "There's plenty of people here, Reverend," he said with tightness in his Southern drawl. "Since you're a man of the cloth, I can give you a generous discount on a small room on our top floor. We even have an elevator."

"Praise God! I tell you this is the friendliest town I have ever encountered," Teddy said as he stamped his hand down on the counter. "I'll take what you got, my good man!"

Teddy was shown to an eighth-floor room that was sparsely decorated. A simple single bed was neatly made against the far wall; behind it, a three-legged nightstand with a small lamp sat waiting for a patron's wallet and glasses. The single window opposite the bed let in the only natural light. But it was clean. Teddy loved it.

"This is not our best room, Reverend, but it's affordable, and I can guarantee you'll have peace and quiet up here. And you can stay here as long as you like; we'll bill you weekly. Just tell us when you're ready to check out. We do serve supper downstairs at seven p.m. sharp."

"It's just what I need, my boy. What did you say your name was?"

The teen looked at him, taken aback. It seemed he expected everybody to know who he was. "I'm Jimmy Arnold. Son of James Arnold."

"Thank you so much, Mr. Arnold. A certain woman, Mrs. Knight, she said, assured me I would find it hospitable here. I look forward to staying here and getting to know your fine town," Teddy said as he set his bag down.

The boy raised an eyebrow to him. "Mrs. Knight?"

"Yes," Teddy said with a smile.

"Another one goes down," he said with a scowl on his face.

Not understanding, Teddy asked the boy to repeat himself.

"Nothing. Nothing at all, Reverend," Jimmy said. The scowl turned into a well-practiced smile. He nodded and left the room.

Alone, Teddy stretched out onto the small bed. He set his wire glasses down on the nightstand and rubbed his eyes. He had about thirty minutes before the hotel dinner was served, and he wanted to rest his eyes after all the colors and sounds he had experienced walking through the city streets. After he ate, he would hit the streets again, looking for the right place to use as his makeshift church. He also hoped to meet more locals.

After a filling dinner, Teddy set out again. The French Quarter was exactly like he had heard. People spoke a mix of English and French, the melodious voices floated in the air along with the sounds of a distant piano being played. Teddy smiled at the songful ruckus. Babies cried, and mothers shushed them while children played in the streets. One group played kick the can, the can landing at Teddy's feet. He eagerly kicked the can back into the game, a smile breaking out onto his face. The entire city was alive, Teddy thought. It lived and breathed all on its own.

Teddy turned left onto another street, and while the scenery wasn't vastly different, the atmosphere certainly was. Jazz music blared, and the sound of a live trumpet blasted through an open doorway. Teddy had heard about jazz music from others. It was the music of sin, they had said. The music of loose women with no morals – let alone questionable morals – and the men who kept them in business. While he had never heard jazz music before, he wasn't sure why it was so objectionable. It was different, soulful, and catchy. It didn't seem to be harmful the way others had told him.

Bistros and music houses behind wrought iron gates were

abruptly replaced with propped up garish gates welcoming in anyone who dared. Now that it was night, he realized he had wandered into Storyville. The red-light district of New Orleans was where legal brothels stood grandly, and nickel hookers littered the alleys behind them. The very street he walked earlier that afternoon without a clue in the world.

A swallow stuck in his throat as he turned a circle, realizing just what kind of buildings stood before him. Teddy was sure his face blanched, and he had to cough a few times to unlodge the lump in his throat. He had intentionally walked into one of these dens of sin to ask for directions. The girls he thought had looked questionable really were questionable – they were prostitutes!

The brightly colored, appealing buildings he had admired that afternoon now looked grotesque in the lamplight. The gingerbread eaves cast foreboding shadows like prison bars. An eerie blood-red glow came from several windows, beckoning men like a siren in the ocean.

As he looked around, a woman called out to him, inviting him inside. His heart thudded in his chest, and he saw spots before his eyes. He hurried past the woman whose tittering echoed after him, confusion and humiliation filling his heart.

Teddy wasn't sure how to feel. He was a preacher, a man after God's heart. He was supposed to avoid people of doubtful repute. Yet, Christ had called him to minister to people such as these. Sinners. People who wouldn't know Him otherwise. Maybe this was where God had called him, a man of the cloth sent to witness to those who made a living taking their clothing off.

He could feel it in his heart. Yes, this is what he was to do. God was calling him to help save the ones the rest of the world had given up on. That was what Reverend Sunday had taught him and encouraged him to do. Was this not what he had been preparing for all along? And he would do it, one sinful soul, at a time. Teddy walked down the block to the Day and Night Spa and stood before the open doorway.

He was greeted once again by the flashy large woman with the near-exposed bosom. The finery of her dress was diminished by the gaudy jewelry and obscene amount of cleavage.

"Mr. Sullivan! You came back to us," she gushed. "I'm so glad. Are you ready for your newcomer discount? Tell me what you're interested in, and I'll help you find what you are looking for." Again, her hands ran down her body from waist to hips. Thick fingers covered in rings tried to draw attention to the woman's curves.

Teddy blushed madly. Single women of his parish back home had flirted with him, but none had outright offered themselves to him. It was completely indecent. But of course, the indecency of it was what made this woman rich.

She sensed his hesitation and nervousness. "Not sure just yet? No, of course not! You've only just arrived." She waved her arm in a circle. "All my girls are well trained in entertainment and relaxation. Maybe a trip to the steam room would help you relax to start? A mere fifty cents for a steam. Make it a dollar, and we will throw in a massage for you. I'm sure you're tired after traveling so far. Did you take the train?"

"The train? Yes," he stammered. He took a deep breath. A steam bath did sound good. But was it a sin to consider a steam in such a place? If he was going to introduce these women to God, he needed to get in their good graces. Time in a steam bath sounded safe, didn't it?

"Yes, Mrs. Knight, I think a steam sounds … heavenly." He smiled.

"It certainly is, sir," she said with a husky chuckle.

She turned and quietly lifted her hand. Immediately, the young brunette girl he had spotted earlier quickly approached and gave a brief curtsy. Her tightly wound curls bounced as she moved. The Madam whispered into her ear, her words curt but breathy.

"Now, Mr. Sullivan, that will be one dollar," she said, assuming he wanted the massage. Without arguing, Teddy pulled a dollar out of his pocket and handed it to Mrs. Knight, who promptly stuffed it between her breasts. "This girl will show you to the steam room. There are dressing rooms for your personal items. Enjoy yourself."

With that, she sauntered off with a wink and left Teddy standing with the petite brunette. She curtsied to him and turned without a word. He obligingly followed, praying the whole way that he would figure out just what to say that might bring this girl closer to the God he loved.

~

She sighed as she led the way to the steam rooms. At least it was a steam room and not a bedroom, she thought. The tall man with the clean-cut look followed her apprehensively. She was used to that, though. Men came from other cities, places where brothels were illegal, to see what Storyville was all about. They would return home to brag about their time in the district, she just knew it.

Madam had called this man Mr. Sullivan. He looked nice, sincere almost. Not like many of her other customers who looked nothing but lustfully at her. Mr. Sullivan did not seem to have that devious streak she was used to seeing. He kept his distance from her and refused to look her in the eye. With dark hair cut short and his face clean-shaven, his bright green eyes stood out behind the glasses he wore. They reminded her of young magnolia leaves. His face and hands were tanned but were not dark and wrinkled like those who labored outside. She guessed he was close to thirty, a good ten years older than she was, but there was no way to know, and she really didn't much care.

Outside the steam room, she turned a small knob, then opened a dressing room door. "You may leave your clothes in here, sir. There's a robe you may put on if you wish. I will meet you inside."

The man nodded and disappeared behind the door. She heard fumbling but decided he would ask for help if he required it. Many men she assisted in the steam room requested that she undress them personally, an act she found to be more intimate than the job she was paid for. A sigh of relief escaped her lips as she closed the door behind him.

She quickly went into her own dressing room and disrobed, putting on a short gown cinched loosely at her waist. She checked the mirror and pulled a few loose tendrils from her bound hair; she arranged the gown so that it exposed her shoulder and a bit of décolletage. Her training had taught her to always show as much skin as possible. She slipped out of the dressing room and into the steam room.

The room was warm, and she immediately felt the dampness on her skin. Despite the heat, she enjoyed the steam room. It was relaxing, and she didn't usually have to give of herself, though she was instructed to offer and give the price. The steam rooms were like a sanctuary since the men could hardly see her, and she could hardly see them. The men usually just wanted to talk and maybe touch a little. She sat on the wooden bench behind the steam and pulled the collar of her gown open a little. Her patron came in slowly, unsure of his step in the dark, misty room.

"This way," she called softly to guide him. He found her and sat on the opposite end of the bench a good four feet away from her. "Do you want your massage right away, or would you like a minute to take in the steam first?" She kept her voice low and soft. She looked at him, his green eyes still piercing despite the lack of bright lighting.

"Um, just a minute, please, if you don't mind," he said. "I just need a minute to collect my thoughts."

She shrugged a little, but he didn't notice. "That's just fine, sir. Let me know how I can assist you. What was your name?"

"Theodore Sullivan, but my friends call me Teddy," he said as he pulled the terry cloth robe closer to his chin. Like every other patron, he didn't bother to ask her name.

"Mr. Sullivan," she said, testing out the name. "What brought you to our fair city?" She scooted a few inches closer to him. She went through all the words and moves by rote, just as she had been trained.

He cleared his throat. "Actually, Miss, I'm a preacher. I just came here from Maryland to start a new church." He looked away from her, embarrassed.

"Oh," she said quietly. Another man supposedly devoted to God, who was more interested in worshipping skin. Sensing his embarrassment, she quietly said, "Don't feel bad, Mr. Sullivan. We get all kinds here, even preachers."

He sat up straight as an arrow and quickly retorted, "I'm not here for that! I can't imagine any man who has dedicated his life to Christ frequenting a … a … bawdy house!" He stood and shook his fist in the air.

"I'm sorry, sir, but you've got to admit … you are here," she said quietly. The outburst didn't surprise her, the embarrassed ones always seemed to get irate.

He looked around the room and at her, his voice calmed. "Yes, I am here. But I'm here to try to save you all from your sin. One person at a time," he said, stepping toward her.

"You don't have to worry about that, Reverend." She laughed. "The priests come weekly to hear our confessions."

"They do?" He seemed shocked.

She giggled again. "They do. They hear our confessions, and then they get the week of sin started again. The priests of New Orleans are some of our best patrons."

The pain and distress were obvious on the man's face. Apparently, there were no corrupt clergymen in Maryland. At least not ones he knew of. She knew that those who proclaimed righteousness were usually the biggest hypocrites.

"That's terrible. I can't believe that. I'm not here for that. I don't even want the massage. I came here so I could talk to you girls, one by one, and tell you about Christ and how he died for you. I want to help you all get away from these brothels. These legal houses of sin and debauchery." The man paced the floor in front of her, clearly upset.

"Mr. Sullivan, I would love to get out of here," she said breathlessly, knowing she shouldn't speak at all on the subject. But for some reason, she felt like she could open up to this man.

The man stood, dumbstruck. "Wait – you don't want to be here? Truly?"

She choked back a chortle. "Who would choose this life? Madam Knight owns us. I hear slavery isn't legal anymore, but she bought each of the girls here. I don't know about the others, but I want to leave."

"I'm baffled," he said, scratching his head.

"Clearly."

"Why not just leave then? Why do you stay?" He sat again and peered into her eyes. He wanted to see her, not just view her for his own merriment. It made her heart race.

"Did you not hear me? She owns us. The only way out of this life is to run and risk getting caught or get married. And last I heard, there's not many men beating down doors of whore houses to marry us. If you have somewhere for me to go where Madam won't come after me, and I won't starve to death, I'm all ears!"

"That woman out there, she owns you? How old are you?" The notion was still registering in his head. She could see the confusion in his eyes.

"I'm nineteen now, but she bought me from my uncle when I was eleven." Looking down, she shared some of her story. "My parents died, and the town preacher gave me to my uncle because he was the only relation they could find. He brought me here and sold me to Madam for two dollars. I saw her give it to him. Then Madam gave me a new name and set me to work."

"That's terribly sad," he said. He looked as though he might cry, but perhaps it was just the moisture from the room.

"That's my life, mister."

"And you ... you sleep with these men?"

"We don't sleep much, Mr. Sullivan," she said honestly.

"Oh, Jesus, help her," he exclaimed. "Since you were eleven?"

"Yes, sir."

"And you had no say in the matter at all?"

"Of course not. None of us did," she said. "Well, most of us, at least. We were bought into it, or forced into it because of circumstances."

"I need to get out of here," he said, rushing for the door and loosening the material around his throat. He grasped for the door, and she followed him, afraid he might faint any moment.

Once out in the cooler air, Teddy Sullivan got his breath back. She fanned him off and offered him a chair, her robe falling open in her haste.

"Please cover yourself," he pleaded, shielding his eyes.

She did as he requested, haphazardly pulling the robe

together and cinching it. Men looked at her body all the time, so she thought nothing of the exposure.

"I'm sorry. I guess I had the wrong notion about these places," he said. "I thought my mission was to come here and save all of you from this life. I thought you all had chosen it with gusto. Never did it enter my mind that you were forced to do ..." He stopped talking and took a deep breath. "Well, I'm sorry."

"It's okay, Mr. Sullivan." She tried to reassure him. "We're used to it. I'm used to it. This is my life. And I like most of the other girls here. We are family."

He went into his dressing room without speaking. She waited for him outside the door, not bothering to change herself.

When Teddy came out, he pressed a coin into her hand. "Please take this," he whispered.

"But I did nothing to earn it," she said with a quizzical look on her face.

"You talked to me. That is all I want. Goodnight, Miss—" He stopped. "I didn't catch your name."

"I never told you. Most men don't ask."

He took a step closer to her and took her hand in his. Her heart beat loudly in her chest with the intimate gesture.

"What is your name, miss?" His gaze changed, and he smiled at her genuinely as his green eyes gazed into hers.

She returned the smile. Her brown eyes welled with tears at his tenderness. "My name is Bluebell," she said, breathless. "But my friends call me Bell."

CHAPTER 2

"*Bell!* Bluebell, come in here right now!"

The bellowing came from Poppy, Madam's head girl. Not even a year older than Bell, she had been at the spa two years longer. She was Madam's favorite by far and made sure everybody else knew it. She kept her yellow hair in shapely curls and wore kohl liner around her black eyes at all times. The men often thought of her as a Grecian beauty with her dark skin, light hair, and faked foreign accent.

Bell rolled her eyes, and they landed on the coin the reverend had given her weeks before. She wondered if he had run back up north with his tail tucked between his legs. She picked up the coin and stuffed it into her pocket, lest anyone else snitch it from her.

It was still fairly early in the morning for their little household. Truth be told, it was probably late morning for the rest of the world, but since they were usually entertaining guests until the wee hours of the morning, lunchtime was their usual hour to rise and greet the day. There were seven girls in the house; couldn't she bellow at one of them instead?

Putting down the bottle of fingernail polish, Bell donned a long robe over her nightdress. Many of the girls wandered the halls in nothing more than their garters, but Bell was more modest and preferred to be covered up unless instructed otherwise.

Bell made her way to Poppy's room and poked her head in. "Yes, Poppy? Did you call me?" She made her voice as sickeningly sweet as she could.

Poppy huffed. "Yes, we are in need of provisions. Find Astrid and the little girl and take them with you to the market and the bakery."

"I'm not dressed, Poppy," Bell said, annoyed that the trivial task was being assigned to her when Poppy was already dressed herself.

"So, get dressed. I would do it, but I am expecting Jack Knowles to come by any time now," she said with a smirk.

"Jack Knowles? Does Madam know you're sneaking around with that Negro boy? You know she doesn't like us taking Negro clients," Bell reminded her.

Madam was happy to have Negros work for her and for them to be friends, but Negro clients were not allowed. She claimed they were dirty and diseased, and Madam only wanted the most elite clientele for the spa. Poppy would be lashed if Madam found out. But Bell knew if she told on Poppy, revenge would be sought.

With eyes wide, Poppy's words floundered, and her true accented drawl came out, "Just go, will you? And keep your mouth shut about Jack if you know what's good for you."

"Fine," Bell agreed. "I could use some fresh air anyway."

Bell left Poppy's room, wondering how long Poppy could keep her secret lover from Madam. Many girls had their own beaus on the side that the madams did not know about. Bell didn't, but she knew many who did. And when they were found out, they had their flesh sorely beaten.

She dressed quickly into an older navy-blue frock that was a little too short for her now. She convinced her best friend and confidante, Astrid, to go with her. Though, truthfully, it did not take too much convincing, Astrid was always happy to walk outside the spa's doors. Astrid's red hair was pulled tight into a bun under her bonnet. The little girl who had just joined their family also took a basket.

Madam had introduced the child as Clover, but little Clover insisted her name was Frances. She was a petite little mulatto girl of about nine years old. Bell felt sorry for the girl who had joined them not two weeks before.

Madam kept Clover busy in the kitchen for now, but soon she would be introduced to the parlor where she would be paraded before their clients for one to purchase her for the first time. Bell hoped the girl would never know the horrors she had experienced when she was first sold to a client.

She could still recall the smell of rotten bananas on the old dock master. His skin had been flabby and pale as he pawed at her. Screams echoed in her head still, so she pushed the memory back into the recesses of her mind before she gagged and retched.

Little Clover walked between Bell and Astrid, too afraid to wander far. Bell tried to coax the girl to talk to them.

"Clover, are you from New Orleans?" she asked.

"My name is Frances. My momma calls me Franny," she said. "But yeah, I's from 'round here."

"You are? Where are your parents? How did Madam Knight get you?" Astrid spoke in hushed tones, but the surprise in her voice was evident.

Clover stuck her finger in her ear and wiggled it around. Bell grimaced at the dirty habit the girl had. She needed to break her of that and teach her some refinement, even if just a little.

"Well," she said after a minute, "my momma is a octoroon.

She real light-colored like you, but my real daddy was a negro. They wasn't married or nothing. My momma's daddy – he was white – married her off to a nice rich white man who didn't know nothing about me at first. When Momma finally told him that the little mulatto girl in the kitchen – that was me – was her daughter, he got real mad and sent me away. Then a few weeks ago, I find out from my foster momma that my momma's husband sold me off to Madam Knight to pay for new stuff for his own baby. A white baby, she told me. I was too black to be with them, she said."

They had stopped walking to hear Clover's story. Tears welled up in Bell's eyes, the pain great for her, but Clover seemed not to notice how tragic her own story was. "I'm so sorry, Clover."

"My name is Frances."

"I know it is," Bell explained. "But when you came to live with us, Madam changed your name. So, you're not Frances anymore. Your new name is Clover."

"Oh," was all she said in response. "Why?"

Astrid stepped in to explain. With a sigh, she told their newest family member Madam's penchant for floral first names. "My name is Astrid. I was born with a different name, but she changed my name to Astrid. Gray is my other name, and I only wear gray. Bell's name is Bluebell, and she can only wear blue. Then there's Zinnia, Jasmine, Poppy, and Daisy. We all have flower names, and we were all given a color. It's the only color we're allowed to wear."

"Forever?"

"Well, until Madam Knight makes you leave," Astrid said with a glance at Bell. Astrid would be twenty-one in a few short weeks and be turned out. They had discussed what might happen to her with no possible solution in sight.

Feeling suddenly ill, Bell hurried them to gather the items on their list and head back to the house. The sun was high overhead, and she knew that once it started its descent back to the west, her busiest night of the week – Friday – would be upon her quickly. Friday was payday for the working men of New Orleans, and many of them chose to squander their paycheck on some of the more esteemed houses on Basin Street.

~

*T*eddy thanked the robust baker at the corner and walked out the door, back onto the thoroughfare. He had completed his shopping list for the day. He had been in the city for almost a month now and was learning the ins and outs of New Orleans. He knew what days were best to shop, where the best places were to minister to eager souls, and where the souls were less than eager. His mind kept wandering to the young girl at the spa with whom he had spoken the month before. Her sad eyes intrigued him like no other had.

He still resided at the Arnold Arms Hotel, and he enjoyed the friendly banter and camaraderie he found with the other patrons. It was better than living alone in a filthy little apartment, and he had ample funds from his trust for the time being to stay there at least another month. Finding a house to worship in was much more important than finding a house to rest in.

A few weeks prior, he had stumbled upon an abandoned furniture store a few blocks from Storyville. It could easily hold about eighty chairs and a small pulpit. Wasting no time, he had mailed his home church with details and asked for donations to rent the space and clean it up. He also asked if anyone was willing to come south and minister with him. So far, no volunteers for that had come forward. Nobody was eager to minister to these soiled doves and their clientele.

But his faith had paid off. One by one, small donations came from parishioners. The Smiths and the Elliotts had sent him five dollars each. Little Timmy Holder had actually mailed him his only dollar as a donation. Teddy was overwhelmed by the small but meaningful contribution, and he knew the Lord could work with any amount. Six months' rent was all he needed to move into the building, and he was sure it wouldn't be too much longer.

As he counted in his head what he would need – chairs, a large stand, a cross (not to mention people) – he nearly walked right into a trio of young ladies who were heading toward him.

"Be careful!" one screeched as she pulled back the young charge with her.

"Oh, I'm dreadfully sorry," Teddy exclaimed. When he looked up, he saw none other than the girl from the spa steam room. "Oh, my. Miss Bell, am I correct?"

The girl studied him a moment, then seemed to remember his face. Her own reddened a little. "Yes, that's right. Reverend Sullivan, I remember. This is Astrid and Clover." She motioned to the girls with her.

"Delighted, ladies," he said as he brought his hand to his head and gave a short bow.

The red-headed girl blushed until her cheeks matched her crimson hair; the dark-skinned girl merely looked annoyed at the delay in their trek.

Bell spoke again. "If you'll excuse us, Reverend, we have errands to run." Her tone was impatient and unyielding.

"Of course, Miss … uh … is it Knight? I'm sorry."

She sighed. "Oh, don't call me by that name, please. Just call me Bluebell or Bell."

"Then you shall call me Teddy. None of this Reverend business. That's my job, not my name," he said with a smile. "Oh, and I should be setting up shop at the old furniture store on Broad Street. I'll come let you know when the doors open. I hope you will come and bring the others with you."

Her head cocked to one side, and she narrowed her eyes. "You mean you want the likes of us to actually come into your church? Is that a joke, Reverend Sullivan?"

She was very wary, like a deer looking to cross a busy road, and he couldn't blame her. Thus far, not many had seemed interested. "Teddy, Miss Bell. And no, I'm not joking. I want to reach out to those who have never heard the true gospel of Christ Jesus. I want you and your friends, here, to be front and center when my little corner of heaven opens up."

"Madam doesn't like us going into churches," Astrid said. "She says we're too sinful for such places. That's why the priests come to us. So, we don't ruin their houses of God."

Teddy scowled. It was talk like that that made him angry. Jesus wanted to reach out to the lepers, not push them aside.

"All sin is sin, Miss Astrid," he said, trying to remain calm. "My sins are no worse than yours. And Jesus welcomes all sinners into his house. I will do the same."

Her green eyes grew wide, and her red hair shone in the sunlight. "Truly, Reverend Teddy?"

"Truly." He gazed at her. She was a pretty girl, but not as pretty as the brooding brunette called Bell.

"Well, Reverend, thank you for the invitation. We really must be on our way now," Bell cut in, her brooding nature all the more apparent. "Come on, Clover." She pulled the little girl by the arm.

The girls departed from him, and he felt an urge to follow them, but he had work of his own to do. As they walked away, he prayed for their protection and for the chance for them to be free of the life of sin they were stuck in. Silently, Teddy made his way back to his sparse room.

As he wrote out another set of letters pleading for funds

to start his church, he thought of the girls he had run into that morning. The pretty ginger-haired girl would have made any man happy to marry her if it weren't for her profession. He wondered how she wound up in such a place. Did her parents die like Bell's? And what of the little mulatto girl? Did the matron of the house sell her body to the highest bidder just like the others? Teddy shuddered at the thought.

"If only there was a way to get them all out of those brothels," he said aloud to himself. "I have no way, but I know God does. Lord, reveal Your plan to me."

Teddy's mind always returned to Bell. Thoughts of her consumed him since their encounter at the spa. She was a beautiful woman, especially with the tightly wound black curls piled atop her head. Black eyes had stared at him from under thick lashes, but they were not lined with kohl like the other district girls he had seen. Surely, she was seen as an exotic beauty as her hair and eyes contrasted with her milky skin, Teddy mused. Her delicate features and womanly curves certainly caught his eye, and Teddy felt his heart leap a little when he thought of her. But her pain affected him more than her comely looks. Perhaps she needed saving most of all.

The need for a church became more and more abundant to Teddy as he thought of these girls and the men who kept them in business. With the Great War in full swing, sailors were constantly in and out of the city. Well, in and out of the district, at least. Different sets of uniformed boys were ferried in and out of the port frequently. Teddy had over-heard some of the crib girls in the district, those willing to work for mere pennies, say they had never made so much money before. He hung his head, desperation filling his heart. He needed to get established quickly.

With determination to get funds locally, Teddy set to the street with a handful of pamphlets to promote his church.

Maybe somebody in the city could donate a sum of money to help him purchase the equipment needed to accommodate nearly one hundred people.

~

*T*hree weeks later, as the heat of summer began to creep into the air, Teddy had an idea. And Bell was at the center of it. He went down to the Day and Night Spa and approached the matron with a proposition.

"Mrs. Knight"—he smiled in earnest—"I would like to hire three or four of your girls for the day."

The keen businesswoman raised an eyebrow. "Three or four girls for the day, Reverend Sullivan? That's mighty lofty. Just what do you plan to do with so many of my girls for an entire day?"

"I want them to paint my church," he said with a satisfactory smile. Honest work for an honest wage, he thought.

The woman's chest heaved as she coughed loudly, the flesh of her bosom shaking violently before settling down. "Paint? You can't be serious? My girls don't paint, Reverend." She guffawed. "They lie on their backs. They don't paint."

"I should like to hire some to paint, anyway. I will pay you, of course. And I would have them home before your evening hours begin, Mrs. Knight. I know you are a businesswoman."

"That's right, I'm a businesswoman. A good one, too," she said as she slapped her knee. "Fine. You can have three girls to paint your church. Might be the only time they're allowed in such a holy house. But they had better be back by four in the afternoon and not be worn out."

"Yes ma'am, I understand," he said as he tried to hide the grin that was creeping onto his face. "Would five dollars be sufficient pay?"

She frowned. "Well, considering they'll be standing, and it's the Lord's work … that will do, Reverend." She stuck out a chubby hand covered in glitzy jewels to seal the deal. Teddy quickly shook it.

"I'll be by at nine in the morning to pick the girls up. Whichever ones you choose is fine by me," he said.

Secretly, he hoped that the raven-haired beauty, Bell, would be among those to join him. Her story fascinated him, and he longed to see her again. But Teddy realized his thoughts had turned to her far too often, and his imagination had also begun to run away with him. The idea of marrying her and carrying her back to Maryland had even entered his mind. He needed to stop concentrating on one girl. But perhaps since she was the first person he conversed with in New Orleans, she now epitomized the lost souls he was reaching toward. Yes, that had to be it. Bell had become his poster child for those needing saving.

He quickly rose and departed Mrs. Knight's parlor to find paint and paintbrushes for the girls to use the next day. He hoped he could show these girls that they were good for more than what their bodies offered. Maybe he could help them find new professions elsewhere.

CHAPTER 3

"Girls, I have an interesting prospect for some of you," Madam said as she began their daily conference before throwing open their doors to the public. "The good Reverend Sullivan was here just a few moments ago and asked for several of you to service him tomorrow during the day." Madam snickered at her own words.

Bell's head snapped to attention. The reverend wanted them for what? He said he wasn't that type of preacher.

"The good preacher wants a few of you to go paint his church for him tomorrow," Madam continued. Bell sighed. Not that kind of service, she thought with relief. "Now, you will not be paid for this if you volunteer. But it will count as repentance in the eyes of God for the life of sin you lead. It's the mother of all Hail Marys. Now, does anyone actually want to volunteer for this task? Remember, that does not excuse you from your duties here."

It was a chance to get out of the walls of the spa for a day, and that was all the encouragement Bell needed to speak up. "I will volunteer," she said quickly.

The thought of seeing the reverend, who never looked at

her like clients did, appealed to Bell. His words at their previous meetings fascinated her, and he was pleasant to look at, too. She recalled how expressive his green eyes were behind his round spectacles. She tried to hide the smile that crept up on her lips.

"I will, too," Zinnia said with an eager hope in her eyes.

Not to be outdone, Poppy also spoke up. "I'll go. I always have extra energy at the end of the night. Maybe if I exert some before the night comes, I will actually get worn out for a change." She cackled at her own crudeness.

"Very well, girls, and take Clover with you," Madam said with a wave of her hand. "Don't wear any nice dresses, wear old ones. And be sure to be back here by four. You'll have work to do."

"Yes, Madam," all three girls said in unison.

"Now, on to our own business," she continued.

Madam went over the clients who had made reservations with girls for the evening. It was a Tuesday, so not many clients were on the list. The girls who had not been specifically requested would lounge in the parlor, waiting for any clients to wander in off the street or entertain the men waiting for other girls.

But Bell would not be a parlor girl tonight, and for that, she was disappointed. She flinched as Madam spoke her name, a chill running through her. Casting a glance toward Zinnia and Daisy, Bell felt the bitter seed of jealousy settle in her heart. They were not in the highest demand, especially not during the week. Even with Zinnia's caramel skin and blue eyes, the quadroon girl's demand did not match her own. Bell was always in demand, her contrasting Scotch-Irish features and flawless skin made her a favorite for many well-paying customers.

It was Tuesday, which meant her evening consisted of entertaining one man, George Barnard. He was a construction foreman who was in the upper part of the working class. He had been coming to the spa for as long as Bell could remember, but in the last year, he only came for her.

George had confessed his undying love for Bell repeatedly in that time, affections that she did not return in the least. How could she ever love a man who had bought her body so many times over? His gaze caused her to feel like she was on fire, and his touch made her shudder. George's bony hands on her caused her to fantasize running away every week. But Bell knew how to be a good girl. She knew she had to endure his affections if she wanted to eat the next day.

In George's desire for her, he had even proposed marriage, and she had considered it. It would be a way out of the spa. But it wasn't so easy to leave the other girls behind, and Bell wasn't sure it was worth trading one bad life for another. When Mr. Barnard had asked Madam for her hand in marriage, Bell confessed that she would rather stay where she was. Madam had told him he would have to wait until she was twenty-one and of a suitable marriageable age before asking again.

But that did not stop him from coming by every Tuesday evening. He paid lavishly for dinner for the two of them in a private room, and then paid for the entire evening with Bell, no interruptions. He tried desperately to woo her, but it was of no use. Bell felt nothing for the man.

He arrived precisely at six, as was his routine. He came into the parlor, and his eyes immediately went to Bell. Rising quietly, Bell glanced at Astrid, who awaited her own client. George Barnard approached her, towering over her. Despite his strength, he was a gangly man. A gnarled hand caressed Bell's cheek, and she closed her eyes, wishing him away. When she opened her eyes, she forced herself to look at him. His mousy-brown hair fell into his eyes, which were also dull and nondescript brown. Crooked teeth showed as he smiled at Bell, and she gave a terse smile in return. He did show fondness toward her, that was apparent, but it horrified her all the same.

"My darling Bell. Aren't you lovely this evening?" he asked as she took his extended arm. "What are we expecting for dinner tonight?"

She grinned at him, only because he insisted she smile all the time. "You'll love tonight's menu, George," she said as she led him back to his favorite room, the gold one with lots of mirrors called The Star. "Sallie made us a wonderful dinner of fresh clam stew and shrimp. I know how much you adore shrimp, George." Bell kept her voice melodious as she spoke.

"I do love shrimp, Bluebell, and I love you," he said fervently. He looked at her with hopeful eyes, always eager she would return his affections, but she never did. Not any more than he paid her to.

They ate, or rather, George ate. Bell would occasionally pick up a shrimp with her fingers, peel off the shell, and gently feed it to him. Mr. Barnard enjoyed the intimate service immensely. The act was silly in her mind, feeding another person as if they were an infant. But he always liked it, and she did whatever she could to hurry the evening along as quickly as possible.

After dinner and small talk, Mr. Barnard ran his long, bony finger along the dipped collar of Bell's sky blue dress. Inwardly she cringed, but he took the raise of gooseflesh to mean interest. Bell prayed to a God she wasn't sure of before she was undressed. Not that any God knew she existed. She bit her lip as she thought about the reverend and his spirited eyes. She would have to ask him tomorrow when she was painting his pious church building. Tomorrow seemed a long way away.

"You look distracted, my pet," Mr. Barnard said with his brow furrowed.

Bell quickly shook her head, a curl popping loose from its confines. "No, nothing, George. How could I think of anything but you?" She forced a pleasant look on her face and put her arms around him as much as she wished to run in the opposite direction. He began to kiss her neck.

Her mind returned to the reverend and his desire to teach people about a God that he claimed loved them. How could his God love her? Surely her sins of the flesh were much worse than any little sin that he might commit. Was there such a thing as redemption for people like her? She planned to ask him that the next day, too.

This day, however, couldn't end quickly enough.

~

*S*unrise woke Bell from a fitful sleep. Mr. Barnard was gone, and Bell sighed with relief. Dressing quickly, she knew the reverend would arrive right on time. The day would be hot, so she tied her thick tresses up off her neck. A quick glance in the mirror showed Bell a young woman who could never atone for her sins with a little paint. But she was willing to try anything once.

The good reverend appeared at precisely nine o'clock with nothing more than a smile to get Bell, Poppy, Zinnia, and Clover to the location of his new church. He said nothing, but led them all single file down the streets of New Orleans to the dilapidated building he hoped would bring the sinners of the city to God.

"So, what's this place called?" Clover asked, the first one to speak. She put her hands on her hips and stared at the bleak building.

"I don't know just yet," the reverend responded. "If you got an idea, I'm all ears."

"I'll think about it and let you know, Padre," she said with a sassy voice. Everybody laughed at her remark, and the mood immediately relaxed.

"Well, girls, I hope you can figure this out. Let's start inside," he said, opening the door for them. "I picked a pretty gold for the inside walls and dark green for the outside. I hope it can make this dirty place look good."

Poppy flashed her pearly smile and winked, "You can make any place look good, preacher man." She gyrated her hips and flicked her yellow hair towards him.

"It's not about me, Miss," Reverend Sullivan said back to her, but he did not meet her gaze. He seemed to be giving Poppy a wide berth. Bell thought he might resist her now, but not many were able to resist Poppy for long. She was the one girl who relished in her position in this world.

"Poppy," she filled in. "I'm Poppy. This little one is Clover. And Bluebell and Zinnia." She pointed to them as she listed their names.

"All names of flowers," the man mused.

Bell rolled up her sleeves as she replied, "Madam has a penchant for floral names. Astrid, Daisy, and Jasmine are still at the spa. And Myrtle and Rose just left us within the last year. I told you she gave us all new names."

Poppy shot her a sideways glance. "When did you tell him that?"

"I entertained Reverend Sullivan in the steam room a while back and told him that Madam gave us all new names."

Poppy frowned, grabbed Bell by the arm, and wagged her finger the same way the madam did. "You should not have done that, Bluebell," she hissed in Bell's ear.

Fingernails dug into her arm, and Bell yelped in surprise. What did it matter if she had told this man about their names? Surely, he didn't think they were all born with flower names. Yanking her arm away, Bell looked to the preacher and watched as his eyes grew large with alarm, but he turned away quickly.

Seldom one to speak up, the shy Zinnia broke up the budding argument. "Let's not fight, please," she said with her waif-like voice. "We're here to paint, let us paint."

Bell looked at the dark-haired preacher, and he led them all inside. He handed each girl a paintbrush and a can of gold paint and set them loose. Each girl chose a wall, Poppy insisting that Clover work with her, and got to work.

It was hot and muggy inside the confines of the converted furniture store. The walls were dingy, and little nail holes peppered them where art had once been displayed. The main room was large, large enough for a small church service, Bell noted. She had not seen the other rooms, but there were a few doors leading to other areas of the building.

It was solid, hard work, and the girls were sweating in no time. Bell noticed that Poppy had shed her outer shirt and was just in her chemise. Bell was surprised the preacher had not objected, but he said nothing. Instead, he focused his attention on helping Clover figure out her brush strokes. Keeping her eyes on her section of the wall, Bell still was not convinced that his intentions were purely of God and not of flesh. She had learned that men usually disappointed, so she kept her eyes ahead so she could not see if his wandered.

As she wiped her brow, Reverend Sullivan approached her with a glass of water. "I appreciate your willingness to come out here, Bluebell."

She greedily drank. "Please, Reverend Sullivan, call me Bell."

"Then you must call me Teddy," he insisted.

With the glass empty, she agreed. "Alright, Reverend Teddy." She smiled at him. He returned the smile, and she felt her heart jump. It had never done that before. Quickly, she spoke, "I have a question for you, Reverend Teddy."

"Of course, Miss Bell." He stood attentively as she dipped her brush into more paint. Her arm was beginning to ache, but she dared not stop or look his way. She feared that her heart would jump again if she looked at him, and she couldn't have that happen.

"You said before that all sin was sin, and none was worse than another, right?" She felt befuddled as she spoke, sure she had said it wrong.

"That is correct," he said. "All sin is sin. It doesn't matter how big the sin is, it's all punishable by death."

All the girls stopped mid-stroke and turned to face the pair. The mention of death was taken seriously.

"Death?" Zinnia asked at a bare whisper. "Will they come to kill us?" Her light-blue eyes grew wide with fear, and she puckered her full lips.

"No, Miss Zinnia," Teddy reassured her quickly; for that Bell was thankful. "But it does mean that all sinners who do not repent of their wicked ways will go to hell and not live eternally with our Lord Jesus Christ."

Stepping closer, Clover asked what they all wondered. "What does living eternally mean?"

Bell looked to the preacher, who thought for a moment and then responded. "It means that when you die here on earth, you get to be alive forever in heaven. But if you don't ask God to forgive you of your sins, then you will suffer forever in hell. Does that make sense?"

The girl's dark eyes grew at the notion of suffering forever. "Am I a sinner, Padre?"

"We're all sinners, Clover. You just have to ask Jesus to come into your heart and make you clean again." He crouched down to the girl's level and gently touched the top of her head. The tender show of affection caused Bell's eyes to tear up, and she had to look away.

Poppy huffed, then immediately barked at Clover. "Stop

asking silly questions, Clover. Come help me paint this blasted wall and stop bothering the reverend with your prattle. Besides, he's not even a priest."

With the spell broken by Poppy's harsh words, Clover went back to Poppy's side like a wounded pup. She dipped her brush into the gold paint and began sloppily applying it to the wall.

Bell continued to paint but whispered to the preacher, "I'm sorry, Reverend. Poppy can be very cruel at times."

"I think we all can be cruel at times, Miss Bell," he sighed but made no show of moving away from her. He leaned his hand onto an unpainted section of the wall and spoke again, "Allow me to ask you a question."

She cast a quick sideways glance at him, his white shirt still pristine and buttoned to the top of his collar. "You can ask me anything. Not much surprises me anymore."

"Do you believe in God, Miss Bell?"

Bell turned toward the man, his eyes pleading for her to say yes, but his brow showing that he knew the answer was no. She studied his face a moment, her gaze looking over the stubble on his chin, the mess of his hair. She so wanted to please him. His intentions seemed so pure. She felt so wicked for wanting to reach her painted hand out to him to touch him.

"Do you, Bluebell?" he whispered, his baritone voice barely audible.

"Move your hand, Reverend," she commanded harshly as she began to apply paint where he was standing. When he didn't move more than a step, she answered with a low voice, "I want to. I want to believe in your God, Reverend Sullivan." She looked up at him and wiped her forehead, leaving a streak of gold paint across her face. "I'm a whore. How could there be a God who would allow anyone to become like me? Look at that little girl over there," she said, motioning to

Clover. "She's nine. Nine years old, and in a few weeks, her innocence will be bought, just like the rest of us. If there's a good God in this world, how does He allow such things?"

The anger in her voice was thick, and she pushed back tears. She did reach out and touch the pastor, but instead of the tender touch she had imagined moments ago, she pushed him aside, tears spilling over her cheek as she dipped her brush into more paint.

Reverend Teddy hesitated, then said, "I don't know, Miss Bell. I wish I knew." Then he walked away, taking water to the other girls in the room.

He didn't speak to her again, even with the sun high overhead and the heat at its apex. Poppy and Clover left to head back to the spa earlier than Bell and Zinnia. At about three o'clock, they had finished the inside of the newly converted church building. Bell and Zinnia were both covered in gold paint, their dresses practically ruined.

"I'm so sorry about your dresses, ladies," the reverend said. "Please let me give you some money to buy new dresses."

"We're not allowed to take money, sir," Zinnia said in her quiet, mousy voice. She attempted to pull gold paint from her light brown coils of hair, but the effort was in vain.

"Surely, for a dress, you can. I've caused you to ruin yours," he said with a smile.

Bell furrowed her brow. "Madam doesn't let us keep any money. If you give us something, she'll search us and take it before we ever set foot in a dress shop."

"Are you serious? How do you earn money?"

"She gives us a little to live on each week. Otherwise, we do our best to smuggle tips that she can't find," Bell said, matter-of-factly.

"I wish I could rescue all of you from that place," he said, looking at Zinnia. They exited the building and began the walk back to the spa. Bell and Zinnia would need to bathe before beginning their evening.

Zinnia just sniffled. Bell took her friend's hand into her own. When the reverend opened his mouth to speak, Bell shook her head. He closed his mouth and didn't say any more.

Back at the spa, Madam Knight ordered the girls to the baths right away. Zinnia scurried off as quickly as she could. As Bell began to follow, Madam stopped her.

"Bluebell, my dear," she said, "Did the preacher give you any extra money?"

"No, ma'am." Her expression remained blank.

"Did he ask you to do anything other than paint? Did he ask any of you to be alone with him?"

"No, ma'am. All we did was paint."

"Very good. Off with you now, you're filthy." She waved her hand, and Bell disappeared into the showers.

The next day, a delivery appeared at the spa. A package each for Bell, Zinnia, Clover, and Poppy. Reverend Teddy had gone to the dress shop and gotten each of them a dress and had it gift-wrapped and delivered with specific instructions to go back for fittings, all paid for by him personally.

"This is highly unusual," Madam Knight said, her hand pressing on the flesh of her hip. "Where is a young preacher getting money for dresses, anyway?" But she allowed the girls to keep their new dresses since it was one less she would have to purchase. She waved the four of them off to try on the new frocks.

Zinnia and Clover slipped into Bell's room with their boxes. Bell opened hers and saw that a note had been left inside for her.

Miss Bluebell,

Please accept this new dress as an apology for the ruining of your other one. Every time I see you, you are dressed in blue, so I hope you like what I have chosen. If not, remember I was a single preacher alone in a dress shop and haven't the foggiest what is in style. The dresses are nothing fancy but hopefully will replace the ones soiled by paint.

My sincerest regards,

Rev. Theodore Sullivan

P.S. – Thank you, from the bottom of my heart, for being honest with my question. I am in constant prayer for an answer.

By the time she had finished reading the note, Zinnia had helped Clover into her new dress. It was a khaki frock a size too big, but she could grow into it nicely. It was cut in the current fashion with a large collar, and the hem hung just below her knees.

Zinnia pulled a cream-colored dress from her box. How had the preacher known they each had to wear a certain color? Had she told him that before? Bell couldn't remember. Zinnia's dress was also simple, the collar coming nearly up to her neck with delicate ruffles along the neck and sleeves.

"Oh, Bell, isn't it lovely?" Zinnia asked, a blush in her cheeks. She quickly tried it on. The dress was a perfect fit for her slight build.

"Did you get a note with yours?" Bell asked her. When Zinnia shook her head, Bell quietly tucked hers under her pillow to hide it. She wondered if Poppy got a note but realized the reverend had probably just written one to her. Her heart skipped a beat, and she looked up at Zinnia.

"Put yours on," Clover said. "Let's see."

"Alright," she said to the young girl. Clover's excitement was contagious, and Bell lifted the dress from the box.

"Oh, Bell, that's so pretty," Zinnia said quietly. "I think that preacher likes you."

Bell shot Zinnia a scowl. "I don't think so, Zinnia. I think I made him angry. Besides, he's a preacher. He'd never actually have an interest in someone like us. He's too good for us."

The cornflower blue color went wonderfully with her dark hair and eyes, and Bell eagerly slipped into it. The bell sleeves came just below her elbow and ruffled slightly, and the neckline was in the shape of a modest V. A look in her mirror showed Bell that the dress revealed not even a hint of her breast. Delicate lace wrapped around the skirt, giving it a beautiful illusion. The dress was much fancier than the one Zinnia had received. Why was her dress more becoming than her friends'? The thought niggled in her mind, but she tried to shoo it away.

After admiring the dresses for a moment, Bell noticed the time. "It's nearly four. Go put these new dresses away and put on something else. Best not to let Madam see them tonight."

The two girls rushed to the room they shared together, their boxes clutched to their chests. Bell redressed in her fancier indigo dress in hopes of forgetting the stunning dress from the dashing preacher. She shoved the box and her unsettling feelings under the bed, but she could not hide them forever.

CHAPTER 4

The bell over the front door chimed for the fourth time that afternoon. Each time it rang, Bell looked up to see if Reverend Sullivan had come to see her. Not just her, of course, but all of them. She tried not to let her face fall when a short, yellow-haired man came in, licking his lips. He took Daisy's arm and pinched her backside as she sashayed next to him.

Bell's mind imagined Teddy Sullivan coming in and asking for her. Would she treat him like any other client? Shaking her head, she reminded herself that he would never come for that. She thought about the way he talked, the confidence he had. She imagined the way his eyes wrinkled up when he smiled and how the dimple in his left cheek would appear and disappear as he spoke.

Why did she think about such things? He was kind, nice to look at, but he troubled her. She felt challenged by him. Maybe that was why she thought of him so much – she felt like he challenged her very existence with the way he spoke of his God's love and forgiveness. As if God would accept her apologies after the life she had been living since being left at the brothel. And He was the one who saw fit to leave her there. God should be happy to have *her* forgiveness.

She stomped around the house as she thought, getting angrier by the minute. Heat rose in her cheeks as she carelessly rearranged the flowers in each vase throughout the house. Soon she was ready to give that preacher a piece of her mind and demand answers; however, she wasn't entirely sure why.

"Bluebell, my dear!" Madam called to her with her shrill voice. Bell took a deep breath and hurried to the parlor. There she found Madam waiting with one of her most vile clients, Nigel Harding. "Mr. Harding has come to pay you a visit, dear." Madam smirked, and Bell had to fight back the taste of bile in her mouth.

His visits were infrequent, but Nigel Harding was a memorable man. Close to forty, he was completely bald and as round as he was tall. Much to her dismay, she was his favorite girl. He owned half of the marina in New Orleans as well, so he flashed his money around at the spa, leaving Madam promising him anything he wanted if he would just leave a portion of his wad of bills in her cleavage.

All the anger Bell had felt for Reverend Sullivan melted away and was replaced with genuine fear. Nigel Harding had a quick and heavy hand.

Bell smiled prettily and curtsied at the man, an uneasy smile on her lips. "Mr. Harding. How pleasant to see you again, sir." Her heart beat rapidly, and sweat already beaded on her neck.

"Of course it is, my dear," he said boisterously. "Don't you look delicious today?"

Bell blushed, hoping she had passed her dread off as being flirtatious.

At that precise moment, the chimes rang again, and Bell looked up to see Theodore Sullivan walk into the room. Her fear suddenly turned to humiliation. The reverend was about to see her take a client back into the locked rooms of the house.

Madam glanced at the reverend, then back at Bell and Mr. Harding. "Now, Bell, you be sweet to Mr. Harding. Don't rough up one of my favorite clients," she joked.

Bell risked a glance toward Reverend Sullivan. He had realized what was going on and looked horrified. She tried to hide the panic from her eyes but knew that he could see her fear. He glanced around, looking as if he was trying to come up with a way to help her, but he came up with nothing as Mr. Harding practically dragged her down the hall. The reverend's bright green eyes were the last thing she saw as she was pulled around the corner.

$\sim$

"*R*everend Sullivan! Do you need more painting done?" Madam Knight asked with a smirk across her face.

Teddy tried to ignore the woman's greeting as he watched a very frightened Bell being led down the hall by one of the fattest men he had ever seen. She couldn't hide her trepidation, and Teddy recognized that she didn't even try to. She seemed to be pleading to him for help. She was scared. Terrified. Why was she scared of that man? But there was nothing he could do … they disappeared before anything came to mind. Quickly, he shot up a prayer for her safety.

"Reverend Sullivan?"

"So sorry, Madam Knight," he said as he tried to smile at the woman who would callously allow such a young girl to be put through such pain and terror. "No, no paint today. I just wanted to see if I may use the steam room and talk to one of your girls tonight. I have my dollar!"

The madam snorted at him and waved him further into the room. "Who'd you have in mind today, Reverend? Astrid is available, as is Daisy. Would either one suit you?"

The redheaded girl stepped forward. "I'll volunteer, Madam," she said. "If that's alright with you, sir." She smiled and showed a set of lovely teeth, a pretty dimple making a quick appearance.

Teddy remembered the girl from when he ran into her and Bell in town before. "Yes, that would be lovely," he said with a smile. Astrid led him back to the steam room as Bell had done the first day he had been in New Orleans. When she opened the door to the locker room for him, he quietly said to her, "Please stay as dressed as possible. I want nothing more than to talk."

In the steam room, Teddy found the girl in a robe similar to what Bell had worn before, but the collar was pulled tight, and the belt cinched firmly around her waist. She wore knee-length knickers under the robe. She wasn't as dressed as he would have liked, but it was a lot more than he knew she was supposed to wear. Teddy himself had fashioned cut-off pants to wear, so as to stay as decent as possible.

"Astrid, isn't it?" When the girl nodded, he continued, "I thank you for joining me."

"You're worried about her," she said boldly, searching his face.

"I beg your pardon?"

"Bell," she said. "You are worried about her. You saw her being led away by Mr. Harding. You have every reason to worry, Reverend. That man is a monster."

Teddy sat next to the tall girl with the flowing red hair. "If he's so bad, why does the madam allow him around you girls?"

"Not us – just Bell. He's quite smitten with her," Astrid informed him. "All the men are quite taken with her. But Mr.

Harding is one of the richest men in New Orleans, and when he steps foot into the spa, Madam's pockets get filled. But he only comes for Bell."

Teddy wished the steam wasn't so thick, and he could see into this girl's blue eyes. "You said he was a monster ...?"

"He's terribly cruel to Bell. He forces himself on her, and he talks to her like she's garbage. But he hits, too. He hits hard," Astrid said, her head hung in shame. "I wish I could help her, but there's nothing I can do. I told Bell I would offer myself to him, but she says no. I just pray each time he comes that he won't hurt her."

Anger boiled in Teddy like lava that wanted to burst forward from a volcano. He wanted to find them. He wanted to open every door until he could get the girl away from harm. But he also knew it would be a foolish move.

"Well, let's pray right now then for her to get away from him. Let's pray that God will spare her this time." He patted the bench next to him, inviting her to pray with him.

Immediately, Astrid turned and knelt at the bench and folded her hands. She began to pray under her breath, her lips moving quickly with petition to the Lord. Teddy was shocked for a moment. He knew Bell struggled to believe that God was real. It seemed that most of the girls on Basin Street had no faith at all. But here was a girl who took immediate action to pray for her friend. After a moment, Teddy himself knelt down a few feet from Astrid and joined her in prayer.

"Dear Lord, please deliver Your child Bell from the hands of that man. Allow her to escape unscathed. Give her peace and calm in your presence, God. Help her to have faith in you. Amen."

Inside his head, he repeated his prayer several times over, *help her, help her*. His breath grew more rapid as he prayed until he couldn't catch it. He got to his feet and nearly collapsed onto the bench from heat and worry. Astrid followed, keeping the space between them.

"Every time I come here, I learn something worse than the time before," Teddy said.

"This is our life, Reverend."

"That's precisely what Bell had told me the first time I came here," he said as he looked at her.

"You like her quite a bit, don't you?" The girl looked amused, her expression genuine.

He tried to think of a way to avoid the question. "You prayed. I have yet to meet a girl in a brothel who so easily knelt in prayer before the Father."

Astrid sighed. "My faith in God is the only thing that gets me through most days. That and Bell's friendship. And you didn't answer my question."

"I'm surprised because Bell told me herself that she had a hard time believing in a God who would allow all of you to be in such a situation. And I've noticed that not many of the ladies I have met in the district have any faith at all." After a pause, he added, "And I do like her. She's honest, and I feel like she epitomizes what I want to save in this town."

They were both silent a moment. Teddy thought about Astrid's assessment of his affection for Bell. He was attracted to her, and the admission to himself was a little alarming. That was not why he had come to New Orleans. He acknowledged that she was one of the loveliest women he had ever seen. But there was more than that. There was something to her that drew him in. But from what Astrid said, many men felt drawn to Bell. Might this be nothing more than an attraction to a pretty face? Regardless, Teddy felt anxious to help the petite girl with the pleading eyes.

He glanced at the door, and Astrid's gaze followed his. She reached out her hand and placed it on top of his.

"We can leave, Reverend, but it's only been ten minutes.

Mr. Harding pays for the whole evening. We can do nothing but wait as we pray." When he sighed, Astrid added, "I appreciate how worried you are for her. It's obvious you care about Bell."

"I care about all God's children," he said, making the argument to himself just as much as to the girl beside him. "Especially if they are in danger. Please, Lord, don't let Bell be hurt tonight." He squeezed his eyes shut, willing time to lurch forward at a faster rate. He stood to pace the room, his feet beating out a rhythm that matched his racing heart.

Astrid smiled at him. It took her a moment, but she finally spoke again. "I'm sorry if I appear happy. I truly am also worried. Bell is the best friend I could ever ask for. But watching you … I see that you feel more for her than liking a pretty face."

"You are a very insightful girl, Astrid. I have to admit that there is something about Bell that makes me think of her constantly. I don't know why God has ingrained her image in my mind and in my heart." He sat and looked directly at Astrid. "Now that I've confessed that, please tell me about yourself. Bell told me that her parents passed away. What is your story?"

Astrid beamed, her rosy lips revealing small, perfect teeth. "Well, as I know Bell told you, Madam changed all our names. The name my momma gave me is Virginia, and I came here from Virginia. I don't know what happened, to be honest. My family was moving from the town of Wytheville to Roanoke. I'm told that's a big city."

"It is, it's a very large city," Teddy interjected.

"My poppa got a new job that moved us to Roanoke," Astrid said without skipping a beat. "On the first night of our trip east, our wagon was attacked. I'm not sure who did it. I don't know if my family is still alive or if they are gone. All I know is that I was tied up in the dark and put into another wagon. After a day, they untied me and would toss me food scraps. We wound up here where Madam got me. I never saw the faces of the people who took me away. I don't know if they were Indians or white men or what. I was thirteen years old. I came in about a year after Bell, and we were instant friends."

"I'm terribly sorry to hear that. I am from Maryland and have connections in Roanoke. If you tell me your father's name, I will see if anyone knows of his whereabouts," Teddy said. He felt compelled to reach out to Astrid, but given where they were, he restrained himself.

"Would you do that for me?" Her voice filled with hope. "I would be most grateful! My father's name was ... is James Manning. My momma is Mary."

Teddy smiled as he filed the name into memory. "I'm happy to check for you. I can't make any promises, but I will write a letter tomorrow."

"Thank you so much," Astrid said, jumping to her feet. "You are a wonderful man, Reverend Sullivan!"

"Please, call me Teddy."

"Teddy," she repeated. "Oh, Teddy?"

"Yes?"

"My momma called me Ginny." A faint blush came over her cheeks.

"That's a lovely name, Ginny," Teddy said with a soft smile. "I will do what I can."

"I appreciate it, Reverend Teddy. Time's about up."

They both exited the steam room and dressed hastily. They hurried to the parlor, where Astrid quietly crept away from him. Teddy knew that many regular customers stayed and enjoyed the chatter of the girls well into the evening.

He spotted Zinnia and made his way to her, sitting in a chair opposite her. The girl's Creole heritage was apparent from her deeply tanned skin and hair that coiled like an

African's. But her hair was light brown and her eyes a piercing blue, making her a beautiful enigma among the girls of the spa.

They made small talk, and Teddy steered the small girl to talk about herself, even though she was prone to talk about others. He had noticed her need to keep the peace and also keep attention away from herself. He wondered what she hid, as it seemed so many of them had secrets. Teddy kept one eye on the hallway, waiting for Bell to emerge.

A few moments later, the portly Mr. Harding came through the parlor. He tipped his hat at Madam Knight, and with a smug smile, he strode out the door. Teddy's fingers dug into the plush seat; it was all he could do to prevent himself from storming after the man and planting his fist squarely against his jaw. Instead, he focused his gaze on the hall, waiting for Bell to come into sight. In the shadows, he saw her figure, but she stayed behind the curtain, darkness covering her. Astrid stood and glanced his way, concern in her eyes. Teddy fought the urge to follow Astrid as she disappeared behind the shadows of the hall.

"Astrid will take care of her," Zinnia's timid voice said.

Her words startled him, and he jumped. All the other girls had disappeared in his mind.

"I ... uh ..." Teddy hadn't realized how obvious he was.

"It's okay, Reverend Teddy," she said quietly. "I noticed yesterday how taken you are with her."

Was everyone else in the world aware of his feelings before he was? "Are you certain she'll be alright?"

"Astrid will take care of her tonight. But she won't come back out if Mr. Harding bruised her. Last time he gave her a black eye," she whispered. "But he paid Madam dearly for giving her a visible bruise. Hopefully, he wouldn't have done that again."

When Teddy's eyebrows rose up, Zinnia quickly continued. "You won't see her tonight. It's best if you go now and come back tomorrow to see how she is."

He merely nodded, his eyes still fixed on the blackened hallway where Bell had not shown her face. Before he could chase down the hall toward her, he left the spa house and headed back to his solitary room, praying for wisdom the entire way.

CHAPTER 5

"Why was Reverend Sullivan still here?" Bell asked Astrid as she applied a cold cloth to her arm. Her anger at him from earlier and Mr. Harding now was compounded. Tears spilled over her cheeks.

"He was very worried about you, Bell," Astrid said as she examined the hand-shaped bruise Mr. Harding had left on her friend. "He came to make use of the steam room, and I went in with him – the most dressed I've ever been in there. We prayed for you, Bell. That pastor really cares for you."

Furrowing her brow, Bell seethed. "Then why didn't he come in to save me? Then why didn't your prayers do anything? Why didn't your God save me, Astrid?" Tears spilled over her eyelashes, burning as they made their way down her aching cheekbone. Bell cried out in pain even though Astrid's touch was as gentle as a mother's.

"I wish I knew," was all Astrid said. "But I do know that Theodore Sullivan thinks much more of you than just a girl in the district. I can see it plain as the nose on his face."

Bell gingerly touched a developing bruise on her shoulder

she would now have to cover. It would take nearly all her make-up to cover it. "I doubt he feels that way, Astrid. And besides, if he did have feelings for me, why didn't he do anything? Why did he wait around, looking to see what that nasty old man did to me?"

"He was concerned, Bell. I mean it. And I talked to him – he said he would try to find my father for me."

Bell paused. Compassion for her friend overtook her own personal pain. "Oh, Astrid, really?"

"He said he wasn't sure what he would find, but he would look for me. He said he had friends in Roanoke."

Bell stretched her battered arms around her friend and hugged her tight, ignoring the searing pain in her body.

"That's the best news I've heard all day." She offered a genuine smile. "If you don't mind, though, I think I'm going to lie down. Will you come check on me later?"

"Of course," Astrid said. Her eyes crinkled in a joyous smile as she left, and Bell struggled to get comfortable in her bed and cover herself.

Bell winced as she moved her arm. The bruise on it would last two weeks, she guessed. The hidden ones on her legs, however, would last longer. And the shiner she once again sported would have Madam in a tizzy. She hoped Mr. Harding would not be welcome again, at least, not for several weeks until she was healed. Madam would need to see her entire body in the morning and determine if Bell was out of rotation for a while until she could heal some. Exhausted and in pain, Bell fell into a fitful sleep, dreaming about the events of the day – Reverend Sullivan's horrified look playing a central role in her looping nightmare.

In the morning, Astrid called Madam Knight into the room she shared with Bell. Bell could hardly move, and every muscle in her body ached. When Madam saw the bruises on

Bell's eye, arms, and legs, she quickly sent Jasmine and Zinnia out for some herbal remedies from the local witch doctor.

"I'll call up that Nigel Harding and have words with him," she said with a scowl. "He put you out of commission at least through the weekend, and he don't pay enough for all that. It will be a long time before he's welcome through my doors again."

While the words were a relief for Bell, she was dismayed by Madam's concern for her loss of income and not her well-being. Nevertheless, it meant a weekend of parlor duty without having to accompany a man back to one of the bedrooms, and for that, she was grateful.

"Rest a little longer, Bluebell," Madam instructed. "But come into the parlor by five sharp and put as much powder on that eye as you can. Maybe cover with a hat or something. I'm glad it's Thursday. Maybe you'll be feeling better before the weekend is up." Then she left with a quick wave of her hand.

Bell doubted she would feel better anytime soon. And if some well-placed bruises were her saving grace, she would welcome that kind of pain. She sighed and played with a dark coil of hair that had been resting on her pillow. Where had the God of Astrid and Reverend Sullivan been last night? Where had he been for the past year? The past eight years? Where was the loving God they spoke of when her parents died?

Her parents had been church-going people. Bell went to church her entire life until her parents died. And she knew her parents were not educated and were not well-to-do people, but they were always happy. They had a wonderful community around them that abandoned her when they were gone. Church-going people were hypocritical as far as

Bell was concerned. The only ones who didn't seem to go back on their word were Astrid, and so far, this new preacher. Even the priests who came to hear confession were hypocrites, and Bell wanted nothing to do with their religious ways.

She closed her eyes, wishing Jasmine and Zinnia were back with the herbs Madam had told them to fetch. She cursed Nigel Harding and Madam Knight under her breath and willed herself to sleep more.

~

*S*weat stained Teddy's shirt as he put every ounce of effort he had into painting the outside of his new church building. Thoughts of Bell had woken him in the pre-dawn hours. Unable to sleep, he had risen and written a letter to his cousin in Roanoke as he had promised Astrid and dropped it at the post office on his way to the old furniture store. Before the sun had crested the trees, he had one entire exterior wall painted as he prayed for wisdom and guidance.

There had to be a way to save all the girls at the spa. Not only Bell, hidden in the shadows, but Astrid, who didn't know if her family was alive, and little Clover, who was still so fresh and innocent. Teddy prayed for God to reveal an answer, something that would get these girls out of this life. Bell had said the only way out was to get married, but he couldn't marry them all, and certainly the younger girls were way too young to even be considering marriage.

As he plodded along and applied more green paint to the outside of the new church, he gave up trying to come up with an answer himself. Finally, he prayed aloud, "God, I give up. I don't have the answers, but I know you do. Just help me!"

"Reverend Teddy?"

Teddy spun around at the sound of his name. The soft, song-like voice belonged to that of Zinnia. With her was one of the girls from the spa he had seen but not yet met. She was a pretty mulatto girl of about fifteen.

"Zinnia, I'm so sorry, I did not see you." He rubbed his hands on an old rag and extended his hand to her and the other girl. "I'm Reverend Teddy. I don't think we've been introduced."

The girl thrust her hand out and smiled. "They call me Jasmine. Like the flower. Your name is Teddy? Like a teddy bear?"

Teddy looked at the girl quizzically. She spoke as if she were much younger than she looked. "Yes, like a teddy bear. My full name is Theodore; Teddy is a nickname."

She grinned wide, revealing a row of clean but crooked teeth. "Sometimes Poppy and the other girls call me Jazz, like the music." Her eyes sparkled as she talked.

"Stand here, Jasmine," Zinnia told her, her voice firm but friendly. "Don't move. I need to tell the reverend something private."

"A secret?" The girl clapped her hands and shuffled her feet. There was something off about the girl, Teddy could see it plainly.

"Yes, Jasmine. A secret. Now stay right here," she warned. Zinnia moved a few steps away with Teddy, so they were out of earshot. Jasmine stayed put. "Jasmine is a little … behind. I'm sure you can tell."

Alarm filled Teddy as he thought of the girl selling herself unknowingly. "She doesn't …"

"No. No, she just works in the house, cleaning or helping in the kitchen. Her mother, a young girl off the streets, gave her to Madam when she was a small child. But when her impairments became obvious, Madam knew she would never be able to ... Anyway, I'm here to tell you about Bell."

Teddy leaned in closer to Zinnia. "How is she? Is she okay?" He licked his lips, unsure if he wanted to hear the answer if Bell were not faring well. Regardless, he needed to know.

Zinnia looked down. Her large, baby-blue eyes told Teddy that she was obviously struggling to tell him what the news was. "She's very tired. Madam said she will only be in the parlor this weekend, which means she must be hurt. Madam wouldn't risk losing income if it weren't serious. She sent us to the witch doctor, Redgood, for herbs."

Teddy's eyes widened. "Witch doctor?"

"Yes, Redgood is an old negro woman. I think her Christian name is Dorcas," Zinnia noted. "But she gives a lot of the district girls herbs so they won't conceive or herbs to help with illness. I didn't see Bell, but Astrid says her legs and arms are black and blue, and she has a black eye. Madam sent us out for some herbs for the pain and some salve. I just thought you would like to know, Reverend Teddy."

Zinnia looked so concerned for her friend, and her compassion was obvious to Teddy. "Thank you for letting me know, Zinnia. You are a wonderful friend to Bell and the other girls, I'm sure. I'm in constant prayer for how I can help you all." He avoided laying his hand on her shoulder, though he felt a strong urge to do so. Teddy just wasn't sure how even the simplest touch would come across to these girls.

"Well," Zinnia said, turning back toward Jasmine, who hadn't moved an inch. "I better get this to Bell."

"Thank you for telling me, Zinnia. Please tell Bell I will be by to see her soon. And would you tell Astrid I wrote to my cousin in Roanoke? I posted it this morning. Hopefully, I will hear back soon."

"Yes, I will let her know. We better be going, Reverend," she said as she took Jasmine's arm. "Have a nice afternoon."

Teddy waved the girls off, but as soon as they were out of sight, he put his paint and brushes away. He hurried back to his room at the Arnold Arms Hotel and scrubbed himself clean. With a fresh change of clothes and his glasses perched upon his nose, he took off for the Night and Day Spa for Men.

It was nearly four o'clock when he walked into the parlor. Madam Knight looked up from her cash drawer as he strode in, but when she saw him, she shook her head and turned her attention back to the money. Teddy took a deep breath and approached the madam.

Before Teddy knew it, he blurted out, "I'd like to marry Bluebell, with your permission, Mrs. Knight."

The piano stopped playing. The room grew quiet, and all eyes turned toward him. What had he just said? Was he serious? Teddy wasn't sure himself. But he knew he needed to save Bell, and if marriage was the way to do it, then that was what he would do.

The robust woman stood from her chaise, though even standing, she barely came to Teddy's chest. "Did I hear you correctly, Reverend? You want to marry one of my whores?"

"She's not a … a …" he stammered. "And yes. I do."

"Why on earth would a good man like you want to marry a girl with so much … previous experience?" She wrinkled her nose as she spoke, as if Bell was a lowly flea. "Do you love her? Does she love you?"

Teddy took a step back. Love had nothing to do with his idea. Should he not marry for love? He was fond of Bell, but then again, he was fond of Zinnia and Astrid as well. But love her?

"I'm not sure how she feels about me, Miss Knight," he

said boldly, though avoiding answering for himself. "But I'm willing to take the chance."

"You're not the first man to be smitten with her beautiful face and body, Reverend. And you haven't even seen it all! Mr. Barnard asks for her hand on a regular basis, and she's still here. What makes you think you're different?"

When no words came to Teddy's lips, she continued, "Do you think Bell would even consider your proposal, Reverend Sullivan? Go ask her. Down the hall to the left, third door." When he hesitated, she shooed him away, "Go! Go ask her yourself." She cackled the way he imagined an old witch would, her chest jiggling as she did.

Teddy staggered backward a few steps, unsure of what to do. Part of him wanted to bolt for the door and never come back. The other part wanted to call Madam Knight's bluff and run away with Bell that very night – if she would go with him.

He turned around and saw Astrid looking very shocked, her blue eyes wide, and her brow raised several inches. She immediately went to his side and led him toward the back of the house.

Once they were out of sight in the hall, she whispered, "I can't believe you did that."

"I can't either, to be honest. But Zinnia came to me and said Bell was hurt. If this is the only way to save her, this is what I'll do. I'll find ways to send you other girls to Maryland where you're nothing but new girls in town. No past to follow you."

Astrid paused in front of the third door down the hall. "Our past will always follow us, Reverend. You know that as well as anybody else. We can't run from it. Only God can pull us out of this pit. I'm trusting that my God is big enough to do that."

"You are very wise, Astrid," he observed.

"She's inside here," she told him, putting her hand on the door. "Good luck."

With that, she thrust the door open and practically shoved Teddy inside. "Bell? Reverend Teddy to see you." She smiled at him, "She's all yours."

~

*B*ell quickly pulled the covers over her shoulders as the door opened. When she heard Astrid say the minister's name, she reached a weak arm out and dimmed her bedside light. Bell turned her face as he entered her room. Scorn filled her. Why was Reverend Sullivan here? To mock her? To pray over her lost soul yet again? Someone had told him she was injured, of that she was sure. Maybe he came to read her the last rites. Well, she wasn't about to let him.

"Bluebell? May I come in?" His voice was soft, but not sappy. When she didn't respond, he came closer until he was at her side. "You're not even pretending to sleep. Zinnia came to see me earlier and said you could use a friend."

"I have friends," she snapped. "Astrid and Zinnia and Jasmine. I don't need you."

Without turning her head, Bell tried to see what the reverend was doing. One thing was certain, he was not leaving. He cleared his throat. "Okay, so you don't need a friend. When I got here just a moment ago, I asked Madam Knight a question. She suggested I come and ask you instead."

Her curiosity piqued, Bell shifted a little in her bed while still keeping the deep purple sheet over her. The bruises on her shoulders and legs made every movement painful, and she winced. With each wince, the eye that now matched her sheet cried out in agony, tiny tears slipping down her cheek without her even knowing it.

Reverend Sullivan hesitated, opened his mouth and closed it again, then finally spoke. "Bluebell, I asked you this the day we met, but I know the answer wasn't the truth. What is your name? Your real name?"

She turned fully toward him. "My name? The one my parents gave me?"

He quickly pulled a small chair up to her bedside. He squinted his eyes when he saw her face. "I can't believe any man would do this to a lady," he said, gingerly reaching an arm out to Bell. But he brought it back to his side before he ever touched her. She watched as he struggled with where to place his hands, eventually just keeping them folded in his lap.

"Nigel Harding is no man. He's a dog, Reverend, that's for sure," she said, trying not to sob any more. "And I am no lady. Just a common whore."

"You are no whore! I am so tired of hearing that crass word," the minister said, heat rising in his cheeks. "Stop talking like that, and tell me your Christian name, Bell!"

"Is that what you asked Madam?"

"What? No. I just need to know it," he said with urgency. "Tell me."

She had never heard him angry before, at least not angry with her. Bell was shocked. She sat up higher in her bed and let the sheet fall slightly off her shoulders. The light chemise she wore only had straps, no sleeves, and the bruises on her shoulders were revealed.

"Do I make you angry, Reverend Sullivan? Or do these?" she said as she painfully thrust her shoulder toward him, her voice exploding with the suffering and anguish she had been going through for the last eight years. Tears fell freely down her cheeks, searing her cracked skin, and wicked away onto her cotton shirt.

The look of fire flamed in the reverend's eyes. He was

obviously not expecting to see her so severely beaten. Bell could hear his breath catch in his throat, and his fists balled up and released several times. It took him several deep breaths for the color in his cheeks to cool.

"I will not let this happen to you again. I swear it to you," he said, tears in his own eyes. Again, he reached his hands out to her, but this time did not recoil. As he took her hands in his, he asked again, this time gentler, "Please tell me your real name."

Bell blinked several times; she could feel the wet on her eyelashes. She could hear every beat of her heart. She could feel warmth mixed with something else radiating off of Teddy's hands. Slowly, she took a deep breath and looked straight at him. His green eyes shone with compassion, and if Bell didn't know better, she might think she saw a spark of love there as well. He did not smile, but neither did he wear a scowl.

In a voice as meek and quiet as a timid child, Bell answered, "Lana. My mother named me Lana."

She let go of her breath, and it felt like the weight of the world was lifted off her shoulders. In eight years there, she had never shared her given name with anybody – even the other girls. Madam had told them their old names were erased, and they were never to go by those names again. Telling someone, finally, meant connecting to her old identity, the person she was *before*. More tears slipped down her cheeks, the pain of her body replaced with the pain of losing her family and her self.

Once she had composed herself, she looked up and saw the reverend smiling, beaming.

"Lana, it's so nice to meet you. My name is Teddy," he said. He slowly and gingerly moved from sitting in the chair to sitting on the very edge of her bed, but he never took his hands off of hers.

Bell smiled in return, the ache in her body and mind slowly releasing. "Teddy," was all she said. "Thank you." She closed her good eye a moment as she began to relax. "Is that what you had wanted to ask?"

She opened her eye and saw Teddy smile wide. "No. I wanted to ask if you, Lana, would marry me."

CHAPTER 6

"*Y*ou can't be serious?" Bell, no Lana, said, a look of pure confusion on her bruised face.

The names wrestled back and forth in his mind. Her old self and her current self, two halves of a broken woman. Regardless of her name, her response cut deep.

"I am completely serious," Teddy answered. "Madam Knight said I should come ask you myself. I can get you out of here. I can save you."

Bell raised her unbruised eyebrow and chuckled. "Oh, you can save me? Who told you I needed to be saved, Reverend? Unless you happen to have a wad of cash in your pocket, Madam will not take you seriously. Besides, you're a preacher. You don't want to marry me, you just want to save me from my profession. And what about the other girls?" She paused and took a deep breath, huffing escaped curls from her face as she did. "If you can't save all of them, you can't save me. Who will look out for the meeker girls? What about Zinnia and Jasmine and Clover? Astrid will be kicked to the street in just a few weeks, and then what for her? If you want to save someone, Reverend, save them."

"But, Bell …" he started. He leaned closer to her, licking his lips. What could he say to make her understand that he did feel like he loved her, even though he knew practically nothing about her? Something inside him longed for her, ached to hold and comfort her.

"No, Reverend Sullivan," she interrupted, putting one hand on her hip and pointing the other toward his chest. "Until someone can truly say he loves me, without my flesh being part of the deal, I will not get married. Besides," she paused, "I'm sure you want to marry a good Christian girl. And that, sir, I ain't. Get away from me. Now."

Bell winced and sucked in a sharp breath as she angled her body slightly away from him. But Teddy was certain her heartache was even more obvious than her physical pain. Those sad eyes called to him, willing him to take on her challenge.

"If saving every girl in this house will convince you to marry me, I will do it. If I have to come here night after night and buy time with you to convince you that my intentions are pure and honest, I will do it," he said as he stood. "Bell, promise me. Promise me that when I get Astrid and Zinnia and the others out of here, you will marry me."

Teddy could feel his heart beating so rapidly he thought surely Bell could hear its thunderous roar. He stood beside her bed and waited for a response. Slowly Bell's gaze lifted to meet his.

"I can promise nothing, Reverend. Because while you're off saving the world, I'll be here, giving myself away. I am no prize, you see." Her voice was small again, defeated. Crushed, Teddy began to back slowly toward the door, watching her turned face via the mirror before her.

She looked up with shame-filled eyes and saw him

watching through the mirror. "If you can get Astrid, Zinnia, Jasmine, and Clover out of here, I will consider marriage to you. But don't expect me to follow your God, Reverend. Tell Madam I am considering your proposal. Nothing more."

A smile swept across Teddy's face. There was hope. It wasn't until that moment he realized just how much he did care for the petite brunette girl who had turned his world around. "I will do just that, Bell. Lana. Bell ..."

A hint of a smile came to her face, "Bell is fine. Were you going to come see me tonight?"

Teddy only nodded and opened the door, nearly tripping over the threshold. He backed out of the room and quietly closed the door behind him. With a smile on his face, he marched right up to Madam Knight, who looked quite smug herself.

"What are you smiling at, Preacher-man? Didn't she turn you down?" The Madam's voice boomed, and the visible flesh on her body shook.

"Mrs. Knight, Bluebell is considering my offer," he said with a flash of teeth. "With your permission, I would like to call on her tonight around six. Please have dinner ready for the two of us. I have no intention of touching her, especially not in her condition, but I do want time to court her." He spoke directly and loudly, so everybody in the room could hear him.

A look of pure shock came across Madam Knight's face. She stood stupefied at his words, her fleshy hand scratching absentmindedly at her upper lip.

"I will return at six," he said when the madam did not respond right away.

Teddy turned and strode for the door. He quickly sighted Astrid and motioned his eyes toward the back of the opulent home, towards Bell's room. When the redhead quickly batted her blue eyes in response, he knew she understood.

Realizing he more or less made a deal to get four of the girls out of that brothel, Teddy knew he needed to act quickly. The longer the girls were in there selling themselves, the worse their situations would become. At least Astrid would be leaving in about two months' time, but from what Teddy had learned, if she did not have a marriage prospect – or even the prospect of being a wealthy man's mistress – she would become a crib girl.

Crib girls had one foot in a bed and one foot in the grave, Teddy knew. They would rent a room with a bed for the night, then try to lure in as many customers as they could to earn back their rent, plus money to live on. Many had diseases they passed on to their partners. He had met several who had children running the streets. Those women had no hope, no chance of getting out alive. Their hollowed, deathly stares had followed him like he wore a target as he moved about the district. Teddy tried to minister to them, but all they wanted was to shed their clothes for a nickel. At least he could talk to the parlor girls in the big houses.

No, he had to do something before Astrid became a crib girl. The letter he sent to Richmond wouldn't be quick enough. Something needed to be done immediately. He quickly jogged to the nearest place with a telegraph and sent a message to three of his ministerial colleagues. He implored them to please try to find the Manning family, formerly of Wytheville, Virginia. If they found them, please let them know that their daughter, Virginia, was alive and in need of them to get her. He gave his information as who to contact if the family was found. Teddy quickly prayed under his breath for the Lord to bring Astrid's family to New Orleans to reclaim and heal their broken daughter.

Next, he composed a letter to his home parish in Maryland. He asked his congregation if any of them were in need of a maid or house girl. If they would pay for the girl's transport, she would work for them until the debt was paid off. Then the girl would be free to pursue the course in life God had for her. Teddy figured Zinnia, with her gentle nature, would make a wonderful governess. He told them there were two girls who needed families – one about sixteen, the other almost ten. He knew of two Negro families in town who would be perfect for the girls.

His messages sent, Teddy returned to the Arnold Arms Hotel and flew up to his room. Soon he would need to vacate his room; he had been there long enough. He planned to move into a back room of his new church building. There was plenty of space for him to set up a simple bed, washstand, and coat rack. The building even had indoor plumbing already, so it was the perfect space for a bachelor like him.

But wait – would he be a bachelor that much longer? Teddy suddenly remembered his proposal to Bell. His Bell. If she accepted his proposal, he could not move her into the back room of his make-shift church. That would be completely unacceptable. Tomorrow he would begin the hunt for an apartment … preferably away from the district.

Teddy's clock chimed five. He glanced outside and noticed the sun already dipping quickly toward the western horizon. Fall had begun; Teddy had noticed a chill in the air that morning, despite the warmer Louisiana temperatures. He quickly shaved and changed his clothes. He wanted to bring Bell a small gift that night to show he intended to court her properly.

He stopped in the local bookstore, though he realized he wasn't sure if Bell could read. Had she been able to read the note he sent her along with the dresses? He knew she didn't lose her parents until she was eleven, so he hoped against hope that she had learned to read before that tragic event, for surely Madam Knight did not encourage her girls in the art of literature.

If she could not read, he would read to her, he thought. He could teach her to read. With resolve, Teddy picked out a small book of the Psalms, the songs of the Bible. He quickly paid for his purchase and walked to the Storyville District, where jazz music blared. Teddy subconsciously walked in rhythm with the music, beating his hand against his thigh as he went.

~

O nce Teddy Sullivan had left her side, Bell had eased her way out of bed. She had intended to jump out, but the bruises hurt too much for such a passionate act. Her body screamed at the simple task, but she pressed on. She quickly tried to pace the floor, willing her muscles to ease and the bruises to fade.

She shook her head and chuckled a little as she recalled the hasty marriage proposal. Teddy Sullivan was not the first man to ask to marry her. But he was the first who had not seen her flesh in its entirety before the proposal. Perhaps he only saw her as a way to get the girls free from this life, and she had somehow become his pet project. Bell stood still for a moment and wondered if he had proposed marriage to any other bordello girls. Her cheeks turned crimson, and her stomach twisted. She tried to shake the feeling, willing herself to think it would be better if he married someone else, and left her to save herself. She didn't need saving, anyhow.

Astrid came into their room softly. "Did you really say you would consider his proposal, Bell?" Her blue eyes were opened wide, and she made no attempt to hide her grin. "He told Madam you were considering it loud enough for the entire room to hear. Poor Poppy about fell over in her chair.

Daisy nearly had to catch her!" She giggled a little and sat in the gold upholstered chair between their beds.

Bell lifted her chin. "I did say I would consider it. But only if he could get you, Zinnia, and Clover out of here first. I refuse to leave while you all are still here." She sat at the vanity desk she and Astrid shared and began to apply face powder to her bruises. She caked it on heavily.

"What? I'll be out of here soon enough, Bell. And how will he get Zinnia and Clover away, too?" Astrid's pale face reddened. "You should have accepted his offer and ran away this very night!"

Bell turned toward her dearest friend. "I can't leave you, Astrid, I love you. Even if you will be turned out in a few weeks, I can't abandon you. And I can't leave the others behind, either. I don't care how he does it; I just want it to happen. What other prospects do you have? Become a crib girl? Or is some rich suitor going to put you up in an apartment as his mistress?"

"Reverend Teddy is going to find my parents. They'll come for me," Astrid said with a smile. "I can't wait to hear my momma call my name again." Her eyes lost focus, and she stared off for a moment.

Bell's face softened. "I hope he can find them, Astrid. One day you will hear your mother's sweet voice again, I'm sure."

She hoped it was true. If her prayers went anywhere other than up in the air, Bell hoped that this prayer would make it to whatever in the universe controlled their destinies.

Astrid crossed the room to her and perched lightly on the vanity. "Let me help you with that. Your eye is very purple, but it will heal quickly." Astrid gently patted the dusty powder on Bell's face. "He really likes you, you know."

"Who?"

"Reverend Teddy," Astrid replied nonchalantly. "He told

Madam he would be back at six o'clock, and he intended to dine with you tonight. He said he wanted to make his intentions known." She sighed. "I think he loves you, Bell."

Bell's heart skipped a beat. Could that be true? Could the handsome man with the bright-green eyes really love her? He had never used her, never even so much as kissed her – could he truly feel love for her?

She knew she had never loved anyone other than her parents and her dear Astrid. She certainly never felt anything close to love for the men who frequented her bed. Disdain, disgust. Not love. Not even a hint of like. Did Bell know how to love a man? She wasn't sure she would recognize the feeling if she did.

Astrid must have guessed what she was thinking because she reached out and gently took Bell's hand. "I don't know what love really is, Bell. But I know he is serious about you. And if your condition was getting us out of here, he will do it. I have faith." She looked down at Bell and put the make-up down. Bell watched as her friend slowly made her way to the door and return to the parlor.

Bell looked into the mirror as the door clicked closed. "What is love?" she whispered to herself.

CHAPTER 7

*A*s the clock neared six, Bell began to watch the door. Just to prove to herself that the reverend wouldn't show up. She just knew that he would never enter through the doors again once he realized he had asked to marry a district girl.

Nevertheless, Bell wore the cornflower blue dress she had received from Teddy. Her arms were stiff as she lifted the dress from its box, and she whimpered as she brought the cool material over her body. It fit like a glove, and Bell felt transformed into a refined woman for the first time since she had arrived in New Orleans. Not a single bruise showed, besides her eye, of course. It was the most modest dress she owned, and she loved it. She had wanted to play with her hair, styling it just so, but the pain in her shoulder prevented it. Instead, she allowed her natural curls to cascade down her shoulders.

While she waited, Poppy positioned herself on the same couch as Bell. "I hear the preacher wants to marry you. Don't think he loves you, Bluebell. I'm sure he'll marry the first district girl who accepts. He's desperate for a lay and can't get one without putting a ring on a girl's finger."

Bell frowned. She knew Poppy was just jealous and trying to make herself feel better. Still, Bell wondered if she was right. She shot a nasty scowl at Poppy, who merely tossed a blonde curl over her shoulder.

"I don't care what you think, Poppy. Maybe Madam needs to know about your off-duty visits with Jack Knowles. Has he proposed to you? You will be twenty-one in a few short months, yourself," she quipped, sliding down the couch away from the vile girl. "Do you think your boyfriend will marry you, or will you be forced to the cribs?"

Bell hated being so nasty, but Poppy brought out the worst in her. A dose of her own medicine should be enough to keep the madam's favorite girl away for a while. Poppy opened her mouth, but no words came out. When the bells on the door jingled, she rose, her black dress rustling as she did. She huffed off just as Teddy came into view.

Bell watched him approach Madam Knight first. They had a quick but heated discussion. Madam eyed Bell several times, but she continuously nodded at the preacher. He handed her an envelope and nodded in return. Bell could only guess there was money in it, but she stayed seated. Where did he get all this money from? Perhaps he was wealthier than other ministers. She knew most of them were too poor to afford fancy dresses and nightly visits at brothels. Surely, his Maryland parishioners weren't paying for him to try to win over a prostitute.

He took a few steps toward her but did not get very close. His hand stretched out for hers, waiting. Bell hesitated for a moment, but the simple smile on his face bade her to come with him. Standing was not an effortless feat for her, but she tried to look elegant. She smoothed the dress and gently took Teddy's hand. He held her lightly, barely touching her, but she could feel his strength in his calloused hands. It was firm and steady; no hint of nerves was given away in his touch.

She did not speak, could not. Her stomach flipped, and she did not think her vocal cords would work properly if she tried to speak. Teddy also held silent, and Bell wondered if he was as nervous as she. His quiet smile gave flight to the butterflies in her stomach, and she did not know why. This was almost like real courting, aside from the fact that they were still in the house, and he had paid for the time. But Bell could sense that Teddy would have paid a small fortune to be with her and not in the way to which she was accustomed. He just wanted to be near her, no matter the cost.

His gaze never left her face, and it made Bell feel like her cheeks were aflame. Of course, no man had ever looked at her like this before. There was no want in his eyes, no lust. Instead, she saw longing, hope, and compassion. The need for intimacy was there, but not the intimacy men paid for by the hour. No, this was the kind of intimacy shared between souls.

Without looking away from her, he led her to the spacious kitchen where Sallie, the house cook and bartender, was preparing the food and drinks for the girls and their clients. In the corner of the room was a small table set for two. The lighting was dark, the chairs a bit wobbly, but hot food steamed off the plates. Teddy pulled out a chair, and she lowered herself as graciously as she could.

Seating himself, Teddy smiled at her. Still silent, he lifted his glass filled with a cheap red wine and held it toward her. Bell raised her own glass and gently clinked it together with his. She took a small sip, unsure if Teddy was much of a drinker, but he swallowed almost half the glass in one gulp. With his glass set down, Teddy began carving into the roast before him.

Bell looked at him, surprised. He wasn't going to insist on

blessing the food? Every pastor, preacher, and priest she had ever seen had always blessed food before cutting into it. Not wanting to be the one to break the silence, she shrugged to herself and slowly began to eat as well.

For the better part of twenty minutes, they ate in silence. Every so often, Bell would look up to see Teddy always watching her. His unfaltering gaze caused her to squirm in her seat, but it was endearing all the same. It gave her the chance to take him in as well, one small glance at a time.

His suit was faded gray. It was probably several years old and had served him well from his pulpit in Maryland, Bell thought to herself. His nearly black hair was in need of trimming, as strands fell straight over his right eye. With a deep breath, Bell could smell him. He smelled faintly of paint, but mostly of manly sweat and a hint of cedar. His hands were large, she had noticed that before. They were stronger than she would expect for a preacher, hard but not rough. She could tell between his hands and his eyes that he had never raised a hand in anger. That impressed her because Bell could remember her father disciplining her as a child with a paddle.

She knew he studied her in the same way. What did he see? The dress revealed nothing, as he had picked it out himself. Did her hands say anything about her as his did? She quickly flexed her fingers and wondered. Soft, yielding, but quietly strong. Did her face or her hair reveal her secrets as his did? Bell had worked very hard to be sure her face only told what she wanted it to, but she felt that this man could see beyond the falsities.

With their meal finished, Teddy stood and approached her chair from behind. He gently slid the uneasy seat from behind her and helped Bell to her feet. He flashed her a quick smile, then led her to one of the smallest client rooms in the house. It was the least favorite of all the girls being much too small for their tastes. They had nicknamed the room "The Hole," but Madam called it the Quaint Retreat. When he opened the door, Bell furrowed her brow. What was he doing? Why were they going into The Hole? Surely he didn't think that a proposal and dinner meant …? No, of course not. Not this man.

Her confusion must have shown because Teddy's smile grew wider, and he finally spoke. "Don't worry, my dear. We're just finding a quiet place to talk. I shall not touch you again."

Bell's nerves calmed as she walked through the doorway. Teddy turned both lights up as high as they would go so that they could see each other fully. Bell had to stifle a giggle. Not many clients wanted it as bright as day in these rooms. Teddy quickly took the large chair in the corner for himself, leaving Bell to sit upon the bed. At least he was true to his word – he could never touch her from the seat he was in.

"I don't usually talk in these rooms, Teddy," she admitted. "I try to say as little as possible."

Teddy cocked his head to the side. "Really? I must admit I'm very curious about what goes on in these rooms – the obvious aside, of course. I have wondered if you talk, if you lounge about, or what you do."

"I do my job. Nothing more than is required of me. I talk to the clients who want to talk. I am silent for those who want quiet. Many men just want someone to listen to them because their wives don't," Bell said as she glanced around the room.

The Hole was sparsely furnished. It was not for entertaining, it was to serve a purpose, a quick one at that. The room reminded her of the crib rooms she had seen before. Maybe that was why none of the girls liked this room.

"So, you are whatever they want you to be?" Teddy leaned closer, resting his elbows on his knees. The light glinted off his glasses, but Bell could still see his green eyes staring at her.

"Yes, exactly. My goal is to be and do what they want, so they are gone all the quicker. Very few have the notion of being entertained in these rooms," she said with a sigh. "George is one who wants to be entertained. He pays for the entire night every Tuesday. We have dinner, I listen to his prattle, then we …" She let her voice trail off, suddenly embarrassed by her actions, even though Teddy knew what she did not say.

"Every Tuesday?" was all Teddy asked. He did not judge her, and for that, she was thankful.

"Every Tuesday without fail. He's not married, though he was engaged to a nice girl from Mississippi. But she passed away just before they were to wed. That was almost fifteen years ago now. George never married, but he has proposed to me several times."

Teddy sat up straight as an arrow. "He has? When? Does he love you? Do you love him?"

Bell laughed at his concern. "Every few months, he tries again to get me to marry him. I always say no. I could never marry someone who bought my body before I gave him my heart. I will never love George Barnard. If he loves me, only he knows that."

Teddy brought the chair a foot closer to her, but still too far away to touch her. "I will never try to buy your body, Bell. You have to know that."

Bell's smile faded as quickly as a storm cloud covers the sun. "I know that," she said softly. "Poppy tried to tell me you only want to get married for a lay. But I told her that wasn't true." She lifted her eyes to meet his. So piercingly green. "Is it?"

He scooted his chair a little closer to her and gazed thoughtfully into her eyes. "I would never marry someone because I wanted their body. I would only marry someone I truly love, who I feel God is leading me to."

"Then why did you propose to me?" Bell did not understand the man before her. Did he love her? Did he really think this deity of his led him to her?

Teddy sighed. "Because I can't stop thinking about you, Bell. I keep thinking I want to save all the district girls, but selfishly I only want to save you. I don't know all the answers. I am a flawed man who makes mistakes. But I do know that when I see you, my world is brighter. When I hear your voice, it's like a song is resonating in my soul." He took a deep breath and closed his eyes.

When he opened his eyes, it was like he could see into her very soul, and Bell's breath hitched. Teddy began again, this time his voice soft but assured, "'If I speak in the languages of humans and angels but have no love, I have become a reverberating gong or a clashing cymbal. If I have the gift of prophecy and can understand all secrets and every form of knowledge, and if I have absolute faith so as to move mountains but have no love, I am nothing. Even if I give away everything that I have and sacrifice myself, but have no love, I gain nothing.'"

Tears sprang to Bell's eyes. "That's the most beautiful thing I've ever heard. It reminds me of something my mother used to recite to me."

Teddy looked at her tenderly. "Do you not know it? It's from the New Testament. First Corinthians. It's a scripture passage about love."

"My ... my mother used to say it to me. I have not heard it since I last heard her say it." Bell buried her face in her hands, tears rolling quickly down her face. It had been so long since she had thought of the comforting sound of her mother's voice.

Teddy quickly moved to her side but was careful not to

lay a hand on Bell. "I am so sorry. I had no idea that would cause you to hurt so."

"No, no," she said, lifting her head. "Oh, now I've made the make-up run, and you can see my horrible black eye."

"I don't care about the black eye," Teddy said gruffly. "Are you all right?"

"Yes, I am." Bell sniffed. "I'm sorry. I haven't thought of my mother's voice in so long. It's too painful. Lovely, but painful."

"My parents are passed on as well," Teddy admitted. "I understand how you feel."

"I didn't know that, Rev – Teddy. How did they die?"

"A mixture of age and heart problems, I was told. They had me so late in life; Mother was over forty when I was born. I was the surprise child, their other children were getting married when I came along." Teddy chuckled. "But I was a mere fifteen when my mother passed from heart failure, and my father went the next year of a broken heart."

"A broken heart? Can people really die from that?"

"Well, the doctors said it was a heart attack. But I think he only had a heart attack because his heart longed to be with Mother again," Teddy said, a small glint of a tear in his eye.

Shifting her head to the side, Bell sighed. "That is so sad. And sweet."

"Would you mind telling me what happened to your parents?" He moved back to the chair, inching it a little closer still as he sat.

Sighing, Bell pulled one stocking-clad foot under the rest of her body, leaving her shoe on the floor. "I was eleven years old and in bed one night when Shep, that was our family dog, came into my room whimpering. I shooed him away and pushed him away, but he would not leave me alone. That's when I smelled the smoke. I ran to my parents' door and banged on it, yelling for them to come out and get out of the house. Shep must have known how dangerous it was because he practically pulled me down the stairs of the house and out the front door. Our neighbors arrived just in time to watch the house collapse in, my parents still inside. They never came out."

Bell wiped more tears from her eyes, careful not to rub make-up into them. "I never understood why they never came out," she said, her voice heavy with tears. "The pastor's wife came and got me and took me back to their house. I was friends with their daughter, Becky. Nobody told me my parents had died. I just knew it." She stopped and took a deep breath. "I think it was two days later that my uncle showed up. I had only seen him two or three times total in my life. He showed up, and Pastor Davis just handed me over to him."

Bell quietly took a pillow from the head of the bed and balled it up in her arms and rested her chin on the top.

"And your uncle brought you here to New Orleans? Why?" Teddy raked his hands through his hair as he thought through her story. Bell's head was beginning to hurt, and the tears were stinging her cheek.

"I don't know. He just did," she snapped. Teddy jumped at her loud words. She hadn't meant to snap at him. "He brought me to several of the madams, telling them I was a virgin in my prime. He gave me to the one who offered him the most money – Madam Victoria Knight. A week later, I was debuted, and that was it. My life was over."

Bell looked up at the man; his face was red with rage.

"I can't believe your own flesh and blood would sell you off to the highest bidder," Teddy fumed. "If I could find that man right now, I would cut him down to size."

"You'd have to get in line, Teddy," she said. "I've already called first dibs on that one." She allowed herself a small smile.

"Your life isn't over, Bell. You're nineteen, your life is ahead of you," Teddy said, trying to sound as promising as he could. "Tell me what you wanted to be before your parents died."

"What I wanted to be?"

Teddy thought a moment. "You know, when you grew up. Did you want to be a teacher? A writer? A seamstress?"

Without hesitating, Bell smiled. "All I ever wanted to be was a mother," she replied.

~

*H*is heart might as well have soared off without him. Teddy had to mentally grab it back before it went to Bell completely. All she ever wanted was to be a mother? And her response was so honest, so pure, it had to be the truth.

He beamed and did not try to hide it. "Oh, Bell, you can still be a mother! If you marry me, we can start a family right away if you like," he said, knowing his voice was full of hope.

But Bell's face fell. "I've been here eight years. Eight years of doing what I do, and I have not fallen pregnant once," she admitted. "Not that I want to, mind you. Not like this. But the way I see it, either she gives us something to prevent pregnancy, or there's something wrong with me."

Teddy's smile fell with hers. He had never considered before that she could have – or should have – had a child by this point. But he did know of many prostitutes who had children. Some had many children. He also knew many a girl who admitted openly to having her unborn child disposed of in the most inhumane way he could ever imagine. But didn't he also hear through the whispers how some madams gave their girls a concoction to keep them from becoming with child? Yes, he had.

"Bell, has any girl here even been with child?"

She thought a moment. "Well, maybe about six years ago, a girl called Violet came up pregnant. Madam kicked Violet out onto the street. Her beau had left her, too. I don't know what happened to her," Bell said, her voice trailing off. "But otherwise, no. No one that I know of has been pregnant."

"Maybe Madam Knight is giving you all something to keep you from conceiving, like you said. There are many old Indian and Creole concoctions for keeping one from having a baby. They would mash it up and put it into drinks and food," Teddy suggested.

It was as if a light had been illuminated over Bell. "Do you think? I have always wondered. Not that it mattered, really, because nobody would marry me – especially if I had a child. But to think that I'm not broken after all is, well, it just makes me feel hope."

"I would marry you," Teddy said. He felt like he was repeating that line over and over. Bell really had no sense of self-worth. It had been drained out of her, one night at a time for the past eight years. He would try to do everything in his power to show her just how precious she was, both in his sight and in the Lord's.

"Oh, Teddy," she sighed. "You might just wear me down if you keep talking like that." She picked at a rogue string on her skirt, her eyes focused on it rather than him. "Did you always want to be a minister?"

"I was raised going to church," he said. "My father was a deacon and expected me to live my life for God. After my parents passed, my older brothers and sisters sent me to seminary. I think it was more to keep me out of their hair than anything else. I was quite the spirited child," he chuckled. "But I fell in love with God's Word and was mentored by an amazing man, Billy Sunday. Through his work, I felt a great burden for those who are lost."

Bell scrunched up her nose. "Lost?"

"Those without salvation," he explained. Oh, how he loved talking about salvation. "I decided I would dedicate my life to bringing people to faith in Christ Jesus." Teddy's heart burst with pride in the Lord, just as he hoped God burst with pride over him.

But then Bell's face fell. He could tell she felt let down by the church, but now he understood more of why she resisted the Lord so much. Not only did her parents perish in a fire, but the very church that should have loved her and protected her handed her over to a greedy man who sold her like a slave. Then the God she had learned about in Sunday school seemingly abandoned her on the steps of the brothel. Her bitterness was apparent to him now. But he wasn't sure how to change it.

"I wish I could turn back the hands of time to protect you, Bell," he said. He still longed to reach out to her, to smooth the chestnut curls on her back. "But know that the people of that church probably thought sending you with a relative was the best thing for you. I'm sure they did not wish ill things upon you."

"I know that," Bell exhaled. "But if there is a God, why did he let my parents die? Why didn't they come out of their room? Why didn't this God protect me from the stream of dirty men who forced themselves on me and called it a good time?"

Teddy shook his head. "I wish I knew, darlin'. I only know that God builds us up the most when we are at our lowest. But this won't last forever. I know I keep repeating myself, but if you would agree to marry me, you could end this part of your pain right now."

She stood and began to pace the floor. Teddy noticed a slight limp on her left leg. "Are you all right, Bell? Please sit back down."

"I'm not all right, Teddy," she cried out. "I'm battered. Last night, a very large, mean man used me as a punching bag before and after he raped me. Don't you see? I'm not all right. This is my life, Teddy. I sicken myself, I can't imagine how much I must sicken you." She paused and looked at him with tears welled up in her eyes, daring to spill over. "I am not good enough for you, Teddy Sullivan. Can you not see that? I will never be the preacher's wife type of person."

Teddy only saw a beautiful and broken woman, afraid to let anyone in. Her scars ran deep, the emotional ones far deeper than any physical ones on her alabaster skin. If she would only let him in, he could introduce her to the healing powers of God. He rubbed his eyes, tired from the emotional upheaval of the evening. If he felt this beat, he could only imagine Bell felt ten times worse.

He stood and quietly spoke, "I will go now, Bell. Please know I did not intend to upset you in any way. My offer still stands." As he made his way toward the door, he said one last thing. "I open the doors of my church on Sunday. Please come, even if you don't intend to listen. I would like a familiar face in the crowd." He silently put the book of Psalms on the chair, opened the door, and slipped out, leaving Bell standing in the center of the room.

Without a word, he slid out of the building and into the chilly night sky. Brooding the entire way back to the hotel, Teddy entertained the thought of giving up on Bell, but that was exactly what she was trying to get him to do. Instead, he prayed.

Lord, what have you dealt me? What is going on in my life? I don't know what your plan is, Lord, and though I know it will always be divinely perfect, right now I have my doubts. Why did I propose marriage to that girl? Is she who you have chosen for me? Or am I being too rash in this offer? It is too late now, isn't it? If she accepts, I must follow through. Though, Lord, I doubt she will accept. How can I save the lost souls of the world if I can't save the soul of the woman who seems to have stolen my heart? Help me, Lord. I have nothing – only your promise to be with me wherever I go. So, guide me, be with me, God. Show me the way, because I sure feel lost now.

CHAPTER 8

eddy managed to stay away from the spa for the past two days. He busied himself getting last minute things ready for Sunday morning. He prayed for there to be standing room only come ten o'clock, but he knew, in reality, he would be happy with a dozen chairs filled. He had made fliers and handed them out like candy to everyone and anyone he passed. He posted them on walls and benches. He handed them to the crib girls as he held his breath from their stench. He stood at the start of Storyville and handed them to the men sneaking into the district.

Yes, he picked more than a few from off the ground after they had been discarded, but he was not dissuaded. He would preach God's truth and love and hope that New Orleans was ready to hear it.

At nine forty-five Sunday morning, Teddy threw open the doors, ready to welcome parishioners in for his ten o'clock service. Nobody was waiting outside, but there was time still. He remembered that he had made a sign to go out front and quickly went to fetch it and set it out along the roadside. It read, "Forgiven Grace Church: All Walks of Life Welcome."

Forgiven Grace Church was proudly waiting for any who would enter. The freshly painted sign hung proudly at the double doors that sat propped open. Teddy waited outside and felt a crisp breeze announce the arrival of autumn as it swirled around him. Then he meandered inside, not wanting to seem overly anxious. He straightened a few chairs, the legs screeching over the hardwood floors.

Minutes ticked by too quickly with nobody entering the oversized doors. Teddy nervously removed his glasses and wiped away imaginary dust. He replaced them and glanced to the door again.

Then he heard the shuffle of feet outside. It was nine fifty-seven. Astrid came in, followed by Zinnia and Jasmine. "Are we late, Reverend Teddy?"

He smiled wide, happy to see them. "No! Girls, come in! I am surprised, pleasantly surprised, to see you here. I think the cool air is holding people up. We will wait a few more minutes." He opened his arms wide, inviting them to sit wherever they wanted.

As the girls filed in, Teddy glanced behind them, looking for anyone else – a certain brunette in particular. Astrid stopped beside him, her feathered hat blocking her face from his view.

"She's coming with Clover and Sallie, don't worry," she whispered. "I think a lot of girls from the spa are coming this morning, and maybe a few others, too."

Sure enough, as the three ladies took their seats, a group of four dark-skinned men he had seen working in the brothels came in. "'Scuse me, sir?" one asked. "Is colored folks allowed in here?"

Teddy gave them a big smile and clasped the hand of the one who spoke. "All God's children are allowed, no matter their color and no matter their profession. Please come in." One of the men leaned back out the door and waved, and two light-skinned colored women hesitantly shuffled in as well. They took seats in the back two rows of the room.

Teddy beamed with pride. Almost ten people. Even without Bell, he felt successful, but he prayed she would show her face. He slowly walked to the front of the room and stood at his homemade pulpit, where his Bible lay open and waiting for him.

Just before he opened his mouth to welcome everyone, another group came in the door. It was Bell. And with her was little Clover and the cook, Sallie, with her two children. He smiled and cleared his voice as they slipped into seats in the middle of the congregation.

"I am so happy to have you here," he said to everyone, but he meant it doubly for Bell. "Thank you for coming for the inaugural sermon for the Forgiven Grace Church. We welcome everybody in our doors, be you white or negro, wealthy or poor, man or woman. God wants us all to come to him – we are no different in His eyes. I am hoping to soon be able to purchase a small organ so we can sing hymns, but until then, we will make do with just our voices. But first," he said with a deep breath, "let us bow our heads in prayer."

The fourteen heads seated before him lowered their heads to the floor. Teddy felt like he was soaring but tried not to let pride get ahead of him. He lifted a quick, silent prayer for the right words, then spoke. "Lord, we come to You this most holy of days to give You thanks for Your divine ways. We may not know the plans You have for us, Lord, but we know they are perfect in Your will. We thank You for sending Your Son Christ Jesus to atone for our sins, Father. We give blessings to You and ask that You bless us in return. Amen."

A chorus of amens lifted from the group, and their heads rose. Teddy looked directly at Bell as she looked up. Her gaze met his, and he prayed for God to touch her heart most of all.

Her eye looked better, make-up now covering an ugly shade of green instead of the purple it had been.

"Do any of you have Bibles?" he asked. Astrid held up her hand, and one of the men he did not know also did. "That's okay. It is not a requirement. I will be reading the scripture anyway.

"Today, we will look at passages on forgiveness, since the name of this church is Forgiven Grace. God longs to forgive all of us for our misdeeds, no matter how heinous they may be. Nobody is beyond reproach if the Lord is with them," he began. He pushed his glasses up onto his nose and checked his place in his Bible.

"Psalm Fifty-One reads, 'Have mercy upon me, O God, according to thy lovingkindness: according unto the multitude of thy tender mercies blot out my transgressions. Wash me thoroughly from mine iniquity, and cleanse me from my sin. For I acknowledge my transgressions, and my sin is ever before me.'" He took a breath and looked out at the people. Did they understand what he said? Did they care? Teddy prayed for it to get through to them.

"Ladies and gentlemen, this means that God can forgive you of your sins. This psalm was written by King David after he had committed adultery – he had slept with a married woman, he himself being married as well. Many times we see a Biblical man like King David and think of how holy he was, how much he loved God. But he made mistakes, too. We all do. None are perfect but can be washed pure as snow with the love of Jesus."

He spoke on, pleading with his congregation to ask for God to forgive them and to sin no more. He had already planned for the next week to speak on the woman condemned by the Pharisees, but when Jesus asked that the one without sin to cast the first stone at her, they all left. He wanted these people to see that everyone was full of sin, but God would give them complete forgiveness.

Bell sat with her eyes fixed on him; Teddy could feel it, even though he did his best to look at the other people seated before him. Once he finished his message, he implored everyone to return the next week and to please bring a friend with them. He also invited them to stay after to talk or have some coffee. He prayed one more time in closing, then stepped down from his pulpit.

The girls from the spa were slow to stand, but the men and women he did not know left quickly. Perhaps the next week they would stay to chat.

Astrid approached Teddy and smiled warmly. "Oh, Reverend Teddy, that was a wonderful sermon," she gushed. "I really felt it speak to me, and it's so nice to have a reminder that we are all sinners but are washed clean by the blood of Christ."

He shook the girl's hand. "Thank you, Astrid. It's nice to know my message got across." He then remembered the telegraph he had sent on her behalf. "Oh, Astrid, I wanted to let you know I posted a letter to Roanoke but then decided to send a telegraph. I'm hoping to get a response this week."

The redhead's cheeks flamed the color of her hair. "Oh, thank you! I have been praying that my family is still out there and still wants me!"

"I can't imagine anyone not wanting you, Astrid. But I promise you, even if we can't find your family, I will get you out of here." If her parents could not be found, he would see to it that the gentle girl was given a proper position somewhere else as a tutor or governess, for she was very bright.

Astrid glanced over to where Bell stood with the young Clover. They were talking quietly with Sallie and her children. Teddy guessed the little boy was close to twelve and the girl not quite ten – the same age as Clover. Astrid leaned closer to Teddy and spoke quietly to him.

"She's been reading the book you got her. I don't know what you talked about with her the other day, but she's been very withdrawn. But not in a bad way. Bell has been very deep in thought. Thankfully, Madam has been true to her word, and Bell has been confined to the parlor this weekend. She has not taken a single client further than the curtains, which I think she appreciated more than the men. And she's stayed covered up. But whatever your plans are for winning her over, you better do quickly. Tomorrow, Madam will put her back to work, still bruised or not."

"Thank you, Astrid. Or shall I call you Ginny?" he asked tenderly.

She beamed and nodded as she bit her bottom lip.

"All right then, Ginny. God has surely blessed her with a friend like you to look out for her."

"Oh, no, I'm the blessed one," she said in reply, then excused herself back to Zinnia and Jasmine.

~

*B*ell glanced up and saw Teddy striding toward her. Her heart began to beat quicker, and she pleaded with it to slow down. She was still skeptical about God, but the words Teddy had spoken resonated within her. The God he spoke of was one of forgiveness and love. Was that God real? Or was it the merciless God who left her to wither away who was real?

As Teddy approached, Bell noticed his suit. It was the same one he had worn the previous Thursday when he had called on her. He did look dashing in it, the gray making his eyes look all the more green. Those eyes were always smiling, it seemed. Bell wondered if they ever showed melancholy.

"Sallie, I am so happy you came today and brought your children," Teddy said, looking at the cook. "Tell me your children's names again? I have a terrible memory when it comes to names."

Bell wasn't sure if she should be relieved or offended that he addressed Sallie first. But Bell did notice that even though Teddy did not speak directly to her, he grinned in her direction, and she thought he gave her a little wink.

"This is my son, Thomas. I'm sure you've seen him around, he runs errands for lotsa people," she said proudly. "And this here is Josephine." Sallie put her hands on the shoulders of her children, a very proud mother.

Bell was pleased as Teddy reached out to shake Thomas's hand. "Nice to meet you, young man. It's a pleasure." The boy nodded back sternly and returned the preacher's firm grip. "Josephine, you are a vision like your mother." The little girl grinned at Teddy.

Finally, he turned toward Bell and Clover, but he again skipped over greeting Bell. "Oh, Clover, you're wearing the dress I sent for you. It looks wonderful."

Clover beamed but for once was quiet. She glanced up to Bell quickly before she and Sallie's children took off running, Sallie chasing after them.

Alone, Bell suddenly felt nervous. Teddy took a step closer. "Thank you for coming, Bell," he said in a voice just above a whisper. "It means more than you can ever know."

Still not meeting his gaze, she replied, "Well, Astrid really wanted to come and bring the girls. I couldn't let them walk alone."

It was a poor lie. Yes, Astrid had practically begged her to come, but she hadn't needed to. Bell was curious about this God

Teddy was always talking about and Astrid constantly prayed to. And she wanted to see Teddy, plain as day. Teddy leaned a hand on one of the chairs, his other hand casually tucked into his pocket. He was so relaxed, Bell thought. Teddy was comfortable while she felt like a fish out of water, drowning in the air.

Teddy looked serious, though his eyes still seemed to smile. "Did you get a chance to look at the book I left for you?"

"I did," Bell said hesitantly. "Thank you very much. I'm sorry I was such a pain the other night. But I do love the book. As I said before, it reminds me of my parents. My father's favorite book was Psalms. I grew up hearing them all the time, so the words were so familiar." Bell finally held her gaze steady onto his. "I didn't realize how much I had missed hearing and reading them."

It was obvious Teddy wanted to reach out and take her hand, but he held himself back. It was sweet, the reverend being afraid to touch her. Instead, he ran his hand through his unkempt hair and stuffed it back into his pocket. "I am so glad you are enjoying it. How are you feeling now?"

With a sigh, Bell gingerly touched her eye. "Well, I'm green and yellow instead of black and purple," she said with a slight smile. "I'm off parlor duty tomorrow. It's been so nice not having to …" she trailed off. She didn't want to talk about work with him.

"It's okay, I understand," he said. "Is your dance card for tomorrow filled?" Bell smiled and giggled a little at his joke, as did Teddy. "Well, if not, I would love to call on you again. I promise I will try not to offend you this time."

"I believe I am free tomorrow," she said coyly. It was nice pretending he was a true suitor. It made her feel more human and less like a piece of flesh. "As long as you have the money for Madam," she reminded him. "I can't imagine you can keep paying for entire evenings with me, though."

"Don't worry about that, sweetheart," he said. "Just be ready for an evening of old-fashioned fun. And every other evening this week if it keeps you from having to earn money in other ways."

Bell beamed. He really was a very respectful man. "I appreciate that. But I'm more concerned for the other girls. Keeping me from lying on my back only brings more of it to them," she said, looking at Zinnia and Astrid. "They don't deserve that. Besides, I have regulars. George Barnard comes in every Tuesday, without fail, just for me."

At that moment, the smile did fade briefly from Teddy's eyes. Jealousy and rage flashed before Bell. His eyes fell to the floor before he spoke.

"I hate this, Bell," he said, his voice low, but the anger was apparent. "I won't lie, I am envious of the time you spend with these men. I don't want you anywhere near them. I don't want them touching you. I feel the same for all the girls of the district, but with you, it's personal."

Bell puckered her lips as if she had tasted bitter lemons. "You made it personal, Reverend," she pointed out. "I've been doing this for years now, and it's never been personal before. I don't like it, but it never bothered me like this before you came into my life. Now I'm even more ashamed of the life I lead."

"My goal is not to shame you, I swear it. I know I made it personal between us, but I could not help myself," he explained. Bell watched his face contort to a scowl, his voice following suit. "From the moment I first saw you through the doorway of the spa, those sad, dark eyes looking up at me, I felt drawn to you. Like God led me right to you. Then as I have gotten to know you, though I admit I don't know as much as I would like, I have felt even more for you. I don't know if it is love, but I know I did not choose these feelings, they chose me."

Tears filled Bell's eyes at his gentle expressions. Oh, if only he could understand that these feelings were not of love, but of his own ego trying to save the world. And right now, she was the one he so desperately felt the need to save. But that didn't stop the words he spoke and the actions he took from taking root in her heart. What had started as tender stirrings deep inside her had turned into near burning longings that spread throughout her entire being. But she could never let Teddy know that. Bell knew that her station in life could never suit the morality of someone like Teddy.

After a pause, Bell shook her head. "Oh, Teddy, you've only made me into your pet project. Why do you feel such a need to rescue me? I welcome your company, but please stop with these silly notions of love."

Teddy only nodded, his eyes downcast. Bell felt badly if she had hurt his feelings, and she almost reached out to him but thought it best to maintain a safe distance. For his good as well as her own. Talking about love seemed as useless as bathing in mud, Bell thought. It only served to soil things more. Besides, if true love did exist, Bell had never seen it.

She murmured a quiet goodbye to Teddy and headed for the door, the other girls shortly behind her. The walk home was silent, and she toiled in her head over Teddy's speech about forgiveness, and then his profession of almost-love. She wanted to believe him but wasn't sure she could – or knew how.

The following evening, Teddy came into the spa, as he promised. When she saw him, Bell felt her heart jump and her pulse race, and she willed it to calm. Why did it do that? She felt the urge to jump up and rush to him, but she made herself stay seated. Eagerness would only encourage his attempts at getting her to accept his proposal.

Her nose stayed buried in her book – the one he had gotten her – while she peered over the top of the pages at him. Before he could cross the parlor to her, Poppy and Daisy approached him, blocking him from getting close to Bell. They spoke in hushed tones, obviously trying to be sure Bell did not hear their advances.

"... both of us together ..." she heard Poppy say. Bell could hear the devilish sneer in Poppy's voice even through the broken fragments of speech.

"... ever so much fun, Reverend," Daisy added, tossing her straight, dark hair over her shoulder.

Teddy shook his head and said no to whatever they were proposing to him, but they did not give up their pursuit. Poppy stepped a little closer and pushed her chest out toward him.

"Come on, haven't you always dreamed ..." Poppy said before her voice became much too quiet to overhear. Teddy's eyes widened, and his face blanched.

Bell could feel the flush in her cheeks as rage flashed in her eyes. She immediately stood and marched over to the trio, ready to give Poppy and her crony the fight of their life for being so bold with a man of the cloth. Her man of the cloth.

Instead, Bell wedged herself between the two girls and flung her arms around Teddy's neck. Without so much as a peep, Bell pressed her lips to his and locked her hands behind him. She closed her eyes and nearly melted at the taste of Teddy's mouth. And as far as she could tell, he was kissing her back.

After a moment, she let go and gasped for breath. Teddy did the same. Bell turned her head slightly toward the other girls as if to challenge them, but instead, they retreated. Bell took the still dumbfounded Teddy by the hand, grabbed her book, and gingerly pulled him back past the velvety curtain that led down the hall.

But instead of going to one of the house rooms, Bell led

Teddy to her room. She released his hand and took a seat on Astrid's bed, allowing Teddy to sit upon her own.

She smiled and almost laughed. "I'm sorry for coming on so strong. But when I overheard a few of the words they were saying and saw how you paled, I felt the need to do something drastic."

Teddy, still dumbfounded, barely shook his head. "All this time, I have taken such care not to touch you for fear of you thinking I was using you, and you just kiss me like that as if it were nothing." His eyes were still wide; his limbs hung loosely at his sides.

"It was nothing," she said flippantly. She waved her hand in the air. "A way to get Queen Poppy and Daisy away from you. You were clearly uncomfortable." Bell didn't see the reason for Teddy's shock.

Slowly, Teddy blinked a few times. "It wasn't nothing, Bell," he said. His voice sounded crushed. "It was something. To me, it was very much something. I have not touched you out of respect and decency, though I have longed to run my hands through your hair and to kiss your mouth. Yet you did just that without an ounce of desire or passion behind it. It was just a game for you."

Bell blinked several times as she tried to understand. She would have never thought a kiss could be so personal. Apparently, a kiss was much more than lips brushing up against one another.

"I'm sorry, Teddy. I did not realize it was so different for you," she stammered. "I was just so angry with what Poppy was suggesting that I felt the need to ... to ..."

"Stake your claim?" Teddy asked, his eyebrow raised.

"Well, yes," Bell faltered. "Um, no. Not like that. I mean ..."

"Mean what?" Teddy smiled at her.

Bell flung her hands up into the air. "Oh, never mind," she

exclaimed. "I don't have to explain myself to you. It was just a way to save you from their wiles is all. I'm sorry if I offended you," she said with a huff.

Chuckling, Teddy assured her, "You did not offend me, dear Bell. I may be a preacher, but I have kissed my fair share of women. Though you are the first to have kissed me. I just thought that with the delicacy of our relationship, it would be best if we did not touch."

"So, you want to preserve your reputation of holier-than-thou preacher in town?"

"I wanted to preserve our relationship, Bell. I didn't want you to think I was only spending time with you because of my physical attraction to you. I want you to know that I am completely serious about my marriage proposal, and I intend to be a complete gentleman when it comes to how I handle you."

Feeling unabashed by her actions, Bell moved to sit next to Teddy. "I appreciate that," she said quietly. "But you don't have to treat me with kid gloves, you know. You can touch me. I won't bite or melt away."

And with that, Bell took Teddy's hand into hers, and she kissed his palm. Then each of his fingers. She moved closer toward his mouth, but he stopped her.

"Bell, stop. Please. This is not how I want us to be. I am not one of your johns who needs to feel you under him. I don't want your body, Bell," he pleaded. "I want all of you. I want you to love me."

Bell sat up straight, "Love is a fairy tale, Teddy. And life is not."

"No, Bell. Love is not a fairy tale. Did you not read this book?" He pointed to the Psalms on the bedside table. "In this book are some of the most wonderful love stories and songs anyone has ever heard. And not only the power of love between a man and woman, but also between us and God.

Oh, Bell, He longs to love you. So much more than I do. Why don't you understand that?"

Bell stood, anger once again rising in her. Why didn't Teddy understand her? "He left me here to die! Don't you remember us having this conversation before? Will we fight over this every time we see each other? Your God left me here!" she practically screamed. "All I have of worth is my body. Nothing else. Love is a luxury I cannot afford; neither is a God that may or may not exist. If He is truly out there, let Him prove it to me."

Teddy took off his glasses, then put them back on his nose as he considered her words. "How can He prove His existence to you? God always rises to a challenge." He did not know what she would say, but he would try his hardest to give her a chance at faith in Christ.

"How do you know that?" She folded her arms and turned from him. Bell didn't believe him, but she wanted to.

"In the Bible, there was a man named Gideon whom God wanted to use to save Israel. But Gideon wasn't too sure," Teddy explained. "So, he laid a piece of fleece on the ground and asked that God make the fleece wet and the ground dry. It happened, and then Gideon asked again for the fleece to be dry and the ground wet. It happened as he asked, so Gideon knew that God was truly speaking to him."

Bell furrowed her brow. "I have never heard that story. It was never in my Sunday School classes."

"It's in Judges. I can show you if you have a Bible," Teddy offered.

"No, I believe it's there," she said. "It's too far-fetched not to be. Let me think." Bell paced the floor around Teddy for a moment as she thought, her skirts swooshing behind her. Suddenly, an idea came to her. "I have it!"

"Name it. God will prove that He is real if you truly seek

Him." Teddy closed his eyes, his lips barely moving. He was praying for her, she realized.

"I hope you know what you're talking about, Reverend," Bell said, "because I don't want to have to disrobe for any man for the next two weeks. At all. If that happens, I will believe that your God is truly out there and truly does care for me and the other girls here. But I promise you this, if I have to show my skin to any man, you will know about it, and you will not be welcome back here again."

Teddy only nodded.

CHAPTER 9

*T*eddy had no idea how he was going to keep Bell from lying with men for two whole weeks. He couldn't afford to pay Victoria Knight to give Bell two weeks off; his personal bank account was not that large. He couldn't stand in the doorway and scare off any men coming to see her – he might be tall, but he was not intimidating.

He also wondered how he would get the other girls away from the brothel. Clover, he had noticed, was spending more time in the parlor. Was the time of her debut coming quickly? And Astrid was inching ever closer to being turned out without a penny to her name.

As he walked back to his room that night after seeing Bell, he wracked his mind for ways to keep Bell from doing Madam Knight's bidding for two weeks. After stating her way of testing God's existence, she then revealed that she might see up to ten or twelve men a week. Most were regulars, but many were not. Teddy tried not to be disgusted with the numbers he added up. They weren't her fault, but he was very discouraged by them.

After much thought, Teddy only knew to pray. God was

the only one who could prove Himself to Bell. But Teddy would do his best to be at the spa as many nights as he could. He fell asleep praying for God to reveal Himself to Bell and the other girls, as she was sure to share her challenge with the others.

He awoke feeling refreshed and eager to start the day. More items were needed at the church, and he hoped to solicit some donations from area businesses. Teddy had heard of a jazz pianist who was a "spiritual sort of man," from what he was told. Perhaps he would be willing to put his gift to use in a more holy way. After washing and praying, Teddy set out on his errands.

When he had completed those, he returned home to change and head to the spa. As he walked, he prayed for the right words to say to Bell and anyone else willing to listen. He begged God to show up in the brothel that night.

He arrived promptly at six, just before the sun began to set behind Basin Street. Madam Knight gave him a warm but pithy smile as he entered the parlor. He was something of a fixture now, and everybody knew why after his previous eruption of a proposal.

The girls looked from him to Bell with a ready whisper on their lips. Poppy and Daisy huddled close together in a corner. Teddy nodded at Zinnia and the young man she was talking to on the couch. Jasmine came around with drinks on a tray, and she flashed her pure-white teeth to him and greeted him warmly. The only person Teddy longed to talk to, however, was Bell.

She crossed the room to him; an air of nervousness was about her. "I don't think this will work, Teddy," she said, her voice barely a whisper as she stepped close to him. She looked down and fiddled with the flowers on the table between them. "George is a regular. He proposes to me all the time as he prepares to leave the bed. He will not take no for an answer tonight, Teddy."

Teddy closed his eyes for a moment and tried to steady himself. "Have faith, Bell. Please, have faith. Pray with all your might that dinner and conversation will suffice tonight," he said, trying to convince himself as well as Bell.

He looked up to her, and she briefly met his gaze. While their eyes locked, Teddy felt Bell's smooth hand flutter over his own. Reassurance for them both and hope for Teddy that perhaps Bell's affection toward him was growing. He smiled at her, both to tell her he cared and that he believed God cared as well.

When the door chimes rang out, Bell's eyes averted from him, and she stepped back, breaking their connection. Her gaze shot over his shoulder, and a warm but artificial smile came across her face. Bell risked one brief glance at Teddy before she sashayed away, and he could see the pleading in her dark eyes. Teddy slowly turned, trying to look casual, as Bell extended her arms toward the tall, skinny man before her.

"Oh, George, there you are! You will love tonight's supper," she exclaimed in a syrupy sweet voice as she linked arms with the man, and they made slow steps through the room.

As she told him the menu with more gusto than anyone had ever described chicken before, she led the man past Teddy. For a split-second, Teddy felt Bell's hand brush his before he watched her skirts swish back behind the curtains – a sign, he knew. She trusted him. Teddy only hoped she trusted Him as well.

He turned, feeling desolate. Praying was the only thing he could do now, despite his urge to run after them or shout that he saw a fire. But really, he just wanted to protect Bell with everything he had, even if that meant landing his fist squarely in the jaw of every other man who even looked at Bell. Instead, he sank down on a chair and raked his hands through his hair and begged God to keep her safe for these next two weeks.

Poppy and Daisy did not approach him; instead, they decided to team up on a newcomer. Madam had slipped away to her office for the moment. Zinnia and her caller were still sitting on the couch, but Zinnia waved at Teddy when he glanced their way. Her expression was inviting and very genuine. Teddy guessed that her friend was more than just a john, and for Zinnia's sake, he hoped that was true as the man nuzzled into Zinnia's shoulder.

About twenty minutes later, Astrid came out from the back of the house with a short but well-dressed man trailing behind her like a puppy. She was wearing nightclothes with a robe covering them, and as soon as she saw Teddy, her mouth went agape, and she pulled the robe up to her neck. She bade the man goodbye and stood about five feet from Teddy, her eyes downcast.

"I am so sorry you are seeing me like this, Reverend," she said. Teddy thought she sounded like she was about to break down into sobs.

"No, Astrid – Ginny," he said calmly. "Do not be ashamed. Remember the woman brought before Jesus caught in adultery? Not one could condemn her, because they were all full of sin themselves. I do not condemn you, and neither does Jesus. Your faith saves you despite the situation you find yourself in."

With that, Astrid fell into a chair in a fit of tears. Teddy did not want to touch her inappropriately, so he settled on smoothing out her straight red hair. He hoped it calmed her without looking like he was trying to manhandle her. Zinnia left her beau and crouched down next to Astrid.

"It's okay, Astrid, really," she said in a hushed voice. "Reverend Teddy is right. Just because we're stuck in this life doesn't mean we aren't washed clean by God."

Astrid looked up. The black liner from around her eyes was washing down her cheeks, and Teddy handed her his handkerchief. As she dabbed her eyes, she nodded at Zinnia.

"I know, I just hate this," she said. "In less than a month, I will be turned out on the streets." She looked up to Teddy. "Have you heard anything yet?"

Teddy shook his head. He had hoped to hear something by now, but he would certainly double-check at the telegraph office the next morning.

"I hope to hear any day now. Don't lose hope, my dear. Listen, just twenty minutes ago, Bell went back there with the hope and faith that she will not have to … perform tonight. I know God will pull through for her and for you soon." Teddy prayed that God would allow his words to become truth.

Before anyone could say anything else, George Barnard came flying into the parlor from the back of the house. "Madam Knight! Madam Knight! I demand to see you at once," he beckoned.

Teddy's eyes flew to the curtains the man had just burst through. Just as Madam Knight appeared before Mr. Barnard, Teddy saw Bell appear in the doorway just inside the velvety red curtains.

"Mr. Barnard, please!" Madam Knight said with her arms waving in front of her. "Whatever could be the matter?"

Teddy turned his attention back toward Madam Knight but then decided to focus more on Bell. He wanted to close the chasm of space that seemed to loom between them, but without knowing what was going on, he knew he needed to stay where he was. He just watched Bell, her nearly black eyes wide and scared and her chest rising with heavy breaths.

George Barnard bellowed at the madam, "I come here

week after week, and I expect my prize – my beauty – to be flawless. And when I comment on the color around her eyes, she tells me that Nigel Harding has made her entire body black and blue? How can you allow such impropriety, Madam Knight?"

Victoria Knight was a businesswoman, and she knew just how to react. "Oh, Mr. Barnard. I was also upset by what that despicable Nigel Harding did to my poor Bluebell. I assure you, he has been properly chastised and will not be allowed into this fine establishment again to lay a hand on any of my beautiful girls."

This, however, was not a good enough answer for the irate Mr. Barnard. "Is that all? A mere slap on the wrist for assaulting the girl I adore?" With that, Teddy returned his gaze to Bell, who stood motionless, staring at the commotion along with the rest of the room. "This is unacceptable, Madam Knight. I will see to Nigel Harding myself," he announced.

With that, George Barnard pulled a pistol from the inside of his jacket and marched squarely for the door. A few of the girls gasped, Bell included. She began to run after the man, but Teddy quickly grabbed her wrist to stop her. If George Barnard was this upset, there was no telling what he might do.

Once the door closed, Madam Knight clasped her hands to her bosom. "Well, wasn't that exciting? Please, everyone, there is no danger here. Please go back to your pleasantries," she said.

Zinnia went back over to her caller. Astrid looked to Teddy and Bell. Madam Knight also looked to the pair and stepped toward them. "Bluebell, what is the meaning behind all this? Is this some sort of joke?"

Bell cast her eyes down. "No, Madam. Just as he said, he asked about my eye. I told him the truth, as I am very fond of

George. When he asked if there were more bruises, I showed him my shoulder, which is still pretty ugly. He became furious, saying nobody was allowed to touch me in such a way. It was very heroic to see, actually. He feels like he needs to defend my honor."

Madam Knight folded her arms, pushing her chest up even closer to her chin. "Hrumph. At least he pays in advance," she said. Then a sinister grin came across her face. "And as far as him defending your honor? He pays for your honor, sweetie. And paying for it and defending it are more than this sack of potatoes does," she said, pointing to Teddy. "He just sits here like a lost puppy, waiting for his mistress to throw him a bone."

Before anyone could retort, Madam Knight sauntered away, howling at her own joke. She retreated into her office yet again and shut the door behind her.

Astrid got to her feet and took Bell's hands into hers. "Are you okay?"

"Yes, I am." Bell smiled. "I can't believe that worked. I put extra make-up on my eye and shoulder tonight – black and brown – so they looked worse. When I told George about Nigel Harding and showed him my shoulder, he really did fly off the handle. I thought it would just keep him from touching me tonight – I did not think he would leave."

She looked to Teddy and sighed, taking one hand from Astrid and extending it to him. The three held hands for a moment, thankful for one night out of fourteen to be put behind them.

Soon, Astrid retired to her room, and Zinnia and her caller had also disappeared, leaving Bell and Teddy alone in the parlor. Only Madam Knight's watchful eye and Jasmine's occasional offer of a drink kept them from being truly alone. Even Hodges, the piano player, was absent.

The pair sat on the couch, burrowed deep in the corner of

the room. It afforded them the most privacy, but Teddy made sure they could be seen if anyone looked for them. He still strove to keep his relationship with Bell as pure and innocent as possible while she was in the house, and that included how they were viewed by others.

"Are you starting to believe in the power of God?" he asked her.

"I still don't know, Teddy," she said, not looking him in the eye. "I'm very thankful and surprised about tonight. And before you came today, I had decided to pray that God would show me how to avoid being with George, and I had the make-up idea. I don't know if God gave me the idea or if I came up with it myself. How do I know?"

"You trust," Teddy told her. "You trust that God gave you the idea. And that he sent that man running from this place. You can't ask for much more."

"I am willing to admit that you might be right. I'm not saying you are, just that you might be," she said, a hint of teasing in her voice. She sighed, then her voice turned serious. "But I still don't see how God cares for a girl like me. I don't see how you care for a girl like me, either."

"Before all the commotion, I was talking to Astrid. She had come out here with a man, and when he left, she broke down over my seeing her like that. I reminded her about the prostitute Jesus forgave. Do you know that scripture?"

Bell shook her head, "No. I didn't know there were whores in the Bible."

She turned more toward him and leaned in a little closer. Teddy could smell the scent of lavender waft off of her, but he tried to keep his mind focused on recalling the verses in John.

"In the book of John, a woman is brought before Jesus," he began. "She was caught in the act of adultery. It is widely believed that she was a prostitute. The holy men of the day brought her to Jesus, saying that the law commands that she be stoned to death for such an act." Bell's eyes widened, and she gasped. "They asked Jesus what should be done. They hoped to get him into trouble one way or another, but that's not the point I'm trying to make. Jesus said to the holy men, 'Let he who is without sin cast the first stone.' That means Jesus was calling them out – they were all sinners, so none could throw the first stone to cause this woman to die. One by one, all the men left. When Christ asked the woman if none of her accusers condemned her, she said no. He told her to go and sin no more."

"Really?" Bell licked her lips with anticipation. "So even though they could have killed the woman, they didn't?"

"That's right. Because Christ challenged them to let the person who had no sin on him to go first. They all had sin, and they knew it, so they left. But the thing is, Bell, that Jesus was sinless," he said. "He very well could have been the one to throw the first fatal stone onto that woman. But he didn't. He let her go because God loves all people regardless of their sin."

Teddy looked at Bell and saw tears swimming in her eyes. She smiled at him and wiped a rogue tear from her cheek.

"Thank you, Teddy," she said. She looked away as Poppy and Daisy came back into the parlor, eyeing them. "I'm going to go back to check on Astrid now, if you don't mind. But thank you so much."

With that, she leaned in and put her hand to Teddy's cheek. Her hand felt warm and smooth against the stubble that had grown since the morning's shave. Bell leaned a little closer still and gently kissed Teddy on the cheek. She allowed her lips to linger beside his skin, and Teddy could feel his heart leap within his chest. All too soon, Bell stood and smiled at him. He rushed to his feet but felt wobbly. She slowly sauntered away and disappeared behind the curtain.

CHAPTER 10

*N*early two weeks later, Bell sat perched on her window seat, looking through the frosted window at the cold day before her. It was still early morning, and most of the house was still asleep. She, however, was not. Astrid was also awake, reading a book and biting into a red apple that nearly matched her hair in color.

As Bell scratched the icy layer off the glass, she thought over what had happened over the past two weeks. The time she had challenged God with was nearly up, and not once had she lain with a man. Either nobody showed up for her, or when they did, they were not interested in sleeping with her. One poor fellow had come asking for her and wound up crying over the death of his brother the day before. She patted his back and talked to him, and he went on his way. To her surprise, Bell found herself praying for the man.

George Barnard had succeeded in searching out Nigel Harding, who had been frequenting one of the many opium dens in the district. He shot the gun into the air, threatened the large man, and got arrested by pseudo-mayor Tom Anderson and his gang of supposed peacekeepers. For his part, Nigel Harding was scared to death, nearly had a heart attack, and decided to give up loose ways for good, returning to his wife in the French Quarter.

Bell and the other girls had been attending services at Teddy's Forgiven Grace Church, and the numbers had grown in just the few short weeks it had been open. On its third Sunday, a crowd of twenty-five graced the pews. Bell smiled as Teddy beamed from the pulpit. When he winked at her, she had blushed like a young girl being courted. She was even warming to the idea of marrying him, and she could feel the embers of budding love growing inside her.

She expected Teddy to come to the spa that evening, as Madam has taken to playing cards at Lulu White's house on Thursday evenings. She left Poppy in charge, but Poppy was usually occupied with her boyfriend, Jack Knowles, while Madam was away. Teddy had come by many nights in the past two weeks to watch out for Bell, talk to her about God, and just spend time with her. He also ministered to the other girls as needed, which endeared him to Bell all the more.

Teddy had struck up a friendship with Jasmine, and Bell thought the girl had a slight crush on the reverend. But he was always very sweet to her and had even brought her some candy one evening. Jasmine had been so excited and walked around with her box and proudly offered all the other girls a piece.

And he was that way with all the girls. He and Astrid prayed and talked philosophy. Zinnia had confided in both Teddy and Bell that she was in love with one of her regulars, and they hoped to get married soon. Even Daisy, Poppy's shadow, had begun listening to Teddy speak openly about the love of God.

Bell, however, was still reluctant. She wanted to believe but felt like something was holding her back. She wasn't sure what. There was something about taking that final leap of faith that scared her. What if she was terrible at being a Christian? What if God rejected her? What if she just screwed up?

And she was unsure about Teddy's marriage proposal. She knew how he looked at her. She could see the passion in his eyes, and that it was true passion – not lust like the other men who gazed at her. Teddy truly felt something for her, but Bell still feared the idea of love. And she wasn't sure Teddy – or his very good Christian friends – would be accepting of a minister with a Storyville girl as a wife. Would he be shunned? She didn't want that to happen to him just because he wanted to rescue a poor prostitute from the life she was living.

Too many things were worrying her this morning, and she rubbed her temples. She needed some fresh air. She stood from her seat and quickly got dressed.

"Where are you going, Bell?" Astrid asked, setting the apple core on a small plate.

"I was thinking of walking up to Franc's Bakery for some fresh scones or pastries. I'll bring some back for the other girls, too, as a treat." Bell wasn't usually one to splurge and spend her money, but today she didn't mind the expense.

Astrid smiled. "Oh, I'll go, too, if you don't mind." When Bell nodded, Astrid quickly jumped up and pulled on an old dress.

The girls quietly tiptoed out of the house and began to walk the few blocks up the street. They passed several cribs, quiet in the morning hours, so the girls who rented them could get some rest before the next night's work. Astrid shuddered as she passed them.

"I don't want to have to do that, Bell," she whispered. "They're so dirty and dark. And just any dirty old man can walk in there for you. At least at the spa, it's clean, and most of the riffraff are kept out."

"Hush, now. You won't become one of them. I promise you," Bell said. "You're the one with all the faith. Are you not confident God will protect you?"

"Even the faithful have moments of doubt, Bell," she answered.

Bell sighed and rubbed Astrid's arm. "I have faith that you will be fine, Astrid," she said with a smile, hoping she looked more positive than she was.

As they turned the corner, the girls ran right into Teddy coming from the telegraph office.

"Girls. What a pleasant surprise," he said as he adjusted his glasses on his nose. Bell thought he looked rather smart with the spectacles he wore.

Astrid looked up at him, hopeful. "Any word from my parents?"

Teddy frowned. "No, I'm sorry, Astrid. I did hear from my friend in Roanoke, but he has hit nothing but dead ends, I'm afraid. He said he would get back to me in a few weeks if anything came up, but it doesn't look promising."

Bell watched as her friend's face fell. "But my birthday is in a few more weeks – and a life in the cribs is right behind it."

Filled with compassion for her dearest friend, Bell tried to reassure her. "It's okay, don't worry, Astrid – "

"Ginny, please. Call me Ginny. That is my real name," she said with a half-smile. Tears filled her eyes and wet her lashes.

"Ginny," Bell repeated. She longed for people to call her by her given name and was so happy her friend was asserting herself. "Ginny, we'll get you out of this life before then. Won't we, Teddy?"

"Where can we take her? Will Madam Knight let her just leave? Where do reformed girls go?"

Bell stared at him. He had been in New Orleans for

months now, and he didn't know there were no reformed girls? Bell shook her head. "There are no reformed girls, Teddy. We don't like this life, but if we're in New Orleans, we're whores. Only the ones who get far enough away have a chance. Unless they get married."

Then, an idea came to Bell. It would work to keep Astrid – Ginny, rather – out of the spa, out of the cribs and safe. With the hopes of finding Ginny's family suddenly dashed, Bell knew desperate times called for desperate measures. But she didn't know if her companions would agree to it.

"Astri-Ginny, you'll do anything to get out?"

"Anything," her friend said as she patted her cheeks dry.

"Teddy, will you do anything to help her get out? Anything at all?" Bell bit her lip and waited for the man she was beginning to love to answer her.

He looked from her to Ginny and back. His eyes met hers with a question in them. Finally, he spoke, "I will do anything in my power to help her."

"Marry her."

~

"*E*xcuse me?" Teddy nearly choked. He felt like laughing, but one look at Bell, and he could see she was serious.

Bell took a shaky breath and laid her hands on Ginny's arm. "Yes, you two can get married. That will keep her safe."

Ginny's red hair shook fiercely as she scowled at her friend. "No, Bell, no. Teddy loves you, and you …" she trailed off. Teddy felt his cheeks redden as the girl spoke. Did Bell love him? Ginny swallowed hard. "It's a silly idea. I'll just … I'll just start walking. Eventually, I'll get out of the city."

This time Bell shook her head. "You can't run and hide. Remember what happened to Sadie over at Madam Anderson's in the spring? She was beaten half to death, and then forced into their hole for a week. No. You will not do that. Getting married is the easiest thing, and nobody would ask questions."

Ginny argued back while Teddy just stared at them in shock. "No, Bell. If Teddy and I get married, what about you?"

"You are more important than anything else," Bell assured her with tears in her eyes.

As the girls bickered, Teddy prayed quickly for God to give him wisdom. Never did he think two women would be telling each other to marry him. Especially two women of ill-repute, regardless of how much he liked them both. Slowly, an idea came to him. Teddy hoped it was from the Lord, because it was the only answer he could think of.

"Can't this work, Teddy?" Bell asked impatiently.

Quickly, Teddy spoke up. "It will. Ginny, let's do it. I'll have it all set up; we can get married tonight."

Both girls shut their mouths, and their eyes grew wide. Teddy nodded, the plans forming in his head. "Tonight," he repeated. "We can marry in the spa. Madam Knight will be our witness."

"Are you serious, Teddy?" Ginny squeaked. She shook her head again. "What about Bell? Don't you love her?"

He did love Bell. He loved her madly. And he loved her even more knowing Bell would willingly give up her own chance at love and freedom for her friend. Bell was exactly what Teddy longed for in a helpmate, but here he was agreeing to marry another woman. Both girls looked to him for an answer, and he met Ginny's gaze, then Bell's. He tried to give each a different, yet reassuring glance.

"Bell is right, Ginny. This is the most important thing right now. Go back to the spa. Bell, I want you to be very angry with Ginny for stealing the man you love away – act if you have to. Astrid, tell Madam that you plan to marry me tonight at the spa. I will be there at five with a man to marry us." Standing, he paced before them for a moment.

The girls were still, confusion on their faces. He leaned in to Ginny and whispered, "Trust me, please." She nodded and turned away, giving him a private moment with Bell.

Teddy furrowed his brow and frowned as he looked at Bell. She looked confused, her eyes lackluster and cheerless.

"This was your idea," he reminded her. He tried to reach out to her, but she shied away.

"I know," she said with a sigh. "But if it saves my dear Astrid – Ginny – then that's all that matters. I do care for you, Teddy, I really do. But she will make a better wife anyway; she already has faith in God." She forced a smile, but Teddy could see the tears welling up in her eyes.

"You are a wonderful friend, Bell," he assured her. "God will reward that, I promise you. I will get you out, too." He prayed she would understand what he meant.

She shook her head, then turned. But before she walked away, she glanced back over her shoulder, her long dark curls falling gracefully down her back.

"Goodbye, Teddy," she whispered. He watched as a single tear slipped down her cheek before she scurried off with Ginny.

Teddy took a deep breath. What had he agreed to? When Bell made the suggestion, he wanted to laugh. But realizing he could get Ginny away from this life so easily – and possibly other girls as well – Teddy knew exactly what to do.

That evening at five sharp, Teddy walked into the Day and Night Spa with a new friend on his heels. He had met William Vereen in a coffee house a few weeks ago as he was in his continual search for various items and people for the church. A shorter man of about 40 years, William would perform the ceremony that would take Ginny away from the hell she had known for the past several years.

Madam Knight met him at the door. "Are you daft, man? First, you propose to Bluebell, and now you're marrying Astrid?" She scoffed. "Poppy was right. You are marrying the first girl willing to lay with you. Can't say as I'm all that surprised, though."

Teddy did not speak to the woman as she practically pawed at her own chest. Her bejeweled fingers rested comfortably on her flesh.

"Well," Victoria Knight continued with a wave of her hand, "since I'm to be rid of the girl in a few short days, I'm not opposed to you taking her out now. It will make room for another girl."

Teddy removed his glasses and rubbed them on his sleeve, ignoring the madam's words. "Is Astrid ready? I have a friend here ready to marry us off. We'll live at the church until I can find us a proper house."

The madam snorted. "From the whore house to the Lord's house. If that don't beat all," she said. "She's ready. All the girls are gathered up inside. Come on."

Inside the parlor, all the girls were lined up in a row, Bell and Ginny at the front. William Vereen walked to the front of the room between the piano and opulent fireplace. Teddy peered into the crackling fire, praying for everything to work out. William spoke briefly and quietly with Ginny, then cleared his throat.

Teddy walked up to William and Ginny and nodded for the ceremony to begin. It was brief, William saying all the right words for a proper Christian wedding ceremony. Teddy placed a thin gold band on her finger and kissed her very lightly when they were pronounced husband and wife.

Ginny whispered her thanks to Teddy before she stepped away from him to embrace Zinnia and the other girls. Bell had stepped back into the shadows of the wall, almost hiding. Teddy didn't blame her.

≈

*T*he newlyweds had left a half-hour before, going back to the Forgiven Grace church where they would be living until Teddy could find a house. Bell thought her room was incredibly cold and empty without Astrid in the bed beside her own. Teddy had said he had moved his things into one of the back rooms of the church to serve as a temporary dwelling.

The next day was the last of Bell's challenge to God, and He had come through. In two weeks, she had not once been intimate with a man in any way. Bell was shocked. She laid in her bed and began to pray aloud.

"Lord, I know now that you are truly out there. I believed in you as a small child, but this life caused me to turn from you. The past two weeks were supposed to help me come to believe in You, and they have. But they were also supposed to lead to marriage with Teddy. And now …" her voice trailed off, and she wiped the tears from her eyes. Bell knew that now she would have to go back to turning tricks and batting her eyelashes at johns and still try to maintain her newfound faith. She didn't know how to do it.

She rummaged through her dresser for the book of Psalms Teddy had given her. She didn't even open it, just held it, the cool leather under her hand. Bell turned to her side and clutched the book to her chest and washed it in her tears. Tears flowed as Bell wept herself to sleep that night.

CHAPTER 11

*L*ife had returned more or less back to the way it had been prior to Teddy coming into her life. Bell entertained her clients with a smile on her lips and discontentment in her heart. She struggled to hang onto the belief in a God who would allow this life for her and her fellow brothel girls in the district. She continued to pray the same rote prayer every time her dress fell to the floor, but she was becoming numb to every sensation.

Madam had picked up a new girl fresh off one of the boats in the dock. She was a pretty young girl who had run away from an abusive husband even though the girl was only fifteen. Madam had decided to call her Anise, and the girl took to her new life with gusto. Seeing as she had been a fifteen-year-old bride, she did not need an introduction into the world of debauchery. In fact, she had told Bell, her nearly forty-year-old husband had been quite the lover, except he whipped her whenever he had drunk too much, so she had run away.

Anise seemed nice enough, but Bell avoided her as much as she could. She would stay out of their room if Anise was in it, and pretended to sleep until after the girl had exited in the mornings. She missed Astrid, her friend and confidante. Conversations with her were what kept Bell going day after day and gave her hope. Now that hope was gone. But Bell considered it all worthwhile if it had saved Astrid, now back to being called Ginny, from going to the cribs on her twenty-first birthday, which was the next day.

Bell had not attended services at the Forgiven Grace Church since the wedding. She couldn't handle seeing Teddy and Ginny just yet. Maybe one day she could bear it, but not yet. Zinnia, however, took Jasmine and Clover with her each week and reported the sermon back to Bell on Sunday afternoons. Zinnia, being the sweet girl that she was, never mentioned Ginny at all, or even Teddy, aside from reporting what he had said from the pulpit.

But she knew she would need to see Ginny on her birthday. It was an occasion worth celebrating, and Bell needed her friend to know she was not angry with her. On the contrary, Bell was so very happy for Ginny despite the agony she was under herself. It was of her own doing, she knew, but it didn't lessen the pain of losing both of the people she loved so hastily.

And she did love Teddy. She came to that realization over the weeks since that night. She had not been able to admit it before, but in his absence, she discovered how much she had come to depend on him, how he made her smile and unwind. He had taught her not only about the love of a decent man who was not after her flesh but also the love of the Lord. And she had missed her chance to tell him that she loved him and to finally accept the proposal he had given her.

As she went through the motions of the day, Zinnia came beside her in the parlor. "Tomorrow is Ginny's party at the church. Please tell me you'll attend," the slight girl said with concern in her eyes.

Bell smiled at her. "Yes, I will be there. I've just needed time, you know."

Zinnia laid her hand on Bell's arm. "I know. Listen, can you keep a secret?" Her ash-colored hair fell forward as she leaned closer in to Bell.

"I'm not much of one for secrets, Zin," she confessed. "But I will do my best."

"You know Jake ... Mr. Ames ... who visits with me frequently, right?" When Bell nodded, Zinnia continued. "He's asked me to marry him. For real. And he loves me, Bluebell, he loves me for real!"

Bell's eye widened. "Are you serious? You accepted?"

"I did. Teddy is going to marry us tomorrow after the party. We're going to leave straight away. I wanted to tell you before I just up and left. And I wanted to ask you to look after Jasmine and Clover, too."

"Of course," Bell replied as she hugged Zinnia close. "I'm so happy for you, truly, I am. Where will you go? How do you know Madam won't find you?"

"Jake is from Tennessee, and he plans to take me back to his family's farm up there. He already has rail tickets for us and everything." Bell could see the light radiating from the girl's pale blue eyes.

"And Bell? One more thing," Zinnia added.

"What's that?"

"I'm having a baby."

Tears welled up in Bell's eyes, and she pulled Zinnia close to her. Bell cried out for joy over her friend's wonderful news. As she cried, the tears turned to those of relief over Ginny and now Zinnia being free from the arms of strangers groping them and finally knowing the love of a single man.

After Zinnia had left her side, Bell scurried back to her room and sobbed. She cried selfish, bitter tears, because while her two closest friends escaped the life of a whore, she sank deeper into it every day.

The next day, she nervously approached the church. She noticed the feminine touches at the door, potted mums lined the walkway, and new curtains adorned the windows. She was not sure what to say to either Teddy or Ginny, but she had resolved to be kind and loving toward them. After all, their marriage had been her idea.

When Bell walked into the building, it took a moment for her eyes to adjust to the lower light. Before she knew it, she was face to face with Ginny, who stood waiting for her, her arms outstretched. Without a word, Bell melted into her friend's arms, and the two embraced until all their current hurts had dissolved. Bell wiped a stray tear away and backed up to look at her friend.

"Marriage suits you," she said. She smiled weakly but knew Ginny would see through her façade.

"Oh, Bell," Ginny said in response. "Let's not talk about it. Let's just celebrate the fact that it's my birthday, I'm not out on the streets, and we are finally together again."

"I've missed you terribly." They held hands as they walked over to a table full of food. Bell got herself a glass of punch and told Ginny about Anise. "She's a nice girl, but nothing like you. She ran away from a much older husband and actually seems to enjoy what she does. It's beyond me."

"We should be in prayer for her," Ginny said sternly.

"Spoken like the wife of a minister." The sting of her idea still smarted.

"Bell, how are you doing?" Ginny changed the subject. Bell didn't mind, except that now the subject was herself.

"I'm fine," she lied. She had never been fine, but especially not after Ginny and Teddy had been gone from her life. She looked around the room, at the wall she had painted herself, and at the wooden cross on the wall.

"Don't lie to me," Ginny said softly as she looked straight into Bell's eyes.

"I miss you. I miss my friend. I miss Teddy and being able to ask him questions any time. I miss talking to both of you. I'm back to disrobing for the terrible existence I'm afforded, and I hate it." Bell knew her tone of voice was harsh, and for that split-second, she didn't care. She fidgeted with the table-cloth under her fingers and looked at her friend from under her lashes.

But when tears filled Ginny's eyes, she quickly spoke again much softer. "But it is worth it to see you free and happy, Astrid – I mean Ginny. You have your old name back. You're the wife of a minister. Has there been any word from your parents?"

Ginny closed her eyes for a second. They fluttered open, and a tear spilled over onto her cheek. "They're gone. About five years ago, they both died from pneumonia. But we just found out that my brother is still alive and living in Virginia. We're hoping we can track him down quickly."

"I am so sorry. I know how you longed to see your parents again." Bell rested her hand on Ginny's arm, but she knew the gesture was of little comfort. "How wonderful that your brother is still around, though I'm sure he'll be happy to hear from you."

Ginny only nodded, then Teddy stepped up beside her. "Oh, Bell, you came," he said. His face spoke volumes more, however. Bell saw relief, anguish, and many other emotions mixed in Teddy's bright-green eyes.

Those eyes bored into hers, as if they were trying to find her soul. Bell wanted to fall into his arms and proclaim the love she had discovered for him but knew she could never do that now. Laughter bubbled under the surface as she realized how easy it was to fall into bed with married men who bought her affections, yet the man who had given and gotten them freely could never caress her skin or hair again. It was a cruel world, Bell thought.

"Let's find our places for Zinnia's nuptials," Teddy said as if he was changing the subject, even though they had not been speaking in the first place.

An alcove off the main room was set up with a center aisle with rows of two chairs on each side. It was cozier than the main space where Teddy did his preaching and where Ginny's party was set up. Bell noticed that her friend had found white crepe paper and decorated the area simply and beautifully for a wedding.

The ceremony between Zinnia and her Mr. Ames was short and sweet. The words and actions differed greatly from that of Ginny and Teddy, but Bell guessed it was just how the two men of the cloth differed in their delivery. Teddy's words as wedding officiant were joyful and well-rehearsed, whereas Teddy's friend had spoken with halted, unsure words.

As Bell watched the two lovers make promises to each other, Bell thought she could see the faintest sign of rounding in Zinnia's slim frame and smiled. Once Teddy announced them as married, they kissed passionately. It was nothing like the kiss that had been shared between Teddy and Ginny.

The love birds took off to wait for a train to take them north on the way to Tennessee, where they could begin life fresh, and Zinnia would have no stigmas attached to her. Bell hoped nobody up in Tennessee would care that she was quadroon.

What would her own wedding look like, Bell wondered? She had begun to contemplate herself with Teddy, but now that vision was gone. Would she even marry? Bell frowned as she realized not many men would sign up to marry someone like her.

Would she ever be saved by a dashing prince like Zinnia and Ginny? Perhaps she would just have to save herself.

Teddy approached her when nearly all the guests had left. Bell was leaning sideways against the wall facing the alcove away from everyone else, but she could sense him behind her. Her spine tingled, and her heart began to beat erratically. He didn't need to say anything, Bell knew it was him.

"Teddy, what do you need?" she asked quietly without turning.

"To know you're okay," he replied.

Bell fought tears and turned her head into the wall, hiding herself further. "I'm fine. As long as Ginny and Zinnia are safe, I'm fine."

"Don't lie to me, Bell, please. I can see the pain in your face. Is it because of us or something else?"

She refused to turn to face him, knowing that if she did, she would burst into tears and not be able to regain her composure. "I sell my body to anyone with a fistful of cash, Teddy. Those two weeks were wonderful, but reality has come back hard. I am praying daily for God to take me out of that place, but so far, nothing."

"You're praying?" he asked; his voice sounded almost exuberant.

"I'm trying to. It's hard believing in God when sex is your profession," she said. "But I pray. I pray for God to deliver me from my hell, and I pray for you and Ginny."

"Thank you," came the simple reply. "Bell—"

She whirled around to face him finally and held up her hand to stop him from saying more. She couldn't stand to hear his syrupy words of hope anymore. Anger filled her, brewing like a storm about to lay siege to the city. She was furious with him and with herself. She was furious, because it had been her idea for Teddy and Ginny to marry, and she couldn't believe they had gone along with it. Like a hurricane, her fury turned to devastation as she realized just how much she really did love the man standing before her.

Her heart beating wildly and her courage surging, she felt the need to speak her heart. Hot tears ran down her cheeks as she made her impassioned declaration. "I love you, Teddy. I know it does no good now, because even if you don't fully love Ginny yet, you will. I know you will, you're too good a man not to. You're married to her. And she will love you one day, I know that, too. But I just can't stand here with you this close and not tell you. I love you. Very much."

Bell didn't even try to wipe the tears away. She looked down at her shoes, unable to meet his gaze. The tears fell to the floor and splattered in a hundred pieces, just like her heart.

Quietly and softly, Teddy spoke. "I love you, too, Bell. Please don't worry." He shifted where he stood, and for an all too brief second, his knuckles brushed against her hand, and then he walked away.

Stealing away, Bell retreated back to the spa. She laid in bed, her eyes wide open as it was almost time for her first client of the evening. It seemed Jimmy Arnold was making a return visit and had asked for her specifically.

Shouts from downstairs startled her, and Bell poked her head out of her bedroom door.

Obscenities were being spewed from Madam's mouth like rapid fire. Zinnia had been discovered missing. "Where is she? Poppy! Call Tom Anderson and tell him to get his men out looking for that little—"

Rushing out into the parlor, Bell feigned surprise. "What's going on? What happened?"

"That little brat Zinnia – where is she, Bluebell? You're friends with her. Did she tell you where she went? Who she was with?"

Madam got so close to her, their noses almost touched. Bell was backed against a wall, literally.

Knowing not to meet the woman's gaze, Bell kept her eyes low and her voice soft. "No, Madam. I have no idea."

"Liar!" she bellowed. Drops of spit landed on Bell's neck. "You will risk a beating yourself if you don't tell me something right now!"

Thinking quickly, Bell fired off the first name that came to mind. "Tyler Sheriff. He was sweet on her, and I saw them whispering last week." With a silent prayer, Bell hoped Zinnia was long gone.

Satisfied, Madam backed away. "Poppy, tell Tom to find Tyler Sheriff. Little Zinnia couldn't have gotten too far this quickly. Bell, you will see to all her clients as well as your own until she is found."

Poppy ran back into the office and picked up the telephone to call the self-professed mayor and lawman of Storyville.

"Yes, ma'am," Bell whispered as she quickly backed away back to her room.

Dread filled her as she considered what it would be like to take on all Zinnia's clients, plus her own. But if it meant Zinnia was safe, she considered it worthwhile. She knew how to turn her mind off and become numb.

Back in her bedroom, Anise was scribbling away in a journal. "What's all the fuss about?" the cherubic blonde asked.

"Zinnia is gone. She's run," Bell told her without meeting her gaze. "If they find her, they'll beat her. I hope she got away far enough." Bell did not mention the wedding ceremony or the church to Anise.

Anise rapped her fingers across the table where she sat. Her shoulders squared as she looked with confusion at Bell. Her eyes were wide with question.

"Who would run from this life? It's great. I can sleep in, I can do what I want. I don't have to cook or clean. And the men who visit me whisper sweet nothings to me all night." She sighed. "I love it here. Didn't Zinnia? Don't you?"

Bell's eyes narrowed as she considered the girl. Surely Anise had problems if she thought this life was so wonderful. Then again, she was not forced into it and found it exciting. In a year, she would feel differently. "I don't love it, Anise. I hate it here. I've hated the past eight years here."

Anise's blonde curls bounced as she shook her head at Bell. "Eight years? Why would you be here eight years if you hate it?"

Fighting back tears, Bell answered through gritted teeth. "Because Madam Knight owns me. And now she owns you, too. The only way out is to go to the cribs or to run."

"Why don't you run then? Why do you risk having to go to the cribs?" Anise had put her book down now and was staring at Bell.

"Because I have to get all the other girls who don't want to be here out first," she said in a rush.

"Girls like Zinnia?"

Realizing the girl might tell Madam what she had just said, Bell spoke quickly. "I don't know where she went with Mr. Sheriff, but, yes, girls like Zinnia."

Anise eyed her as she picked her book back up, but she didn't speak again.

Back in the parlor, Bell discovered Zinnia's scheduled john boiling with anger. "What do you mean she is gone, Madam Knight? Zinnia is my favorite with that dark skin and genteel nature," he said, poking Madam in her ample bosom.

"We have many other girls suitable until Zinnia can be found, Mr. Johnston." Madam Knight tried to gloss over the situation.

At that moment, Jasmine carefully walked into the room with a tray of sandwiches and drinks. She always concentrated very hard when she carried a tray. No sooner had she come through the curtain, Mr. Johnston knocked the tray from her hands, liquid going everywhere. He grabbed Jasmine by the waist and groped her body. Jasmine froze in fright.

"Fine then, I'll just have a helping of this little negress. She's shapely enough," the man bellowed.

For as callous as Madam Knight was, she had a soft spot for Jasmine. She immediately grabbed Clover and shoved her toward the man. "How about this one? She's still a virgin! She goes to the highest bidder tomorrow."

Without thinking, Bell jumped into action. "Stop!" She took a deep breath and approached the nasty man who held onto her dearest Jasmine. "You don't want them. They're inexperienced and can't please you. You want a girl who can show you a proper good time. Don't you?"

She ran a finger along the man's arm and tousled his greasy hair. Inwardly, Bell cringed and cried out for her body to stop, but she had to keep Jasmine safe. Anything to keep her friends safe.

Johnston released Jasmine and took Bell by the wrist. He looked at Victoria Knight and spat in her direction. "I'll take this one. For free, since Zinnia isn't here."

Madam only nodded, and Mr. Johnston pushed Bell harshly through the curtain. As the door closed behind them, she repeated over and over to herself, "Anything to keep the girls safe."

In the hours before dawn, Bell snuck from the house and hurried down to Teddy's church. She had to make sure Zinnia and Jake had gone as far from Storyville as they could.

She banged on the green door of the Forgiven Grace

Church until her hand hurt. Finally, the door unlocked, and a sleepy-looking Ginny opened the door. "Bell? What are you doing here?"

Filled with panic, Bell didn't care about finding Ginny in her nightclothes. She slipped inside the door quietly.

"Did she get away okay? Did Zinnia and Jake get on the train? Madam is furious and has sent Tom Anderson looking for her," Bell said hurriedly.

"Yes, as far as I know. But you were probably the last person to see her." Ginny yawned, but her eyes were wide open. "They should be safely to Atlanta, getting ready to head to Nashville by now."

Ginny looked a little more closely at Bell and saw the bruise on Bell's wrist. "What—?"

Hiding her hands behind her back, Bell sighed. "I was so worried. I hope Zinnia is safe." Then she looked Ginny up and down again. Her friend's hair was disheveled, and her dressing gown had been thrown on haphazardly. "I'm so sorry for intruding. I'll go now and leave you and Teddy ..."

"Bell, it's—"

"No, I'm sorry. Forgive me. Listen, tell Teddy I need to get Clover and Jasmine out now. A man tried to attack Jasmine last night, and Madam offered Clover to him. I had to give myself to keep them safe. I'm sorry. Goodbye." She made a hasty exit before Ginny could say another word.

Bell ran all the way home, tears stinging her eyes as she went.

~

inny was waiting for him when he came back to the church later that morning, worry in her eyes.

"Oh, Teddy, there you are! Bell was here this

morning." She bit her nails, a nervous habit of hers Teddy had noticed.

"Bell? Here?" he asked, then remembered to add, "Why?" His mind raced with thoughts as to why Bell would show up so early.

He had been contemplating going to her and telling her the whole truth, but he had promised to get Ginny out of the district, and that had not happened yet.

"Zinnia was discovered gone yesterday. Madam Knight sent Tom Anderson and his thugs looking for her. Bell came to make sure Zinnia had gotten away."

"And?"

Ginny paced in front of him, her new yellow frock swishing behind her. "I told her Zinnia and her new husband had safely boarded the train for Atlanta. She quickly apologized and ran right back out. She said she was sorry for interrupting us."

Teddy almost wanted to reach out to her, almost. But he didn't. "Ginny, it's okay."

"It's not okay, Teddy," she cried. "I hate this. I saw she had more bruises when she came."

"More?" Teddy's heart leapt into his throat. How? Why? He could do nothing in the moment. But his plan was slowly taking action.

"I'm hurting her for my own selfishness."

"You're not, Ginny," he said with a smile. "Look what came in the mail. A letter for you from your very own brother." He took the envelope out of his breast pocket and waved it around before handing it to a now blanched Ginny.

"Really? My brother? My own brother, Edwin?" Her face lit up. She sat down with the letter in her trembling hand and ran her fingers over the return address reading Edwin Manning, Williamsburg, Virginia.

"Go on and read it. I'll give you a few moments of privacy," he said before he stepped away. He went into his office to put his other letters at his desk.

As he sat in his chair, Teddy could see Ginny gently open the envelope and take out the letter. Her shoulders trembled, her fiery hair shaking. Teddy prayed it was good news.

As Teddy watched, he thought about all he and Ginny had been through since their hasty wedding ceremony. He had taken her shopping as she had come to loathe the color gray, the color the sadistic madam had assigned to her. She bought dresses and cloth in bright colors like pink, green, and the yellow she now donned. Ginny had dutifully sat front and center at every service of the Forgiven Grace Church and had even ministered to some of the crib girls who had come through their doors, telling them about the love of Jesus. Ginny even relished in the act of cooking meals and cleaning not only their living area but the church as well.

But she was not happy. Neither was Teddy. Though Bell might have been right – Ginny was very well suited to the role of minister's wife – they did not love each other. Teddy's heart beat for God first and Bell second. Oh, he was fond of Ginny and loved her as a sister in Christ, but he was not in love with her. He felt no passion for her. Thoughts of her did not consume his waking thoughts or his dreams. That position was already filled by the petite brunette with the sad eyes.

Ginny was giving him a quizzical look when Teddy snapped out of his daydream. "Thinking of Bell, again?"

He did not even try to hide his thoughts from her. "Yes," he admitted in defeat.

Ginny frowned. "I'm sorry, Teddy. She said something else this morning I did not tell you. She said Jasmine and Clover needed to get out of that house right away. Clover's being sold to the highest bidder today, and someone assaulted Jasmine. Bell is scared for them. It's desperate."

Teddy rubbed his temples. He, too, had been thinking of a way to get the two younger girls out of the spa. His requests for help in that area had gone unanswered; his parishioners only offered prayers for the two mulatto girls, but none wanted to take them in. Anger at their passiveness flamed up.

"I don't know what to do, Ginny," he admitted. "I'm praying."

A wide smile broke out onto her face. "I have a solution," she said. When Teddy cocked his head to the side and raised an eyebrow, Ginny sat before him. "Edwin wants me to come to Williamsburg. I'll take the girls with me as my maids. We just need to arrange a way to get them to the train station before Madam knows and can come after them. I will make sure they find families or jobs."

Ginny's eyes were alight with the idea. Teddy was more skeptical, but perhaps this was the path God had laid out for them. "Alright," he told her. "I will take you, Jasmine, and Clover to Williamsburg to see your brother. But the girls cannot return here, you know."

"I know. Oh, Teddy! I'm going to see my brother!" Ginny flung her arms around Teddy and embraced him.

Teddy was thrilled for her but dreaded trying to get the other girls away without Bell knowing or incurring Victoria Knight's wrath.

Since word traveled that Teddy married a reformed prostitute, the church had been flooded with girls and the men who worked inside the houses as well. Teddy had not given up on his ministry to the lowest of the low in New Orleans. If he was now going to make a trip up north, he would need someone to step in for him while he was absent from his post.

He called upon his friend William Vereen to fill his shoes in his absence. Never mind that the man had never delivered a sermon before in his life. William could fake his way through it, Teddy was sure.

"Very simple, William," he explained. "At ten o'clock, you greet the parishioners, you say a quick prayer. Then read out of the scriptures I have marked here, and then talk about them. You know how it goes."

"Yes, sir," William said, slapping him on the back. "You really taking that girl up to Williamsburg?"

"To her brother, yes," he responded. "I plan to be gone two weeks at most. But if you could stay here for me, protect the place, and pray with anyone who knocks on the door, I would appreciate it."

William smiled and nodded.

They quickly packed their bags for a hasty departure, for time was of the essence. Teddy had purchased four tickets to Williamsburg, two coach class and two servant class for the girls. He wished he could have gotten them coach tickets with him and Ginny, but because they were mixed blood, they had to ride in the servant car. Teddy longed to have found Bell before departing to tell her his entire plan but knew he couldn't. If Bell knew anything at all, it would endanger her. Instead, he wrote her a letter that explained nothing, but he hoped it would encourage her all the same.

Dearest Bell,

I regret not telling you our plans. I hope you can see that your knowing would have only endangered you. I feel that with the girls of the Spa disappearing as they are, you are in enough danger. I pray constantly for your safety and deliverance from the hell you are in. I will do something about it soon, please trust me.

Jasmine and Clover are heading to safety. I will not tell you where, in case this letter falls into the wrong hands. We

are traveling to see Ginny's brother. Yes! We found her
brother, and he wants to see his sister badly. Ginny was so
excited, but I think she will write you her own letter
explaining that.

The girls are going with us as Ginny's maids and will not
be returning to New Orleans. Ginny said when you came by
yesterday that the girls needed to get out of the house quickly,
and when Ginny told me this idea to take them with us, I
could not say no. I pray they will have a wonderful life where
we are going and will never know the pain you and Ginny
know all too well.

I will return in two weeks' time, and I hope I will be able
to speak with you then about all that has transpired. I know it
is hard now, but it will all be worth it in the end, both here on
earth and when we are rewarded with eternal life in our
Savior Christ Jesus.

Until then, Bell, I remain your humble servant.
Love,
Mr. Theodore Sullivan

The letter and a prayer went into the envelope. Teddy
even pressed a kiss to the seal in hopes it would reach Bell.
Ginny also wrote Bell a letter and placed it with his. He
wanted to read it, but since Ginny did not offer it to him to
read, he did not pry.

He sent Ginny to the train station and made his way
quickly to the Day and Night Spa for Men. Jasmine and
Clover would be coming in and out of the kitchen all night,
and he prayed he would make it before Clover's innocence
was sold. Around the back door, he saw the cook, Sallie,
working fiercely on something in a big stew pot. She spotted
him and smiled, beckoning him to enter.

He stood just outside the screened door and whispered to

her. "I'm getting Jasmine and Clover out, Sallie. I'm taking them away. But please don't tell anyone."

Sallie scrunched her brow but nodded slowly. When the door kicked open, Teddy hid behind a column. He heard Bell's voice fill the room, and he longed to run to her, to tell her everything and, more than that, to tell her he loved her. But he restrained himself, fighting every impulse in his body.

As Bell began to leave the kitchen, Sallie called after her, "Tell those lazy bones to get in here. I got work for Jasmine and Clover both. They need to wash up these here dishes."

"Okay, Sallie," Bell replied. The door swung shut again, and Teddy checked to be sure it was clear.

Sallie glanced up at him. "I know what you're doing and why, but I will miss those girls in here. They's like my own, you know. 'Specially that Jazz-girl. I's raised her from a young'un you know."

"I know Sallie, but I'm going to take them somewhere where they can be ladies' maids or find themselves a fine man to appreciate them one day. I know they won't forget you," Teddy assured her.

Sallie smiled, a mix of sadness with her joy, showing pearly white teeth next to spaces missing their toothy occupant. "I knows that, Reverend Sullivan. I think the entire whole of the district is declining. I think in a few years, ain't nobody gonna be left here. So, it's best to get them girls gone now while you can. How's my Astrid?"

Teddy whispered, "She's fine, Sallie. She misses you all, especially Bell. Don't tell her it was me who took the girls, please. And, if you don't mind …" He took the letters written for Bell and handed them to Sallie, who stuffed the envelope in her pocket. Teddy ducked again.

Just then, the door opened again, and Jasmine and Clover stumbled into the kitchen. Sallie hugged them tight and kissed both on the temples.

Always filled with sass, Clover pushed away and twisted her face up. "Why'd you do that?"

"Because I can, young lady. I need you—"

"Sallie!" Madam Knight burst through the door, hip first. Her garish red dress flashed, and Teddy flattened himself as best as he could against the shadows, his heart racing.

"Ma'am?"

"What are you doing with these two?" Madam Knight said with a heavy breath. "I need someone to change the sheets in the Parisian room. And Clover needs to ready herself."

Teddy listened, willing his breath to stay silent. Sallie promised that the girls would be out in just a minute, and Victoria Knight's voice disappeared back into the house.

The porch door creaked as it opened just a few inches. She looked the girls in the eye and gave them instructions. "You two stay together and listen to what you're told."

"What do you mean?" Clover asked.

At that moment, Teddy appeared in the doorway, still slightly hunched in case he needed to duck again. "Come on, girls, we're going on a trip," he said matter-of-factly.

"Why? Where's we going?" Jasmine asked. Teddy knew her simple mind didn't see the wrongdoings going on around her.

But Clover saw it and embraced the idea with gusto. "I know why we're going. And I don't care where we're going, just lead us out of here, Padre!" She grabbed Jasmine's hand and pushed through the screened door.

Teddy held his finger over his mouth to show them to be quiet. Then he took each by the hand and quickly stole away from the spa before they could be noticed as gone. He prayed Sallie would keep her word and not give away who took the girls or when.

They made it to the train station in record time, and

Teddy got the girls into their car. "Now listen, if anyone asks you your name, use the one your Momma gave you, okay?"

The young girl looked excited. "You mean I get to be Frances again?"

Teddy smiled at her. "Yes, you do, Frances. Do not tell anyone the name Clover again, okay?"

"No problem, Padre," she said with a grin.

"I ain't got no other name, Reverend Sullivan," Jasmine said as she scratched her head. "I's only been Jasmine."

Teddy thought a moment. "Okay, let's play a game then. Let's pretend while we're on the train that your name is … Martha. Okay?"

"'Kay. I like the name Martha, she's in the Bible," she said.

Teddy sighed with relief. "Good, Martha and Frances. Do not get off this train without me, do you hear?" The girls nodded. "Frances, if the conductor asks, tell him you two are sisters, as you look like you could be. And tell him you're the maids of Reverend and Mrs. Sullivan in the other car." She nodded again.

Teddy left them in their seats as the train's whistle blew loud and clear. Ginny waited and prayed in the coach car for him, and he joined her with a sigh of relief. He told her the new names of their 'maids,' and bid her to rest until they made their first stop in Atlanta in about twelve hours. As the train lurched forward, he only prayed it was enough time to distance themselves from Madam Knight and the brothels of Storyville.

Two days later and weary from their journey, the four-some arrived in Williamsburg. As they descended from the train, Ginny began to scan the crowd for her brother, Edwin. But before she had looked too far, a baritone voice began to call her name.

"Ginny? Ginny?"

Teddy watched as the girl spun around, and he spied the

one calling to her. A man just a little younger than himself, nearly six feet tall with the same wild red hair, came running toward them.

"Ginny? Is that you?" The man was breathless, his blue eyes filled with tears, searching the matching ones before him. Teddy could not help but smile, and he could feel his own tears welling up at the happy reunion before him.

"Edwin!" It was all Ginny could say before the man whisked her up into his arms and spun her around, squeezing her tight. Ginny's sobs lifted up toward the heavens as she clung to the brother she thought she would never see again.

"Oh, my baby sister. We thought you were dead – killed by the men who had raided our camp," he said as he pulled away from her. "But it is you. You look just the same as you did when you were a lass of thirteen. When you and Darla Smith were taken, our family was crushed. Father never stopped looking for you."

"He didn't? Oh, I miss him and mother so much. It nearly killed me to hear that they were gone. But to see you, my dear Edwin, I'm home," she sighed. She looked at Teddy and laughed through her tears. "I'm home, Teddy, I'm home!"

The tall man finally looked up at the trio with his sister. "You came with an entourage, Virginia." He extended his hand to Teddy, and he happily shook it. "Thank you for bringing my sister back to me, Reverend."

"Call me Teddy, Mr. Manning. And it was my pleasure."

CHAPTER 12

When Jasmine and Clover were discovered missing that night, just a day after Zinnia, Madam became irate. She slapped Bell across the face and screamed at her, spittle landing on Bell's red cheek.

"You did this, you traitor," Madam seethed at her. "You helped them run away, didn't you?"

Shaking her head, Bell shook with fright. "No, I didn't, I promise. I know nothing."

Her cheek stung, and Bell could feel a trickle of blood run down to her jaw. One of Madam's rings had cut into her flesh. The woman grabbed her by the shoulders and shook her violently.

Finally, Bell suggested that if Zinnia had helped the two run away, they were still close. Like a predator after its prey, Madam Knight pursued every avenue she could think of to regain her property.

Madam Knight sent Daisy and Poppy over to the church to be sure Teddy and Ginny weren't hiding them. Bell could only pray that the two were far from New Orleans and not in the church.

Forbidden to leave the house, Bell was trapped to wait and hear what happened. She paced her room while Anise primped in front of the mirror.

When Poppy and Daisy returned, they told Madam that the reverend and Ginny had left town, going for a belated honeymoon to Baton Rouge. Henchmen were immediately sent after them to see if they had taken the mulatto girls with them.

Shattered, Bell left the parlor. There was nowhere safe from her thoughts, though. Ginny and Teddy were off on a honeymoon. Were they the reason Clover and Jasmine were gone? Had they taken the pair with them? While she could never be upset that the girls were free of the spa, she was tormented to be the one still there, alone.

As she passed the kitchen, Sallie called her inside the sweltering room. "I know you's not too happy right now, Bluebell, but I promise you will rejoice before this is all over."

Picking at her fingers, Bell didn't look up to the woman who cared for all the girls. "What do you mean?"

Without another word, Sallie pulled a crumpled piece of paper from her pocket and shoved it toward Bell. "Go. Now."

It was an envelope. Bell's eyes widened, and she hurried from the kitchen. Inside their room, Anise was primping for the day; going in there was not an option.

Locking herself in the privy, Bell ripped open the envelope and scanned the letter. It was from Teddy. Relief flooded her body. She knew he had to have taken Jasmine and Clover. His letter did not disclose where, and for that, she was grateful. She was confused by the letter, both by his words and her own raw emotions, but she did not mind this time. Ignorance would be bliss in the following weeks.

Another envelope was included, and she ripped it open as well. Ginny's handwriting stood out on the page.

Dear Bell,

Forgive me for not telling you goodbye. Forgive me for not sharing the letter I just received from my dear brother, Edwin. And forgive me for lying to you.

After you left here, telling me Zinnia was discovered missing and that Jasmine and Clover needed to get out, Teddy returned to the church and handed me a letter from my brother. He was beside himself with excitement over finding that I was alive and well. He told me to come to him as quickly as possible, and Teddy was eager to comply. I immediately told him we should take the girls with us to – well, Teddy told me not to tell you where we were going in case someone else read my letter to you.

He agreed, and tonight we will take them with us. I wish we could take you as well. Really, I do. I hope you don't hate me forever for not bringing you. I know this will be so hard on you, as you will be left with Madam, Poppy, and Daisy.

I love you dearly, Bell. Please know that. We will find each other again, I pray for it.

Until then, I am forever your friend,
Ginny

What did she mean that she prayed they would find each other again? Wouldn't they return soon as Teddy's letter said? Bell reread Ginny's letter just as she had Teddy's. Perhaps they did not intend to return at all. Teddy had saved several girls from the life they lived and married the one most suitable for him. His mission was complete then.

The letters safely tucked into her waistband, she came out of the powder room and made her way back to the parlor. A fire was roaring both for warmth and ambiance. The chilly November air was making its way inside as more men also sought a way to warm themselves. Bell decided to toss the letters into the fire before anyone could find them and read them. She balled them up and threw them deep into the flames.

As she watched the glowing flames lick the paper, Madam rushed over to her. "What was that, Bluebell? What did you throw into the fire? Word from that crooked reverend and his whore of a wife?"

Bell blocked the fireplace. "It said nothing, just that they had left to Baton Rouge, just as Poppy told you," she said. She did not attempt to mask the tear that fell. "Trust me, Madam, I have no loyalty to them anymore. I wish them nothing but good riddance."

The woman eyed her cautiously. Bell scowled, but not because she was lying to Madam Knight, more because she thought she was telling the truth.

"It's about time you realized the truth about that minister. He was only interested in getting a girl into his bed, Bluebell. I hope you see that now. He married the first girl willing to take him." Madam turned and shook her head as she walked away.

Bell was beginning to believe that now. They may have taken Jasmine and Clover with them, but they still ran away from New Orleans, away from her. Would they come back? Even though their getting married had been her idea, Teddy had certainly jumped on the idea. Perhaps he was just looking for the first girl who would take his name so they could warm his bed. Maybe she hadn't loved him quickly enough.

Her thought was broken as the sound of heavy footsteps came into the room. Bell looked up to see a very handsome, well-dressed man enter the parlor. He looked to be about thirty years old, had silky blond hair, and dark, brooding eyes. Bell could practically see his biceps through his shirt.

Before anyone could greet him, he eyed her. "You there, girl," he said gruffly. "You will do."

Madam came out into the parlor with a smile on her face, ready to give the newcomer her welcome speech, but the man simply put a small sack of money into her hand and said, "I'll take the brunette by the fire."

He strode to her and wrapped his arm around Bell's waist. She had heard stories of damsels in distress being swept away, but nothing like it had ever happened to her before. Just as she was feeling her worst, the most handsome man she had ever seen had chosen her. Her heart fluttered at the attention, while also screaming at her to get away because she loved another.

The man motioned for her to lead the way, and she silently led him down the hall. In that moment, she gave up on love and allowed the numbness to take over yet again.

With the door closed firmly behind them, Bell helped the stranger remove his jacket. "Welcome to the spa, sir. May I ask your name?"

"Ian," he said succinctly. "I'm not interested in a lot of chit-chat, girlie."

Bell nodded, and she hoped her hands did not shake as he watched her. There was something about this mysterious man. "Of course. Just let me know what interests you."

Ian came close to her and towered over her small frame. Bell willed herself to stop thinking about Teddy and his kind green eyes as the black, passion-filled eyes of the stranger took her in. He leaned down close to her, and Bell stood as still as a statue being viewed in a stuffy museum. She took a deep breath and continued to meet the stare of the man before her.

"I'm interested in nothing but you," he said as he crushed his mouth onto hers.

Suddenly Bell was lost and an empty, hungry soul was left

in her place. Just as Ian had said she would do for him, she thought he would surely do for her.

Four days later, Ian was coming in nightly for trysts with Bell. Daisy fawned all over him the second he came through the door. Poppy wore dresses that revealed more and more cleavage each night and placed herself provocatively on the couch. Anise doused herself in perfumes and elaborate accessories and batted her long eyelashes at him.

For her part, Bell wore modest dresses and let her dark hair fall in natural curls down her back. She wore no makeup, no perfume, only her passive disinterest in life. Ian never glanced at the other girls, never spoke to them even if they spoke first. He simply approached Bell, took her into his arms, and retreated behind closed doors with her.

He did not say much, but Bell had gathered he was not from New Orleans. By his accent, she placed him in the Carolinas somewhere. He was very somber but also very gentle. He never hurt her, but he also was not overly kind.

On this night, he removed his coat, but then sat on the settee at the end of the bed. Bell stood expectantly before him.

Ian dug around in his coat pockets for something and asked her, "How long have you done this, girlie?" He still had not asked her name, something Bell was used to.

She stammered and looked to the floor. "I beg your pardon?" She began to fiddle with the ruffle of her sleeve.

"How long have you been sleeping with men?"

Feeling a little panicked and wanting to tell him the truth, she confessed, "Madam brought me here eight years ago. I've belonged to her ever since."

"Belonged to her? Like a slave?" The man grimaced. He sounded angry, but Bell wasn't quite sure at what.

Meekly, she answered, "I've never thought of it like that, but yes. We are not allowed to leave the district."

"So, you did not choose to be a whore?"

She shook her head, unable to speak. Would this upset him further? She hoped not. Just as Ian used her body, Bell used him in return as a way of numbing herself. She hoped the salve that was his kisses would not cease.

"You did not choose this life, you cannot run from this life," he said, a look of confusion across his face. "Yet you embrace me. You do not seem to take great pleasure in it, but you are eager and willing all the same. You perplex me. And I don't even know your name. You consume my every thought, and I can only think of you as my Little Somber One."

Tentatively, Bell sat beside Ian. She felt compelled to share her real name with him – the name her parents had bestowed upon her – but she held back. "My name is Bluebell."

Ian nodded as he wiped his face with a broad hand. "Bluebell. Bluebell with the dark hair."

"Everyone here calls me Bell, though," she added as an afterthought.

The man stared at her for a long minute. "Bell. Thank you."

"For what?" Her voice was naught but a whisper.

"For bringing me back to life."

He said no more, and Bell did not ask. Instead, she took his hand in hers. She meant to lift up a silent prayer, but instead, she kissed his hand – every inch of it. When he looked at her with sadness in his eyes, she kissed his mouth, not caring, not thinking, just doing.

≈

*R*ight on schedule, two weeks after his departure from New Orleans, Teddy returned with a much lighter load. The reunion between Ginny and her brother had been therapeutic on so many levels. Teddy was thrilled at how God was working to take a girl destined for the cribs and reunite her with her long-lost brother. He marveled at how quickly they seemed to fall back into the rhythm of older brother and younger sister. Edwin's young bride welcomed the lot of them into her home and showed nothing but the kindest mercy.

He was also happy that Jasmine, who had adopted the new name of Martha, and Clover, who went back to her preferred name of Frances, had been able to stay in Williamsburg right in the home of Edwin and Felicity Manning. The wife said she would be thrilled to keep both girls on in their own home, assisting their cook and looking after future children. Though Teddy guessed the future would be upon them soon if the woman's deep blush revealed anything.

The only thing Teddy wanted to do was get to Bell and tell her the news about the girls. But it was early morning, and he knew they would not yet be receiving visitors. He hoped Bell would be open to receiving a visit that evening so he could explain everything, though he would have preferred Ginny do it if she had returned with him.

Teddy decided a rest was in order before seeing Bell at the spa. Refreshed, shaven, and in clean clothes, Teddy set out for Basin Street. The whole way, he prayed Bell would kindly receive him and his words. He wanted nothing more than to put the past behind them both.

At the front door, he hesitated. Would Madam Knight know he helped the other three girls escape? Would police be waiting on the other side of the door? Of course not, he reasoned. Nobody knew he was back in town. But that didn't mean the vulgar madam wouldn't call the police to arrest him the minute he entered the building. It was worth it, he argued, for their freedom from this house of sin.

He walked in cautiously, quietly. He prayed for Bell to be in the parlor so he could speak with her right away. Sure enough, he spotted her dark curls on one of the couches. She was facing away from him, talking to a tall, blond-haired man standing before her. Bell did not even turn when the chime on the door rang. Teddy was not familiar with the man before her, and he felt anger and bile rise up inside of him. He clenched his fists as he heard Bell's familiar giggle rise up and carry across the room.

Before he could call out to her, she stood, her back still to him, and linked arms with the unfamiliar man. She coyly led him back behind the curtain and disappeared. Teddy blinked back shock. Surely, he did not see what his eyes thought they saw. Surely his Bell had not laughed with another man and willingly led him back into one of the rooms.

Despite knowing that her living was made lying with men, Teddy had hoped Bell had fought tooth and nail to preserve herself. But he quickly realized she had watched him marry Ginny a full two months prior. Bell's two weeks of reprieve were long up; God had fulfilled that promise and not a day more. And Teddy himself had brought Ginny into his home, not Bell. If only he had married her at the end of the two weeks, she would not have just led some strange man back to a waiting bed.

Then again, if he had married Bell that day instead of Ginny, only Bell would be free from the brothel. Because he had married Ginny instead, now four girls – Ginny, Zinnia, Jasmine, and Clover – were living a good life outside the whorehouses. Despite that understanding, Teddy still found the deal a loss with his precious Bell still inside.

"Well, look what the cat dragged in. We all thought you'd skipped town," a familiar voice called, pulling him from his thoughts. Poppy sashayed up to him in her sleek, black dress like a cat waiting to pounce. "Bored of the little missy, huh? I knew it," she said. "If you're looking for Bluebell, she has a new man to save her. Named Ian. Big strapping fellow, he's been here every night since Jasmine and Clover left and will only see her. Don't know why, though. I do way more things than she does."

Teddy glowered. "You're crude, Poppy."

"And so much more, Reverend Teddy. Wanna find out?" She licked her painted lips and raised her eyebrows.

"No. Don't tell Bell I was here," he said and turned out the door. He knew Poppy would probably gloat over seeing him to Bell, but he hoped she wouldn't.

As he walked away, he replayed the scene he had just witnessed in his head. Who was this man, and why did he only see Bell? If the stranger had been coming nightly since he had left town, that was two weeks with his Bell. The thought disgusted Teddy.

Not his Bell, he chastised himself. She had never been his. Even though the night of the party she had confessed her love to him, she had not been his. Teddy thought himself a fool for going along with the plan to marry Ginny. He thought himself even more of a fool for not including Bell in on his own plan.

He kicked a pebble in the road as he wondered. Jazz music from another brothel floated out to greet him, trying to entice men into its doors. Teddy ignored the lure of the sirens in the windows, his only thought being what a fool he had been to let Bell think his wedding to Ginny was genuine.

He was a fool for going along with the blasted plan, and for lying to everyone, especially Bell. Then, he thought, maybe they had both been fools for putting their own plans before God's.

CHAPTER 13

*I*an took her hand and placed it over his heart. Bell felt heat rise on her cheeks and her own heart speed up, as the act was incredibly intimate. The last fortnight with him was completely different from the past eight years with all the other men she had seen. Was it he who was so different? Or had she changed?

She quickly realized he was not much of a talker, and that did not bother her. But he had begun to tell her his story in bits and pieces. They shared a home state of South Carolina, but he had been raised in Charleston as the son of a wealthy businessman. Madam Knight's pockets were lined with cash, proving the fact. Each night he had given her money as well, more in a week than she had scampered to save in the past two years. Ian had been in love before, that much she knew, but why he was not caressing the skin of that girl, she was not sure.

Bell didn't care, though. Ian Davidson had shown her more affection and concern than any man had before, save Teddy. But Teddy never showed it physically, and that was the only way Bell knew. But now Teddy was showering his affections on Ginny. She pushed the thought from her head, willing thoughts of Teddy to disappear altogether.

"Why are you scowling?" came the gruff voice beside her.

"Hmm?"

"You're scowling, Bell," Ian said, running his finger along her jawline. "I like you better smiling."

Instantly she smiled, eager to please him. "I'm sorry."

"What made you frown like that?" Ian propped his head up in his hand as he looked at her.

Bell peered into his dark eyes. "Nothing at all, Ian."

Now he scowled. "Don't lie to me. You're thinking about some other man. You must have a boyfriend who doesn't pay to see you like I do," he said, his voice sounding distant and sad.

"No. No boyfriend," she said, maintaining her smile. "You're the only man I've seen or wanted to see since you first came."

"And prior to that?"

Bell licked her lips. "Doesn't matter," she said with a smile, even though her stomach flipped as if in pain. The lie gnawed at her stomach.

Ian's frown burst into a smile. "Now, that's the answer I wanted to hear."

She wished it was the real answer; she would do her best to make it so. Bell felt an intense attraction to Ian, even more than she had felt toward Teddy initially. But she knew it was nothing but physical attraction, and for now, that was fine with her. There was something about him that made her want to be completely consumed.

Before leaving, Ian reclined on the settee and watched Bell as she dressed. This was not something her clients usually paid attention to, but Ian always did. She felt self-conscious as he watched her roll her stockings into place and affix them to her garter. She then stood before the little mirror on the wall and looked at him through it as she re-pinned her hair.

"Do you leave the house much, Bell?" he asked as he leaned forward, his elbows resting on his knees.

"A little, but no, not too much," she admitted. "Madam isn't too keen on us going out, especially now that several girls have run away. She's afraid I'll be next."

Ian seemed to consider that for a moment before speaking again. "Would you run away? Or leave?"

Bell sighed and turned toward him. "Honestly? I would leave. All the girls I was fond of are gone. Aside from Madam not allowing me to leave, nothing is keeping me here."

"Nothing?" He stood and took a few steps toward her but did not come too close.

"This was not the life I envisioned for myself when I was a child. Who would look at this and be envious?" She chuckled a little. More from discomfort than anything else.

"Tell me what you wanted then, my Bell," he commanded, but his words were soft.

She looked down at her hands as she thought, then looked back up into Ian's striking eyes. "A childhood dream is all. I was just a little girl from the mountains. I wanted a happy life, a good man," she said. She did not know why she was admitting all this to a virtual stranger. It had taken her much more to confide in Teddy.

"And now?" Ian finally stepped forward and took Bell's hand into his own. It was so much larger than hers, calloused and strong. Bell felt protected, but also in danger as well. She liked the mix of emotions.

She spoke honestly. "I don't know what I want. Aside from living comfortably without selling myself, I don't know."

They heard a clock chime from the hallway, and Ian

looked up from Bell. "I need to get going. I have an early morning meeting. I will be back tomorrow."

Bell sighed and risked asking, "Why me?"

He ran his thumb along her jawline, and she swallowed hard and closed her eyes.

"Because from the moment I saw you, I knew you were the one I needed. Not wanted, Bluebell, needed. To heal me. And you have, my dear." He kissed her lightly, then quickly left her standing, her heart beating loudly in her ears.

"And you have healed me, too," she whispered after him.

Once she caught her breath, Bell straightened up the room and went back into the parlor, all sign of Ian gone. She sat on one of the golden couches and sighed, running her hands over her upper arms to keep warm, even though she was not cold.

Poppy slowly walked to her and gazed at her strangely. "Who are you daydreaming about, Bluebell? Your newest, most attractive client? Or maybe that no-good minister who ran off with your best friend?"

Bell frowned at the blonde-haired girl and snapped, "Give it up, Poppy. Where's Jack, huh? You know you'll be kicked out when you turn twenty-one in a few weeks. Think we don't know? We do. Madam won't keep you here. Why doesn't your lover rescue you?"

Poppy leaned over Bell. "What makes you think he's not going to? Maybe we have a plan just like Astrid and Zinnia. Plans to get married and run off with men who want us. And here you are, all alone – no man thinks you're worth hanging around for too long."

A fierce ache came over Bell's whole body. "Go away, Poppy. Go bug Daisy and Anise." She closed her eyes, trying to shut her out.

"Gladly," she said with a turn. "By the way ... your reverend came here tonight looking for you. Got here just in time to watch you head to the back with that Ian Davidson. Boy was he steamed to see that," she gloated. "It's almost as if he forgot he had married someone else."

With that, Poppy began to walk away, just in time for the door to open and a pair of sailors to come through. She quickly approached them, whispered to them both, and held out her hand. When they both handed her a fistful of cash, she quickly thrust it into Madam's office and led them both away.

Bell had to turn her head away, as Poppy's actions made her want to be sick. Even worse, she realized she had led Ian back through the curtains, her hips swaying as she went. Had Teddy really shown up at the spa looking for her? And why wasn't Ginny with him? Was she unwell? If she could sneak out of the house, she could go check on them. But she knew it would be nearly impossible. Bell had only thought she was a prisoner before – now she really was.

~

*T*eddy had stayed away from the spa for another two weeks, using the excuse that he was too busy to stop by. He had poured himself into the church and counseling those seeking to get away from the life they had in the district. With each turn of the door handle, Teddy prayed God would bring Bell into his midst, but she still had not come. He didn't know why.

Did she not want to see him or Ginny? Though before leaving Virginia, Ginny had warned him Bell might be too upset to visit for a while. He tried to respect her boundaries, but he needed to explain everything to her.

Teddy knew why Bell had not come. It was the new man in her life, Ian Davidson. Teddy had heard about him around town. He was a wealthy man from Charleston, South

Carolina. Not even thirty years of age, and he had made his fortune in a string of restaurants across the south. The word in New Orleans was that following the death of his fiancée last year, he had sold his restaurants and began traveling, looking for a new place to settle down. Many hoped New Orleans would be it, as he had the potential to make many people rich and happy.

Including Bell, Teddy thought. Teddy had also learned, through asking more questions than a preacher need ask, that the fiancée the man had lost, a girl named Maggie, was a petite girl with curly brown hair and dark eyes. Just like Bell. Davidson had found a replacement for the girl his heart had lost.

For two weeks, Teddy had been working in the church and in the community, but his mind had been with Bell. He prayed for her to arrive at his doorstep. His walks brought him past the spa where he craned his neck to see her, but she never emerged. Ginny would have laughed at him if she had seen him, and she would have told him to go knock on the door. He wasn't sure why he didn't do just that, but he held back.

A local orphanage where the abandoned children of prostitutes and the poor were taken to keep them off the streets took up a lot of Teddy's time as well. He had been reading to the children, ministering to the older ones, and hoping to encourage some to go into more virtuous lines of work. Today he was hoping to talk with the headmaster there about sending one of the older boys off to Maryland to attend seminary. He felt the boy was ready and willing to take on the challenge and would work to earn his keep.

Yet once again, as he passed the Day and Night Spa, he paused and waited a moment to see if he could catch a glimpse of Bell. He didn't see her in the doorway, but her familiar silhouette sat perched in a window, peering onto the street.

Quickly, he jogged across the street toward the window. He smiled and waved at Bell, whose sad eyes revealed much more than her bogus smile. She looked miserable.

"I've missed you," he said through the glass.

Tears immediately welled up in Bell's eyes. "You shouldn't," she said. "Where's Ginny? Is she okay? Poppy said you came by a while back."

Blast that Poppy, Teddy thought as he pulled his coat up closer to his face. A cold breeze blew past, making the winter air even more frigid.

"Ginny is fine," he said coolly. "But I really need to speak to you, please. It's very urgent. Why not come out and walk with me?"

Bell placed a bare hand on the cold window. "I can't. I'm housebound. After Zinnia left, and Jasmine and Clover ran away, Madam suspects I helped them. I'm not allowed to leave at all. She knows you helped them, so she would never let you escort me, either."

Teddy was shocked. He figured the madam knew he was the one who helped the other girls, but never thought it would mean Bell would be confined to the house like a captive. Maybe he had misinterpreted everything.

"I had no idea. I am so sorry, Bell. Please, I need to speak with you. It's very important."

He lifted his hand and placed it on the same spot Bell held hers on the window. It was the one warm spot on the cold glass. Bell quickly removed her hand and looked away. Teddy brought his face closer. "Please, Bell."

"Go home to Ginny. Please, Teddy," she said through the window, a tear rolling down her cheek.

He breathed heavily and pressed his forehead to the

window the way a child would at a candy store. "Ginny isn't here, Bell."

Her head snapped up to look at him, a puzzled expression on her face. "What do you mean? Where is she?"

Teddy glanced around. "Come to the kitchen. Let me tell you without a piece of glass between us and the world able to see."

She nodded and quickly closed the curtain as she rose. Teddy hurried to the back of the brothel where Sallie's kitchen was. The Negro cook was always happy to help him, and he prayed she would allow him and Bell to talk openly. At the back door, Teddy stayed out of the window until Bell came into view. She whispered to Sallie, who nodded and peered out the window, looking for him. He waved as Bell pushed through the screened door as quietly as she could.

Bell wore a dress of robin's egg blue; it was stunning against her nearly black hair. Around her shoulders was a deep russet shawl to protect her from the cool winter air. Her hair was unbound and fell in ringlets over her shoulders. After a month of not seeing her, the ability to reach out and touch her was almost too much for Teddy. His heart surged as she looked over her shoulder and tentatively took a seat on one of the wooden chairs.

"Where is Astrid? I mean Ginny," she said, concern in her eyes. "Is she well?"

He smiled and nodded, "Quite well, last I saw her," he said. "We went to Williamsburg, Virginia, as you know, to see her brother, whom a colleague of mine had located."

"So where is she now?" Bell questioned.

"With her brother, Edwin, still. She decided to stay with him in Virginia," Teddy told her.

"For how long?"

"Forever, I would assume." Teddy chuckled.

Bell did not smile. "You dismiss your own wife so easily? How could you do that, Teddy?"

Teddy leaned in closer, closing the gap of space between them. "I would never do that to my wife, if I had one. Ginny and I did not actually get married, Bell. It was a sham to get her out of here."

Bewilderment came over her face as she tried to grasp what he told her. "What? I was there. You took her into your home for several weeks."

Teddy took a deep breath. This was not the place where he wanted to explain everything, but if this was the situation God gave him, he would take it. "I spoke with Ginny privately after I agreed to marry her. We could fake a wedding to get her away from the district. The man who married us, William Vereen, is not a minister. He's just a good actor. We signed no legal documents. Ginny and I slept in different rooms in the back of the church. Regardless of finding her family, the plan was to get her somewhere up North, where nobody knew her. Then I would return for you. My intention was always to come back for you and marry you, Bell. I love you."

Bell's face fell as she realized everything. "Why did you not tell me, Teddy? Why could you not confide in me that the wedding was a sham?"

"We feared others would find out if either of us breathed a word about it. Please believe me, our intention was not to trick you, but to get as many of the girls away from here as possible."

"So, you left me here? You saved the rest of them and left me here? This place has become a prison within a prison." Her face blanched with the shock, and her hands began to tremble.

"That was not my intention, Bell, please know that. You are the strong one. I knew you could hold your own," he pleaded, but she turned her face from him. "I can see how hurt you are. That was not a part of my plan. Though I have realized that maybe I should have followed God's plan and not my own."

When Bell remained silent, with tears in her eyes, he spoke again. "Tonight, Bell. Tonight, I will come take you away. We'll get right on the train and head north to Maryland. I'll close everything here and take you away. I'll find someone else to take over the ministry here." When she still refused to meet his gaze, he added, "I'd do it for you, Bell. Tonight."

Without looking at him, she shook her head, and she simply said, "You're too late, and I'm not worth it, Teddy. I'm a whore, and I need to stick to my own kind. I have a very rich man coming to see me now, and I'm going to ask him to take me away. Maybe I can be his mistress. You don't belong here, Teddy. Go back to Maryland with your high and mighty church people."

As she spoke, the words sliced right through Teddy's heart. She wanted to remain in the house? She wanted nothing more for herself than to be a replacement mistress for a rich man? Teddy prayed for God to give him some magic words to say to convince her to go with him. When nothing came, he decided to use his own words, which he knew was probably not a great idea.

"You're just a replacement," he said plainly.

"Excuse me?" Now she did look at him, her eyebrows arching upward.

"You're just a replacement for that man. He had a fiancée before – a small brunette with curly hair. You are just a replacement for that girl. She died."

Bell stood, horror on her face. "Oh, poor Ian! I knew he was pining after a girl he no longer had, but I did not know she had died." She shook her head. "But you. You are callous and rude. Who are you to judge? Didn't you preach on not judging others? You're a hypocrite, Teddy!"

With that, she stood and swirled around, her skirt and hair following behind. She marched through the door without another word to him and slammed it behind her. Teddy stood from the chair, defeated. He knew he should not have spoken, and he realized he had just driven the woman he loved further into the arms of a man who was up to no good.

CHAPTER 14

*I*t had been a month since Bell had moved into the apartment with Ian. Well, not with Ian, he lived in a much more luxurious place Bell had never seen, but he came to her almost every night, and the apartment itself was much more elegant than her own room at the spa. And she had it all to herself to decorate and come and go as she pleased.

It was a small but tidy second-floor apartment where other mistresses were kept in the city. It was between Storyville and the French Quarter. Not quite a whore, but also nothing like a wife. A few of the ladies had children their man supported as well, and Bell liked the sound of children's giggles around her.

She had a spacious bedroom she decorated herself with a four-poster bed, soft, cream-colored sheets, and cheery yellow curtains. The room was finished with a cozy settee and an ornate oak wardrobe. Her living room was small, but it had beautiful views of the square across the street, with trees reaching to the sky and people milling about. Yellow furniture made the living space cheerful and happy. Dozens of books sat on a small bookshelf waiting to be picked up and thumbed through. The kitchen was meager, which suited her fine since she was not an accomplished cook anyway.

And since she was able to do what she wanted with her apartment, she had banned anything the color of red or gold – the colors Madam Knight had loved and used the most. Bell wanted her home to be cheery and inviting for polite society, even if she was one of the mistresses of New Orleans.

After Teddy's last visit to her at the spa, where he revealed he had not actually married Ginny, Bell decided she had had enough. She was strong. She was above being a common whore in a common brothel. That night, she had quietly approached Ian and convinced him that if he took her out of the house, he wouldn't have to share her with any other men who might come in.

The next morning, he met with Madam Knight and whisked Bell away to the apartment. She never asked what he said to the madam, nor did she care. He gave Bell a handful of cash and told her to decorate however she wanted and to buy herself clothes that were not blue. Bell had nearly squealed in delight and wished she had Ginny or Zinnia to shop with her.

Now she could roam the streets of New Orleans of her own free will. She didn't have Tom Anderson's men following her. She wasn't reduced to standing around a parlor all evening, waiting to see if some unknown man would decide he wanted her. She was so much freer.

Except, Bell now thought, she was still a slave to Ian. He would send word that he either would or would not be joining her for supper on a particular evening. If he wanted to show her off, she was to be ready at a certain time to be picked up and taken to wherever he wanted her. Once or twice, she felt like a trained poodle, but still, that was a far cry better than being in a brothel and ending up in the cribs. Ian would take care of her for life, she was sure of it.

This particular evening was Fat Tuesday. Mardi Gras. The entire city had been abuzz with anticipation, men and women preparing for the festivities. Bell had no idea how to make a King cake, but Ian had insisted she have one ready when he came to get her that evening. She had placed an order with a local bakery, telling them to make it as opulent as they could and charge Ian Davidson's account. The man behind the counter was all too happy to do so.

Bell had shopped for a new dress as well. A bright turquoise gown with a dipping V-neck that plunged far too low beckoned to her. The tiered skirt rustled as she moved and ended right at her ankles. A gathering of aubergine-colored lace adorned and accented her tiny waist and pushed her bosom upward.

She dressed and looked into the mirror. Perhaps she should wear her hair up, but it was a festive party after all, so she opted to allow her curls to find their own way. She pulled a few strands of hair from her face and used a splendidly colored comb to hold them back. With her mask in hand, she waited for Ian to pick her up for the festivities.

When he arrived, he held her at arm's length and took a long look at her. He surveyed every inch of Bell's body – attention she was used to, though she did keep her eyes down and batted her eyelashes a little.

Ian took a deep breath. "You will be the most gorgeous woman there, Bell."

She looked to him, happy he was pleased. "Do you think?"

"All the other men will want you for themselves. All the other women will be jealous," he said with a smirk.

She stepped toward him and kissed him lightly. "I only care what you think."

She grabbed the king cake and her mask, and they headed to their destination along the French Quarter. Bell had no idea where they were going or whose party it was, but she did not care. She was just happy to be out and on the arm of one of the newest and most prominent men of New Orleans.

At the party, a uniformed Negro man took the king cake and her cape as they entered. Ian held her on his arm as if she were a prized possession. After so many years of being nothing more than an expendable commodity, Bell was in awe of her new position. She held her head high and smiled until it almost hurt, but she was determined to make Ian proud of her.

"Ian Davidson, you cad! You made it," came a call from across the room. A man about the same height and build as Ian approached them. His hair was tucked up into a hat, and his piercing-blue eyes shone from behind his mask.

Ian had not yet put his mask on, and Bell could see confusion turn into recognition as the man got closer. "Lou? Lou Walters? My good man, it's so nice to see you. I had no idea you were coming this way for Mardi Gras," Ian said, an easy smile on his face.

Lou Walters pulled his mask and hat off to reveal shocking red hair and freckles to go with his blue eyes. Bell thought he wasn't near as handsome as Ian, but not terrible looking, either. As he approached them, a small, blonde woman squeezed her way beside him.

"Ian, this is my fiancée Nora LePare. Nora, my old college chum, Ian Davidson," Lou said as he pushed his bride-to-be between him and Ian.

Ian shook her hand. "Charmed. Allow me to introduce my friend Bell … Knight," he said.

Bell blanched. Ian had to search for a last name for her … he had never asked what her parents' last name had been. So instead, he used the name of the notorious madam's house she came from? She was appalled. Perhaps his friends would not make the connection.

She shook hands gently with the girl, then the strapping red-headed man. "I'm pleased to make your acquaintance," she said slowly and with purpose. She had been practicing more genteel ways since leaving the spa.

"Knight, huh? There's a madam in the district by that name. Not that I would know, mind you. But my brother goes there a lot," Lou said with a chortle. "Where are your people from, Bell Knight?"

She sputtered a moment. She was unprepared to answer personal questions about herself. "Carolina," she finally said, "South Carolina."

Lou's eyes lit up; Ian's darkened. "Are you from Charleston? Surely I would remember you if you were from Charleston," Lou asked.

"No, Mr. Walters," she said as she tried to regulate her breathing. "I'm from the mountains, I'm afraid."

The man smiled, but then he looked behind Bell, and his face lit up again. "Hey! There's ol' Moody! Come on, Ian." He tugged Ian's shirt, and they made their way to another man about their age.

Bell thought it was no wonder Ian had come to New Orleans. It seemed he already had a network of friends in the area.

The blonde girl Lou had introduced as Nora took a step closer to her. "What brought you to New Orleans?"

Bell felt perspiration come up on her forehead, and she was suddenly hot despite the winter chill. "My uncle brought me here a few years back," she said. It was the truth as she didn't have time to concoct a plausible lie.

"Ah. Did you go to one of the boarding schools? You look like a boarding school girl. I had to go to school at home in Charleston," the girl chattered. "It was nice enough, and I could visit Mother and Father often, you know. How did you meet Ian? Lou and I met in Charleston. He lives here now, and I'll move once we're married. We'll be married in April, you know. You two should come up for it. Do you think you and Ian will get married?"

Bell just smiled and nodded as the girl prattled on with her deep, Southern drawl. Bell began to think she wasn't ready for all this. Nora thought she was Ian's girlfriend, perhaps future wife. How did one introduce themselves as a man's mistress? She was a soiled dove, as the term went, not a girl from boarding school with an upstanding family back home. Bell had no home, no family.

She resolved to go back to her apartment and quickly sit down and construct a new story for herself. She would stick with coming from the boarding school where her uncle in South Carolina sent her. Now the story was out, she needed to maintain it.

Ian glanced over at her, and she waved. He winked back. Bell noticed his friend, Lou, squint at her, but then he smiled wide. At first, Bell thought he was smiling at Nora, but she was still talking and not even looking at her fiancé. The smile was for her. She timidly returned with a nod. Something about Lou Walters made her uneasy.

After the party, Ian took her back to her apartment. He said he had some business in the morning, so he could not stay with her. Bell understood, and truth be told, she was so tired she didn't really care if Ian stayed that night. He promised to have dinner with her the next evening and excused himself after a lengthy kiss goodbye.

With the door closed behind him, Bell sighed and removed her shoes.

She gently undid her dress and slid the turquoise material off her shoulders. She glanced in the mirror and looked at herself in just her underclothes. She held her hair up on her head and let the curls tumble down her back. She considered cutting it into the new short fashion. She would ask Ian about it the next day.

Suddenly she heard a knock on the door. Bell grabbed her robe and threw it on over her underthings, figuring Ian had forgotten something he would need the next morning.

She flung the door open, "Forget something, Ian?" she asked.

"I'm not Ian, but I did forget something," said a husky male voice.

Lou Walters was at the door, and Bell could smell the stench of many different kinds of alcohol on him. He leaned on the door frame and smiled at Bell, his fiery hair falling into his eyes.

She gathered her robe closer to her neck. "Ian's not here. You can find him back at his place," she said quietly.

Bell tried to close the door, but Lou put his foot in the way. The door bounced back open. Bell shoved it closed again, but Lou was much stronger than she was.

"Ian told me all about his new girl. His latest Maggie-wannabe," he slurred.

"Maggie?" Bell questioned. Then she recalled Teddy's words from before. Ian's former fiancée was a small girl with dark curls, just like her. She must have been Maggie.

"You know, after Maggie died, Ian went from whore-house to whorehouse, looking for someone to replace her. And you could be her twin. Except Maggie was from a rich Charleston family. You're nothing but a district harlot Ian's keeping until he's ready to move on."

Tears fell down Bell's face at Lou's harsh words. But she held firm. "That is none of your business, Mr. Walters. Please leave now." She tried again to close the door.

And again, he blocked it with his large frame. He came through the threshold and closed the door behind him without taking his eyes off Bell the entire time. His sinister stare frightened her as she backed away. But he caught her hand and held tight, covering her mouth with his other hand before she could scream.

∼

*T*eddy had returned to the Day and Night Spa a week after Bell had walked away from him. But Madam Knight herself greeted him and took great pleasure in telling him that Ian Davidson had taken Bell away, leaving a hefty sum for the madam. The spa had gained two new girls that very day, and Teddy walked away, shaking his head. No matter how many girls he helped get away, the madams would always find more young, warm bodies to display for the men.

Davidson had taken Bell as his mistress, but Teddy wasn't sure where. There were a few apartments that housed the mistresses of wealthy tycoons in New Orleans. But he couldn't very well knock on each and every door to find Bell. And Forgiven Grace Church was in need of his attention. He tried to turn all his focus there.

About a month after learning of Bell's departure from the brothel, Teddy escorted a young man from the local orphanage to seminary in Maryland. After a brief visit with his family and old church, he had traveled a bit, speaking at different churches along the eastern seaboard about his ministry in New Orleans and the people of its red-light district. When Teddy returned to the gulf-port city, he had more than enough funds to pour into his church and try to forget about Bell.

But of course, she was always just a thought away. And he thought of her often. Teddy tried to focus on God, to do things for God. But whenever he pictured his ministry in

New Orleans, Bell was the first thing that came to mind. Her sad, dark eyes were the very first thing he saw in the city. Bell had become something of a symbol for Teddy's entire cause. She had become his entire reason for continuing to reach out to the people of the district, and he knew that was dangerous.

Correspondence with Ginny remained constant. He had written her the very day he had told Bell about the fake marriage, asking for her advice. She only said to find her and get her out of whatever situation she was in before she was lost for good. Bell appreciated honesty but also needed time to adjust to change and come around. Ian Davidson's presence had changed things. Bell had not taken time to think, then come around – she ran right into that man's arms and never looked back.

~

*N*early a fortnight after Easter, Teddy stood on the edge of Basin Street. To his left was Storyville and the ornate houses of bordello madams. To his right was the edge of the French Quarter. Behind him were many hotels that did not rent rooms by the hour, including the Arnold Arms, where he had stayed in his first few months in New Orleans. There were also many apartments there as well, and Teddy knew Bell was housed in one of them.

Teddy turned around and faced the apartments before him. A prayer to find Bell and get her away from Ian Davidson pushed past his lips. He didn't know what was going on, but he knew something was very wrong with that man. Davidson was an opportunist and knew how to run a business, and now the man was seemingly squandering his wealth and taking up with a girl who closely resembled his deceased fiancée.

Before he could even take a step from his spot, a woman in a flowery yellow hat walked right into him. Her dark eyes looked up and met his – Bell. God had delivered her right into his path. It made Teddy smile, but Bell did not.

"Bell! I'm so sorry, are you all right?" He asked with a smile on his face.

"I, um, Reverend Sullivan. I am so sorry, I wasn't looking where I was going," she said, keeping her eyes down.

His smile faded immediately. "Reverend Sullivan? Are we reduced to that now?"

"I haven't seen you in nearly three months. I didn't think we were really friends any longer." She nervously looked over her shoulder.

"Oh, Bell … I heard you were away from the spa. I am so relieved. Where are you living now?" He hoped his question didn't seem too prying, and she would easily answer, but he wasn't sure how she would react.

"I have an apartment. I'm doing well," she stammered. "Ian takes good care of me." A single tear slipped down her cheek as it burned crimson. She wiped it away with a gloved hand.

It ripped Teddy to shreds to see her in such torturous pain. Regardless of how Davidson took care of her, she was obviously not happy and not doing well. He studied her as she looked around nervously. Her eyes looked more sunken, her cheeks more hollow. She wore a coat pulled tightly around her.

"May I walk you somewhere?" he offered, still hoping she would show him where she was residing.

"No, thank you. I really better go before anyone sees us," she said.

"Would that be a problem? A preacher speaking to a former parishioner? I just want to know how you're doing."

Bell swallowed hard. She spoke low and quickly. "I need

to go now, Teddy. I am sorry. Please don't look for me anymore. Just forget I ever existed, please."

With that, she quickly brushed past him, skirting down the next street and disappearing entirely. Teddy balled his fists, anger boiling inside him. Every fiber of his being knew Bell was not safe in whatever her situation was. He needed to get her out regardless of cost.

As he walked toward the church, he prayed for God to show him how to reach her. He prayed for God to deliver her from whatever hell she was in, and he could tell she was in one. Could she possibly think her situation was better now than it was before at the bordello? Teddy supposed not having to cater to different men all the time was one plus, but what did she trade for that?

Back at Forgiven Grace, Teddy sat at his desk and began to respond to the letters awaiting him. Thank you letters for those who sent donations both to the church and the local orphanages. Letters updating those already supporting him as to the church's progress in the community. Teddy was happy to boast a weekly attendance of about fifty regular parishioners with anywhere from five to fifteen new faces each week. About one-third of the regulars had begun to tithe, which amazed Teddy.

Sadly, the district girls who came weekly were still district girls. It was a life nearly impossible to leave without leaving town and getting as far away as possible. He had been formulating a way to get those girls into another state where they could begin again as governesses, maids, and cooks – anything but lying on their backs. He hoped to devise some-thing similar to the Underground Railroad employed during the War Between the States some fifty years earlier. A chain of people willing to help the girls get from one point to another on their way to freedom and a life without debauchery.

But thoughts of saving dozens, even hundreds of girls forced into selling themselves – the task Teddy felt God calling him to do – paled in comparison to saving Bell. Even if it meant leaving the rest of his ministry behind, he had to get her away from this life.

Days later, Teddy was heading into a meeting with Arnold Arms Hotel owner Jim Arnold to ask if he would help sponsor sending more of the area orphans north and east, just as he planned to do with the district girls. If it would work with orphaned children, it would work with the girls. And it would help the little girls of New Orleans get away before becoming a crib girl was ever a possibility.

As he waited in the lobby, a tall man with blond hair exited Mr. Arnold's office. Teddy immediately recognized him as Ian Davidson. He watched as Davidson shook the older man's hand and smiled.

William, the concierge, told Teddy Mr. Arnold would be with him in a few minutes. Teddy nodded, keeping his eye on Davidson. Was this the opportunity he had been looking for?

As the man walked through the lobby, Teddy stepped in front of him, blocking his way.

"Excuse me, Mr. Davidson, is it? I wonder if I may have a moment of your time," he asked, his breath short. He hoped it was not obvious.

"Can I help you?"

"I understand you are something of a restaurant connoisseur and a wonderful businessman," Teddy said, hoping the immediate compliment would liken the man to him. "I am looking to do some fundraising. I was wondering if you might be able to help me."

Davidson smiled. "I see my reputation precedes me. I would be happy to speak with you, Mr.—"

"Sullivan. It's Reverend Sullivan, actually," he said with a smile. "I'm looking for ways to help the orphans of New

Orleans and would love some expertise in raising and managing funds the way you have, Mr. Davidson. May I call on you this week for a meeting?"

"Of course, Reverend," he said, obviously pleased that he was well-known already in the city. "Come by my new restaurant on Thursday morning, if you can. I'm free then."

Teddy nodded briefly. When Mr. Arnold's office door opened, he excused himself and went into the office to speak to the hotel tycoon.

"$\mathcal{I}$'m very excited to see your new restaurant, Ian," Bell said, scurrying behind him like a lost puppy. "What did you decide to call it?"

He turned toward her, his face gruff. Ian's brows were bunched, and the color in his face was high. "Maggie's. Now get out of my way."

"Oh," was all she managed as she stepped to the side.

Maggie's? He was naming his new place after his dead fiancée? Bell wanted to pout, but Ian had been prone to a temper lately, and she didn't want him to slap her again. Perhaps when she shared her own bit of good news later tonight after dinner, his mood would improve greatly. She wished it to be so.

Bell had completely given up on praying and had turned to wishing. She wasn't sure what the difference was, just that she was sure now that the God Teddy claimed loved her had abandoned her yet again. And what good was it, praying to a God who hated you anyway? He was likely to do the opposite of what she asked. So instead, Bell had turned to making her own way and trying to take control of the situations Ian allowed her to control.

"Are you ready, Bell?" Ian stood at the door, the scent of aftershave wafting around the room.

"Yes, Ian," she said as she quickly got to the door and took his arm. They went downstairs to the waiting car.

Ian insisted on arriving at his new restaurant in style, which meant hiring a car. Bell hadn't been in a car but a few times in her life, and she felt very important. The slick black seats shone, and chrome accents adorned every surface. She was on the arm of the most important man of the evening, riding in a real motor car – Bell thought this was what she had been waiting for her entire life. She had beautiful clothes and plush furnishings. And she was showered with attention, gifts, and even money. She finally had what she had been waiting for since she came to New Orleans. To be somebody to someone. To be loved.

Sure, she admitted Ian wasn't always the perfect gentleman. He had slapped her a few times, but Bell reminded herself she had been in the wrong. She had raised her voice or had a differing opinion. And he often came home drunk or high, only to pass out as he was pawing all over her. On a few of those occasions, he had called her Maggie. But from what she was told, they did look an awful lot alike, so he couldn't be blamed for missing his lost love. Right?

His attention wasn't all Bell received. Lou Walters had also been giving her attention as well. More than she liked. Shame had filled her, but self-preservation was her forte, and she clung to it the way a baby clings to his mother.

But this night would change it all, Bell thought. Ian's new restaurant was having its grand opening, he would be happy, and that would make her happy. And Bell had her own surprise for him planned this evening as well that should make him overjoyed.

She looked over her outfit for the evening, a jewel-toned turquoise dress with pink accents. The neckline was straight across but was cut low, and the top of her chest was exposed. It was a little much for polite society, but nothing as severe as district girls wore on a daily basis. The bright dress would surely stand out this night amidst a sea of dull colors, Bell hoped. Her hair mostly loose, with the top pinned back, fell in a wild frenzy down her back.

The restaurant was buzzing with activity when they arrived. Ian's staff had things running smoothly, something he demanded of all his employees. There were two bartenders wearing bowties, their hair slicked back, ready to pour drink after drink. Waiters in tuxedos stood along the far wall, waiting to be beckoned by a patron. A stage waited at the front for entertainers to please the crowd, the lights ready to come to life at any moment.

Bell could smell the heady aroma of French herbs swirling around with the scent of warm bodies and hot conversation. Maggie's was packed full of people, most of whom Bell did not know. But she didn't care; everyone was looking at her, vying to talk to her – the woman on Ian Davidson's arm. The former whore-turned-mistress, and she hoped soon perhaps her status would change again to wife.

As Ian released her arm to correct an out of step waiter, Bell turned full circle, taking everything in. She barely felt the hand on her arm for all the people close by, but the voice she recognized right away.

"Hello, Bell."

It was Lou Walters. Bell froze in fear.

After he attacked her a month prior, Bell had pleaded with Ian to have Lou arrested, to send him away … anything. But Ian had refused. He said that as a district girl, she should be accustomed to people having their way with her. And he accused her of being too beautiful for her own good; that she must have led Lou on in some way. When Bell cried, Ian told her that Lou was welcome in the apartment whenever he wanted for whatever reason he wanted.

"He's getting married soon, Bell. He needs an outlet before that chirpy he's marrying gives it up," Ian had said with a sinister laugh that caused gooseflesh to pop up on her arm.

And Lou had made good on Ian's offer. He had forced his way into the apartment and onto Bell on a weekly basis. Out of fear, Bell reverted back to her own self-preservation mode when he was around. She became like a rag doll, letting the brute handle her how he wanted so he would leave all the quicker.

"You can't touch me in public, Lou," she seethed.

"Maybe not," he said as he ran his hand up and down her arm. "But that doesn't mean I won't later."

She did not turn to face him. She refused to acknowledge him publicly. Instead, she whispered, "You won't touch me again."

He snickered and sauntered off toward a group of people Bell did not recognize. Despite the heat in the room, a chill ran through her, and her stomach turned.

She fought her way to the ladies' room to retch.

Feeling only slightly better, she scanned the dining room for Ian. The entertainment and meal would be starting soon; she needed to find him. And find him, she did. He was standing only a few feet away, talking to Teddy Sullivan as if they were old friends!

She made her way over to the pair on wobbly feet, and when the men saw her, they both broke into smiles. Bell smiled tentatively.

"Reverend, this is my lady friend, Bell Knight," Ian said as he brought Bell very close and wrapped his arm around her middle. "Bell, this is Reverend Theodore Sullivan."

"We've met, actually. She graced my church with her presence once or twice in the past," Teddy said with a smile. He nodded to her, "Nice to see you again. Miss Knight, was it?"

She merely nodded, unsure what to say. She was thankful to Teddy for not revealing their past to Ian. It would only anger him. But she could not deny the pull she felt as she looked at Teddy.

He was about as tall as Ian, but that was where the similarities ended. Ian had full blond locks that fell into his dark eyes when not slicked back. His body was sculpted like a statue, and his expression was almost always stern. Teddy, on the other hand, kept his near-black hair cut shorter, and his green eyes were always happy. While he was also very fit, he was softer than Ian. His personality matched – it was kind, joyful.

"Mr. Davidson has been helping me with a project I've taken on, aiding the orphans of New Orleans," Teddy continued. "And Forgiven Grace Church and those rescued children appreciate your generosity, sir."

Ian puffed up the way Bell knew he always did when someone praised him. The man lived for accolades. "Well, I am always happy to help those less fortunate, aren't I, Bell?"

Called upon, Bell replied at once. "Yes, Ian, you are very compassionate. I'm sure the pastor and your other beneficiaries are very grateful."

Ian peered off in the distance. "That's not right," he said, releasing his hold on Bell. "I need to fix this. We will begin in five minutes. See that you're seated in time, Bell."

"Yes, Ian," she said. But he didn't hear her as he stormed off to berate another employee in the wrong.

Bell debated running off, away from Teddy, but knew tongues would wag if she was not a gracious hostess. "I didn't know you and Ian were acquainted," she said.

"I met him about two weeks ago and asked him for help in raising funds and managing money," Teddy said. "He has been most helpful with that, and he donated a nice sum to help some of the youngest of the children in the orphanage get adopted by families in Mississippi and Alabama. I'm surprised you didn't know about it."

Bell shook her head, the curls piled on top shaking along. "No. I had no idea. Ian doesn't discuss business with me." She trailed off and looked at her fingernails for a moment. "Are you enjoying your evening?" She wasn't sure what else to say to the man she thought she had given her heart to months before.

"I am now," he answered.

"I should get to my table," she said, looking away. She saw Lou Walters standing right in her path. He was staring at her with hunger in his eyes. She gulped and felt ill once again.

"Bell? Are you all right? You've gone pale." Teddy glanced at where she was looking. "Is it that red-headed man? Is he a former client?"

Bell barely whispered, "No. Not former." She reached her hand out and grasped Teddy's arm. "Please, Teddy, please escort me to my table. Please don't ask questions."

Teddy looked at her, and Bell risked a glance at him. His lips were drawn tight, and his eyes tried in vain to read her face. She loved that he was concerned, that he was always looking out for her and others. But that was the past, Bell thought. Right now, she just needed to get around Lou Walters.

"Don't worry, Bell. No matter what, I will always protect you," he murmured to her under his breath. He looked away from her and led her to her chair, pulling it out for her. As she sat, he bowed low and repeated himself. "No matter what."

She gave him a curt nod, and he walked away. Something

inside Bell stirred, and she wished she could run after him. Risking being seen, her eyes followed Teddy as he moved through the crowd. The desire to erase the past several months was overwhelming. She wished she had married him instead, she wished she had accepted his God as her own. When she was with him, she felt something good and wonderful and freeing like she had never experienced before. The desire to run to him and run away was alighting in her feet, but she stayed planted where she was. With Ian, Bell only felt free from Storyville; the wonder she felt with Teddy was noticeably absent.

The chair behind her scraped against the floor, startling her. She jumped and turned to see Ian taking his seat, smiling at her.

"Why are you so jumpy?" he asked as he kissed her cheek.

"Sorry, I guess I'm just excited for you," she explained.

"As you should be. Maggie's is a hit! It will be all over the papers tomorrow, I'm sure," he said, clapping his hands together. "The liquor is flowing, the food is about to be served, and the entertainment is top-rate."

Bell forced a smile at him. Despite his flaws, Ian was hers. He was what she deserved. It wasn't happiness, but it was something. "I can't wait," she said.

The waiters moved forward with trays in a sort of procession, a show in and of itself, Bell thought. She and Ian were the first ones served, front and center. A meal of canard à l'orange was set before her. She only knew the name because Ian had told her it was an exotic French dish. He had told her it was like duck in orange juice, which sounded strange to Bell, but she knew nothing of French cuisine, so she had simply nodded at the explanation.

As she ate, the lights went down, and a spotlight came up on the stage. A garishly dressed man appeared and announced the start of the show. He narrated as a dozen scantily-clad girls lined up on the stage. He said the show came straight from Paris and was part of an old French dance, the Cancan.

Bell stared ahead, aghast. The girls' ample skirts were lifted higher and higher with each kick of their leg as they revealed layers of petticoats and stockinged legs. The crowd around her roared in approval.

This was barely above a bawdy house, Bell thought. The girls may not be sleeping with the men in their midst, but they were putting on quite a show for them, selling themselves with the jut of a hip instead of in bed. Bell was embarrassed to be front and center, and because she was with Ian, she could not get up and leave. She thought of Teddy and hoped he had left before the glow of mesmerizing sex commanded his attention.

When the show ended an hour later, the announcer appeared again, front and center. The crowd howled with applause. Bell looked at Ian, who was beaming in light of his success. The announcer told the crowd that the dancers would be doing shows at nine o'clock nightly, and that dinner would also be served. Two shows would be featured on Saturdays and Sundays. He exited the stage, and the lights went dark for a second before the house lights came back on.

Men clamored around Ian to congratulate him. Bell quietly said she would return momentarily, but she doubted Ian heard her or cared. She ran to the ladies' room once again, her stomach still knotted tight. Once she voided her evening meal, she returned to the main room.

She went to the bar and asked for some seltzer water with lime. Bell took a long sip, hoping the bubbles would calm her stomach. Teddy approached her where she stood and took a seat next to her. He motioned for the bartender and asked for seltzer water as well.

"Some show," he said without looking at her. "I can see

you were not prepared for the content, either."

Bell shook her head. "No, I was not. This was hardly any different from the shows in the district, except the girls are not offering themselves to men afterward. At least, not that I know of …" She sighed and took another drink. "I sincerely hope this did not offend you."

Teddy smiled and chuckled a little. "I have seen worse in my ministering to the girls of New Orleans. I have been praying with ladies when a caller arrived. I have seen them half-clothed as I preached the love of Jesus to them. There isn't much I haven't seen. So, no, the show did not offend me."

Bell nodded and still did not look at Teddy.

≈

*T*eddy had been horrified by Ian Davidson's show. He agreed with Bell that it was not much better than what happened in the bordellos several blocks over but did not want to tell her that. He strove to be calm and covered in peace as he spoke with her when, in reality, he wanted to gather Bell in his arms and carry her out of that place that instant.

"I need to get back to Ian," Bell said as she finished her drink.

"He's surrounded by people, Bell. He won't miss you if you need a few minutes to regain your composure."

He looked over to his left and saw the entrepreneur still basking in the praise of his peers. Davidson probably had no idea his girlfriend had even vacated her seat.

Now Bell did turn her head to look at him. A lush, dark curl escaped from its holds and fell across her forehead. Teddy longed to brush it away, to feel her skin. The want was almost too much for him.

"What do you mean by 'regain my composure?'" she asked.

"The food did not agree with you. Am I right?" He hated calling her out on being sick, but this was the second time she had emerged pale from the washroom. "Or perhaps it's merely nerves over such a big night?"

"No, it's not," she said. She grimaced at him, trying her hardest to be genuine. "I need to go."

Before Teddy could ask her what she meant, she slipped from her seat and walked over to Davidson. The crowd around him had lessened, and only a handful of men now stood talking. When Bell approached, he extended his arm toward her and smiled. She quickly attached herself to him and nodded as the men around them spoke to her, the bits of sequin on her dress glittering in the light.

She was nothing more than an accessory for Davidson, Teddy was sure of it. Davidson only wanted a beautiful young woman on his arm to make him look better. The position was supposed to have been filled by the business's namesake. Bell had fit the mold and only served a purpose for the young man. He did not love her. Teddy wondered if Bell loved him.

Teddy stayed only a few minutes longer and prayed for Bell's happiness, regardless of how it came about. Then he slipped out unnoticed and made his way back to the church.

He was still living in the back rooms of Forgiven Grace, having given up his hotel room during his sham marriage to Ginny. It saved him a good bit of money each week, and for that, he was grateful. He had everything he needed – a bedroom, small washroom, and kitchen. He cooked meager meals of red beans and rice, toast, and fruit for himself.

He was always on call if someone needed him. And occasionally, a knock had come on his door in the middle of the night. Once, it had been a girl seeking to run away from her life. He had given her some money and gotten her on a train headed west toward Texas after praying with her. Another time it was a Negro man seeking help for his family; they had not eaten in almost a week. He gave the man all the food in his cupboards and told him to come back for more if he needed it.

He sat down at his desk before retiring for the night and ran his hands through his hair. He tossed his glasses onto the pile of papers before him. He had thought God put Ian Davidson in his path for two purposes. First, to benefit the orphans. That had been fruitful. With the money Davidson had donated alone, four young children were sent east to be adopted by willing families. Second, Teddy hoped to get into the man's inner circle to gain access to Bell. It was a work in progress, but after the evening's so-called entertainment, Teddy wasn't sure he would be able to buddy up to Davidson after all.

He thought over what Bell had said that night. Aside from her poorly covered illness, Teddy was bothered by her words and actions that night. What stuck in his head most was something she said in passing. When she had spotted the large man with red hair, she had become very apprehensive. Bell had said he was not a *former* client. Teddy wondered what she meant by that. Perhaps he was reading too much into it, but there was something going on there, and it alarmed Teddy more than he cared to admit.

He bowed his head and prayed. He prayed first and foremost for the salvation of the people at the party he had attended, especially Bell and Davidson. He prayed for Bell's safety, both from her benefactor and the brutish man she had seemed so afraid of. He asked God to guide him in helping her and the other ladies of New Orleans.

When he lifted his head, he reached for his Bible. Replacing his glasses, he thumbed through the pages, waiting for a particular one to call out to him. Finally, he allowed the page to fall open.

The eighty-second psalm faced him. He read through it and was immediately convicted. *How long will you defend the unjust and show partiality to the wicked? Defend the cause of the weak and fatherless; maintain the rights of the poor and oppressed. Rescue the weak and needy; deliver them from the hand of the wicked. They know nothing, they understand nothing. They walk about in darkness; all the foundations of the earth are shaken.*

Teddy was awed. Was he defending the wicked by standing idly by? He surely was doing nothing to stop it. But that was not true. He was ministering to those who allowed him. He had gotten a handful of girls and small children away from New Orleans and into better situations. And he had tried to get Bell free. Maybe he hadn't tried hard enough.

But then Teddy realized something. It was not him at all. It was God. God had used him to get those others to safety. It had been God's plan, and Teddy had just been who God had used to accomplish the task. When it came to Bell, Teddy had forgotten about God and relied only upon his own power – of which he had none. He needed to allow God to work and be ready at His call. Only then would *Lana* be freed from the life and the lies she had wrapped herself up in.

The psalm was right – Bell was walking about in darkness. She did not know any better, and her world was dark and cold. She was void of the light and warmth of human love and of Godly love. Teddy had tried to show her human love as a means of showing Godly love. But he had been backward. Only with Godly love could Bell then come to love others.

Teddy headed to bed that evening, feeling renewed. He prayed as he readied himself for God to protect Bell until His master plan could play out, and she could realize just how much she needed a loving Lord and not a cruel master.

CHAPTER 16

*B*ack at her apartment, Ian was once again a doting and affectionate man. With the door locked behind him, Ian kissed her neck and tickled her arm. The knots in her back released as she relaxed and snuggled in beside Ian. Bell could smell his aftershave mixed with the smell of his earlier cigar.

She was ready to put the entire evening behind them. And it was finally time to reveal her surprise.

A quick glance told Bell Ian was feeling content. She took a deep breath. "I have something for you. I hope it will be the perfect end to the evening for you," she said, almost singing. She beamed and nearly jumped with excitement.

Ian smirked and bent his head to one side. "You have something for me? After all the success of tonight, I can't imagine it getting any better, but I'm sure if anyone could improve it, you could." He pulled her close in front of him and wrapped his arms over her shoulders and rested his head next to hers.

"Oh, Ian." Bell sighed. "I have not been this happy in a

long time. I have never known freedom in my life, and you have given me that."

She turned to face him and swallowed hard. Bell couldn't help but bounce as she smiled. "And with the freedom you gave me, you also gave me a new life. And together, we have created one." She could feel the light coming off her; she knew she was glowing. Her whole body felt warm and contented.

Bell waited with bated breath for Ian to leap for joy, to express his undying love, and to promise to care for her and their child forever. She had suspected a month earlier that she might be with child, but it wasn't until another cycle was missed that she was certain. She carried Ian's baby, and she could wait no longer to tell him.

Except the expression on his face was not one of pure adulation. It was not even a look of amusement. Bell took a step back and smiled at Ian, sure he was processing what she had said.

"Ian? I'm carrying our child. I think I will be due around October." She held his hands in hers. "Aren't you excited?"

"You're a whore!" Ian roared. He jumped to his feet and sent a glass lamp flying to the ground, where it shattered into hundreds of pieces. "A dirty little whore! How dare you!" He raked his hands through his hair and paced the room.

Bell felt her face flush, her eyes wash over in tears. "I don't understand. Ian? This is our child, conceived nearly two months ago."

"You expect me to believe I fathered your bastard child? I should have known better than to bring a filthy harlot into my home," he spewed. "I know how you threw yourself into Lou Walters' arms. I even saw you cozy up to that minister tonight. You've probably sold yourself off to anyone willing to pay."

"No!" Bell shouted. How could he be saying this? "No.

Lou forced himself on me, Ian. You know that. You gave him permission. And the minister ... well, he's just a decent man. He would never touch me." She begged and pleaded, promising she had never lain with another man willingly.

Tears flowed down her face, her spirit crushed under the heel of Ian's accusations. He was supposed to be overjoyed, lifting her up, and spinning her around. This was not how it was supposed to go. She had thought he loved her, even a little. Ian looked at her with disdain, nothing more. No love, no affection, no compassion. How had the man who gently caressed her skin moments ago turned into such a monster?

"I want you out of my life," he said, his teeth clenched. "And out of my apartment. Pack what trash you brought with you and get out!"

"No, Ian, please!" Bell pleaded for her life and the life of her child. "Don't turn us out. We can be a family. What about your son or daughter?"

Ian spit at her, wet drops landing on the bodice of her dress. "No child of a tramp is a child of mine. You have thirty minutes to get out before I call Tom Anderson over here to haul you back to the cribs."

Ian stormed out of the apartment, slamming the door behind him. Bell jumped at the clap of wood hitting and splintering against the frame. She stood still for a moment, wondering how her amazing news had suddenly left her homeless and alone.

Jumping to action, Bell turned to the bedroom and began to throw her things onto a settee. The blue dresses she had brought with her, taking care with the cornflower-colored one Teddy had gifted to her. She hesitated and considered taking the rest of the clothes as well but realized in her condition they would not fit soon anyway. She grabbed the book of Psalms and another book she had purchased not long ago.

Bell looked around the room. Ian had bought everything else. She would take none of it. She crossed the room to the bed and reached under the mattress. There she kept all the riches she had. Wisely, she had not spent her own money while living under Ian Davidson's roof. Perhaps subconsciously, she had known this would not last.

She pulled a carpetbag from the closet and tossed all of her belongings inside. The cash she tucked into her bosom, and the coins went into her pocket. Glancing at the clock, she realized she only had about five minutes before Ian would return – perhaps with enforcement. She grabbed her bag and left the building without as much as a glance back.

On the street, Bell scurried away from the apartment, walking briskly for several minutes before sitting down at a trolley stop bench. She glanced around, making sure nobody was near her before she pulled the money out of her dress. There was enough for a one-way rail ticket, but that was about it. She would only be able to feed herself a day or two. Leaving town was not an option at this point – she would starve, and it would harm her child. And she knew she would never go back to her old life.

Or maybe she could get out of New Orleans. She would have to swallow her pride, but she knew of many girls who had done it before. Bell stood, resolute. Her days of selling herself were over, she decided. She would take her bag, her expected child, and her wounded pride to Teddy and ask for help getting back to the Appalachian Mountains where she belonged.

As she walked toward the church with purpose, Bell formed her plan in her head. She would go back to her hometown. Now she would be Widow Knight, left alone with a baby on the way. Surely someone she used to know would take her in. She could be a governess or maid. Or maybe an old widower with children would find her suitable and marry her. She could only hope.

At the door of the Forgiven Grace church, Bell hesitated. It was nearly one o'clock in the morning. Teddy would be asleep. Perhaps she should wait until morning. As she shuffled about in the cool air and debated in her head, the door swung open.

"Who's there?" Teddy said with a gruff, sleepy voice. "What do you need?"

Tears began to fall from Bell's eyes. "Only a friend, Teddy. Please, I need a friend." She began to bawl now, her entire body shaking.

"Bell? Are you all right?" Teddy was suddenly alert. He put his arm around her and took her bag, leading her inside.

Between sobs, Bell managed to speak, "I know it's late … I just need a place tonight … I'm going home tomorrow."

Teddy stood firmly. His face was stern but not hard. His eyes were compassionate through the sleep. But he spoke firmly, "You are not going back to Ian Davidson, Bell. I will not allow it."

"We're done," she said. "I mean, I'm going back to South Carolina. I'm going back to where I lived with my parents. Maybe somebody I used to know will take pity on me." Her wailing slowed, her breaths ragged.

"What will you do once you're there?" was all Teddy asked.

"I'll tell them I'm a widow now, come home to find work," she explained. "But Teddy, I just want to sleep now. Can I sleep?"

He smiled at her and crouched down to look her in the eyes. "You can sleep here as long as you need to, Bell. You can take my bed. I will sleep on the couch."

She nodded as Teddy led her to the modest make-shift bedroom with a small bed and night table. Bell did not even think to remove her shoes before lying down, fully clothed, on the bed. She faintly felt her shoes tugging off and felt relieved. Within minutes she was out cold.

~

*T*eddy wondered what had happened. Was this not his every dream come true? Bell lying in his bed? Though she was not his. And he knew he needed to stay away from his room until she woke and felt better. He grabbed his glasses and a change of clothes for the morning before exiting.

But as he turned back to look at her, he found himself entranced. Bell looked as an angel might, her flawless skin shining in the moonlight. Mad fits of curls fell across the pillow and spilled over the edge of the mattress in a disheveled array. She still wore the dress she had on at the party, the turquoise color still bright even in the dark. Teddy watched as she breathed in and out, her chest rising and falling. Then he quickly diverted his gaze and left the room as he felt a desire to caress her collar and kiss her lips.

The next morning, Teddy awoke with a start. Had he dreamed Bell showing up at his doorstep in the middle of the night? He was asleep on his office couch. Sitting up, he put on his glasses and tried to focus. Then he heard footsteps coming from another room. He must not have dreamed it. Someone else was there.

He listened as a door opened and closed. It sounded like the washroom door. Teddy quickly dressed and tried to tame down his hair. He waited a moment to see if his visitor would come into his office. When nobody knocked on his door, he went in search of his charge.

The washroom was empty, but the odor was unmistakable. Someone had been ill. He crept back to his bedroom and cracked the door open to find Bell once again passed out on the bed. Her hair was matted down to her forehead, her cheeks flush.

She was ill, Teddy thought. Maybe that was why Davidson had thrown her out? Surely, not because of an illness, though the thought of having something as serious as influenza in his church made his stomach roll. He left the girl sleeping and returned to the washroom – cleaning agents and rags in hand.

Two more days went by, and still, Bell rose only to retch. He left crackers and seltzer water by her bed, and he only knew she ate some because they would disappear. She slept through an entire Sunday service, and Teddy thought even if she had not attended, maybe just being in the church would give her healing. Sunday afternoon, Teddy decided to fetch a doctor.

Doctor Smith looked over Bell and examined her though she slept through most of the procedure. When he pressed lightly on her stomach, Bell's eyes flew open, and her hands clutched her stomach.

"Who are you?" she demanded. "What are you doing?"

Teddy stepped forward so she could see him. "This is Doctor Smith. You've been so ill for the past few days I decided I had better bring him," he explained. "Please don't be alarmed."

Bell backed away some, jumping as the man attempted to touch her.

"It's all right, Madame," the doctor said calmly. His graying hair fell into his face, and Teddy thought the man looked trusting. "Reverend, would you mind my having a moment with your … wife?" He turned to Teddy and raised an eyebrow. He was asking more about their relationship than he was for privacy.

Teddy nodded silently and stood outside the doorway

with the door pulled closed behind him. He heard muffled voices, first the doctor's, then Bell's. When the door opened again, the doctor exited, bag in hand. Teddy gave the man a handful of money for his services, unsure what he should be paying. The doctor tipped his hat and excused himself, leaving Teddy and Bell alone.

Afraid to enter the room, Teddy stayed at the door. "Are you well? Can I get you something? Did the doctor prescribe anything for you?"

Bell sat up and drew her knees up to her chest, the thin blankets covering her from shoulder to toe. A few fresh tears slid down her cheek, and again, Teddy had the urge to reach out and touch her – to wipe them away.

"I will be fine soon enough, he said," she told him. "I am sorry for being such trouble. I meant only to stay one night."

"You are welcome to stay as long as you wish," he assured her. "Are you sure you are well? I've been terribly worried about you."

"I am sorry for that," she said, wiping a stray hair from her face. "The doctor promised me the illness will be gone soon. I can't wait. It's been terrible."

"How long?"

She looked up at him; her large, dark eyes seemed to be hiding something that she was not ready to reveal. "He says it's just from nerves. I should be completely well in a few weeks. But I do feel much better. I will gather my things and go today." Then she thought a moment. "Only I need some help."

"Anything you want." He meant it.

She looked so small and helpless. Teddy would give her the world if she asked for it. Her long, dark hair was now knotted up on her head, and dark circles lined her eyes from fitful sleep. Bell's skin was as pale as the sheets she held around her. Still, gazing at her took his breath away, and he longed to right any wrongs in her life.

"Once I get back to South Carolina, I will have no money left for lodging or food for a while. Until I can find a job," she said. "If you can help me out, I will send money back to you. I promise."

"You would never need to pay me back," Teddy said with a sad smile. So she was still intent on returning east? "What waits for you there? Or do you just mean to escape New Orleans?"

She raised her head. "Of course, I mean to escape. I have always wanted to get away from here," she reminded him. "And now, with what happened with Ian, I need to leave all the sooner."

Teddy finally entered the room fully and took a seat in the chair across from Bell. "I have not heard of him looking for you around town. I think you are safe. Would you like to talk about what happened the other night?"

He knew not to push her, she would only clam up. Had the man harmed her? She had no visible bruises or wounds. Had Davidson turned her out or had she left of her own accord? And why did she knock on his door in the middle of the night? Perhaps this was just a lover's spat, and she would return to him. Teddy's blood boiled at the thought of such a delicate lady going back to a rake like Ian Davidson.

Bell sighed long and deep. She relaxed her shoulders. "I should have known better, Teddy. He was too good to be true at first and proved the goodness I saw was not true later. I was a fool – that's what happened." She ran her thin, long fingers through her hair, realizing just how matted it was.

Teddy nodded. She was not revealing any more at the moment. He checked his watch and said, "Oh, I have a meeting to attend. Please, stay here until I get back." He stood up and looked down at her. "There's a shower in the bathroom, please help yourself to it, and make yourself some coffee. I won't be long, and then we will see what we can do for you."

Bell managed a weak smile and nodded to him. Before he left, he looked at her tersely and grabbed some ledgers and his coat. Walking out the door, he prayed for guidance as his mind whirled.

Ian Davidson was waiting for him behind a magnificent desk in the restaurant office. Teddy had to restrain himself from planting his fist squarely in the man's jaw when he walked into the room. Instead, he smiled nervously. It had been three days since the party and since Bell had arrived on his doorstep. This meeting had been planned since before everything had happened. He wondered if Davidson would say anything about his missing lady friend.

"Reverend Sullivan. Right on time," Davidson said as he stood. He did not extend a hand to Teddy. Teddy would not have taken it if he had.

"Mr. Davidson." Teddy nodded as he studied the man's longish-blond hair. He, too, had dark circles under his eyes. "I appreciate the invitation to your grand opening the other night. It was quite a ... spectacle."

The man beamed, thinking Teddy's words were a compliment. "Wasn't it? I took a risk on the Parisian-style show – this is the Paris of the States, is it not? A grand success."

"It was. Everyone seemed to have a wonderful time. And it was nice meeting your lady friend as well," Teddy said, testing the waters. Would Davidson realize his tactic to draw out information?

"Oh, Bell," he said, his face scowling. He sniffed the air as if something putrid had entered the room. "Well, she is no lady, and no longer a friend, I'm afraid." Teddy tried not to show his ire while the man continued. "You are a man of the cloth, are you not?"

Teddy nodded.

"May I take a moment to speak to you personally?" Teddy did not respond, but Davidson continued. "I realize you probably disapprove of the relationship I had with Miss Knight. But I discovered that night she had been unfaithful to me. And after I had taken her from one of the whore-houses and set her up in an apartment, too. Was I wrong to make her leave, or wrong to have taken her in in the first place?"

Teddy felt his face turn red. He hoped the man across from him thought it was from embarrassment and not anger.

"Well, you should not bring a woman – regardless of former profession – into your home and into the role of a wife without marrying her," Teddy said with a calmness that surprised even himself. "But are you sure she was unfaithful?"

The man sat back in his plush chair and kicked his lavishly-shoed feet onto the table. "I am sure. I heard it from the man – a friend of mine – myself. She admitted it as well. And now she claims to be with child, telling me it is mine, when I know she has given herself to other men."

Teddy tried to control himself. Bell was pregnant? Is that why she was so ill? Is that why the doctor spoke with her privately? Teddy no longer wanted to discuss Davidson's right or wrongdoing. He wanted to rush to Bell's side. But he knew he had to hear the rest of Davidson's story.

With a deep breath and a silent prayer for the right word, Teddy spoke. "I certainly hope the offending man is no longer your friend, just as Miss Knight is no longer your … um, houseguest. As for her condition, if she does carry your child, you should do the honest thing by her," he said, imme-diately wishing he had not said it. What if the man began to search for her, begging her to return?

"What if it is not my child?"

"I'm afraid to that I cannot attest," Teddy said, shaking his head. "You would need to speak with the woman."

"I have looked," Davidson confided with a forlorn sigh. "I acted rashly and turned her out, and now I cannot find her."

Was the man sincere, or was it a ploy to get back what he thought of as property? Was he truly concerned for Bell? As much as Teddy loved her, he knew if she was pregnant by Davidson, he should be honorable and marry her. But what if the child was someone else's?

Their attention returned to their ledgers. Teddy recoiled at thinking he was using Davidson's dirty money. But then again, money was money, and God used it all, clean or dirty. And Davidson was a brilliant businessman. Teddy would be able to move more people out of the city with the tactics he was shown.

He returned to the church a few hours later, carrying a bag of food with him. His favorite delicatessen happily prepared him two sandwiches, one he hoped Bell would be up to eating. But he could not stop thinking about her being with child.

When he entered the dimly lit kitchen, he found Bell sitting at the table, her hands wrapped around a cup of steaming coffee. Her eyes were brighter, her skin pink, and her hair was clean and shone brilliantly. She wore an older navy-blue frock, but Teddy thought she looked fantastic.

"Can I get you a cup? I know it's still chilly out there," she said as he sat the bag of food on the table.

"Thank you," he said as he removed his coat. He watched Bell reach up in the cupboard and pull down a heavy mug. She filled it with black coffee and turned to him. "Sugar, no cream," Teddy said, anticipating her question. She smiled and plunked two cubes of sugar into the hot liquid.

As she handed it to him, Teddy imagined what it would be like if this was their daily life. Eating deli sandwiches for lunch, Bell making him coffee every day. They could have a nice little existence, maybe have a few children. Then his smile faded as he recalled Davidson's words. If he was right, she had skipped over part of that dream already.

"Teddy? Are you all right?" Bell said, looking at him with a smile.

"Yes, I'm sorry," he said. "My mind got away from me. I hope you're hungry. I got us both sandwiches from a little place down the road." He pulled the paper sack apart and pulled out two paper-wrapped sandwiches.

Bell's eyes brightened, and she quickly took a package, unwrapped it, and took a big sniff of the fresh bread, meat, and cheese. Teddy handed her a red apple as well.

After blessing the food, Teddy looked Bell over and thought to his prayer the night of the party. Was this a part of God's master plan? For her to become an unwed mother and her child to have no father? Surely not. But Teddy recalled that no child was a mistake to God – each was carefully handcrafted by Him as a gift to their earthly parents. But this poor child's earthly father had rejected him and his mother. Would Bell do the same?

After finishing their meal in relative silence, Teddy could hold his questions in no longer. "I met with Ian Davidson today."

Her eyes quickly met his, fear rising up in them. "Why? Why would you do that? Did you tell him where I am? Don't let him find me, Teddy, please! And don't let Lou Walters know where I am either!"

Teddy frowned. "Who is Lou Walters?"

"The red-haired man from the party, the beast who stared at me like a piece of meat all through the show." She ducked her head down into her hands, the long curls hiding her delicate face from view.

"Did he hurt you, Bell?" Teddy tried to remain calm for her sake.

She nodded just slightly.

"How?" he demanded.

"He forced himself on me many times since I first met him several weeks ago," she confessed as tears slipped down her cheeks. "I told Ian, asked him to keep Lou away, but he said Lou was a friend and could do what he wanted with me. And I just let him!" Her silent tears turned to wails.

"Wait, wait," Teddy said, standing. He pulled Bell up and took hold of her shoulders, not caring about keeping his distance at this point. "Ian invited this man to come and rape you repeatedly?" Bell nodded. Teddy only had one more question. "Who is the baby's father?"

~

*W*hat had Teddy just said? How did he know? Bell slowly raised her tear-stained face to look at him. His face showed disgust. For her? For her child? She had hoped to not tell him and secret away before he found out. But if he had met with Ian, Ian must have told him. Why? Did Ian miss her? Did he regret forcing her to leave?

Teddy repeated himself. "Bell, who is the father of your child?"

With a gulp, she quietly answered, "Ian is." She dreaded his response. Would Teddy hate her forever? She never thought she would be ashamed of her child, and here she was, the child recently conceived, and she was already ashamed.

"Are you sure it's not this Lou Walters'?"

"I'm at least 2 months gone by now," she said. "Before the first time Lou kicked my door in with Ian's permission. Did Ian tell you? Did you tell him I was here?"

Teddy released his grip on her but did not move. Bell wanted him to keep holding onto her, to tell her everything would be fine, even if it was a lie.

"Nobody knows you are here," he reassured her. "When I met with Mr. Davidson, he asked if he could discuss a personal matter and claimed that you were unfaithful to him and then told him you were with child." He paused and wet his lips. "So, you are with child?"

There was no use hiding it any longer. "I am. The doctor confirmed it for me," she said with a sigh. "I guess we were right all those months ago. Madam Knight was giving us something to keep us from conceiving. But this was not how my dreams of motherhood were supposed to go," she said as she laid her head on Teddy's chest.

For once, he did not shy away from her. Bell's heart mended a little as he put his long arms around her and held her tight.

CHAPTER 17

*S*till in New Orleans a month later, Bell was uneasy all the time, not to mention still queasy in the stomach. She refused to leave the back rooms of the church building, sure that even being in front of a window would alert Ian to where she was. Why had she allowed Teddy to convince her to stay? She didn't need to answer that. He did not force her. She had stayed for him.

And she had stayed because she knew there were more women who needed to get out. She had seen crib girls on the street, their skin hanging from bare bones. The more she thought about getting away, the more she thought about who she could take with her. Maybe one day she could help Daisy, and maybe even Poppy and Anise, flee from Storyville.

Even though she refused to attend his church service the next Sunday, Bell had peeked out into the sanctuary. A good fifty heads were lifted, and voices sang hymns. White and black, man and woman, young and old. There were even some well-to-do-looking people sitting to the left with several crib girls off to the right. They were all together. Bell smiled as she realized Teddy's dream was a reality. He had created a church that broke down all the barriers – or at least, was starting to.

Each night that week, the pair had prayed before supper. Then Bell would rise and begin to clean the dishes, even though Teddy had never asked her to. As she washed one night, he began to tell her of his sermon for the upcoming week. It had continued since. He would talk about his sermons, asking how he should word a particular point or if something made sense to her. Bell found herself truly listening to scripture for the first time.

And the words were beautiful.

She still occupied the bedroom, with Teddy sleeping in his office at night, tucking the bedrolls away come morning when he might have visitors. In the quiet of night, Bell turned her lamp up and read from the Psalms. She also began reading the small leather Bible Teddy had left for her one night.

In fact, one restless night, she lay staring at the ceiling, counting pockmarks, when the door unlatched. Bell had closed her eyes and stayed motionless, unsure what Teddy was doing coming into the room. He never spoke, but he stayed standing over her for a few seconds, took a hefty sigh, and placed something on the nightstand beside her. As quietly as he could, he disappeared again, closing the door softly. Bell gently rolled to look at what he had put down and saw the Bible. She traced the embossed letters with her fingers and fell asleep with the cool leather under her hand.

She had only been there a little while, but already she felt everything about her changing. Finally, changing for good. This was not the lateral shift she had made from whore for the masses to whore for one man's amusement. Teddy was a gentleman. He would kiss her on the forehead the way an older brother might. He might lay his hand on hers briefly but always removed it just as quick, leaving Bell wishing for the warmth to return.

But more than that, Bell felt a stirring inside her. Not the babe – it was too early for that still, she knew – but in her chest. In her heart, it seemed. She felt as if someone was calling out to her, asking her to reach out. Was it Teddy? No, she accepted him already. This was something else.

Bell worked up the courage to ask him about the feeling. "Teddy?"

He glanced up from his notes and morning coffee. "Yes?"

"I feel … something," she said, unsure how to describe it. And she feared he would laugh at her.

"The baby? Already?" He sounded excited. Bell sighed at his endearing ways and the hope his eyes showed.

She shook her head to clear it. "No, no. I mean here," she said, placing her hand over her chest. "Well, not in here, not a pain," she explained. "Like a calling. Like someone is looking for me and calling me. Does that make sense?"

Teddy beamed and put his notes down. "Perfect sense," he said happily. "Like someone has looked into your very being and called you out to join them?"

"Yes!" she said with a grin. "That's it exactly. What do I do?"

Teddy stifled a grin. "You answer the call, Bell."

She cocked her head to one side, a curl falling loose of its pin as it was prone to do. Bell bit her lip and fidgeted with her apron. She had talked on a telephone before but was not sure how to answer a call from within her.

Teddy spoke again. "It's Jesus calling you, Bell. He wants you to let him into your heart. Into your life. Give him control, Bell," Teddy urged her. "It is so much easier with the Lord in control. I promise."

She scooted her chair around the table, so it was next to his. "What do I do?"

She looked at him very seriously. She was ready. No more fooling around. If Jesus was calling her, she would answer Him. She was tired of messing up her life. She trusted Teddy. If he said life was easier with Jesus, she would believe him.

Teddy cautiously took her hands into his. Warmth radiated from them, and Bell felt the warmth reach her heart. "We pray," he said as he bowed his head. Bell bowed hers in return. "Heavenly Father. Perfect and wondrous. We are sinners who fall short. But we are your children, and you are our Abba Father. We come crying to you the way a child would cry to his mother and father. And you are there. Ever ready to draw us up to you. Ready to heal. Ready to forgive. Ready to bring redemption.

"You know your daughter, Bell," he continued. Bell sucked in her breath at the mention of her name. She wanted with everything she had for God to know her. "You know her plight. You know her road to recovery. She seeks you, Lord. Enter her in earnest. Bring healing to her mind, spirit, and body. Lord, we ask Your protection over the babe she carries. May it know nothing but its mother's love and Your grace. Amen."

She looked up and found Teddy looking intently at her. "What now?"

"Now we set to making things right," Teddy answered. "You attend church, you serve the people of God however you feel called. But the biggest thing is being obedient to God's will for your life."

"And how would I do that?"

A joyous smile erupted on Teddy's face, and his eyes welled with tears as he looked at her. "You pray, you read the Bible. At some point, a voice will come into your head and give you direction. Then you have the faith to carry it out, even if it seems impossible."

Bell sighed and furrowed her brow. "I thought you said it

was easier with God. This sounds hard. I don't want to do the impossible."

With a slight smile, Teddy reassured her. "No, you don't do it. God does it through you. You are just his vessel. And I promise you, when you do things God's way, it is easy. Trust me."

She smiled at him, "That I can do." With her hand still in his, she nestled close to him and rested her head on his shoulder.

A small voice inside her head spoke to her, almost like it was whispered on the wind, but it told her to never forget where she came from. But what did it mean? Not to forget that she had come through the agony of life in a brothel? She would bear those scars forever. Or not to forget her parents? She could hardly forget them.

A faint touch on her shoulder brought her back to attention.

"Teddy?"

"Mmm?" he said, not moving.

"Teddy, I don't"—she paused and licked her lips—"I don't think I want to be Bell anymore." When Teddy lifted her away from him, she took a shaky breath and had a hard time finding her voice. "I want to be Lana again. I want to be who my parents intended for me to be, and that includes my name."

Teddy took her hand in his, easing her apprehension. "I think that's wonderful. Lana is a beautiful name."

Joy filled her. No longer would she be Bell, the prostitute. Never again. Now she would be Lana, a woman to make her parents proud.

≈

*T*he next day, Lana began anew and decided her first calling was to clean the building of the Forgiven Grace Church. She timidly moved inside the main sanctuary and closed the door behind her. The room was cool but inviting. Teddy worked in his office no more than a quick cry for help between them. With a duster, she set to cleaning off all the surfaces before moving onto tackling the never-swept floor.

After an hour of hard work, Bell stood and swept her forearm across her brow. She had made good progress in the large room. Perhaps she should step outside and sweep the front area as well, just for good measure.

She was outside and nearly finished the chore when she realized she had not stepped outside since arriving at the church. She had been confined to the interior all those days. Lana took a moment and stood tall, filling her lungs with fresh, crisp air. It made her feel better, less nauseated, and for that, she was thankful.

"Taking up housework, have you?" said a voice behind her. Lana spun around, dreading who she was sure to see. "Trying to atone for your sins by cleaning up the church, are you Bell?" Lou Walters stood several yards away.

She uneasily put her hand on the doorknob, ready to run back inside the church and lock the door – if there was a lock. If nothing else, she could scream, and Teddy would come to her rescue.

"Don't worry, I won't touch you," Lou said, noticing her apprehension. "I heard from Ian that you were in a family way." He snickered as he spoke and rubbed his own stomach. Lana thought the gesture lewd and looked away.

"It's not your child, Lou, mind your own affairs," she said dryly. But on the inside, her heart was hammering, and she felt like she might be sick to her stomach.

He took a step closer to her; she stepped closer to the door, willing it to swallow her back to the inside. "I don't care if it's my bastard seed or not, Bell," he said. "I don't want it. Nobody wants it. Why don't you just go down to the witch doctor and get it taken care of?"

Instinctively, Lana put a hand around her midsection, as if to protect her tiny babe. "I want this baby. I do. Now go, leave me alone, Lou."

With that, she thrust open the door and ran inside, the door slamming in her wake. She knew Lou would not follow her. His days of dominating her were over. But she did fear that Ian would show up on the church steps soon – the very steps she had just swept free of dirt.

"Teddy!" she cried out as she rounded the corner into his small office. She stopped in his doorway, chest heaving, cheeks flushed.

Teddy stood immediately and tossed his glasses on the desk before Lana fell into him, holding him tightly. "What's wrong?" His arms tensed around her, making her feel safer.

"I was outside, sweeping the entrance," she said, her chest heaving. "And Lou came up to me. He'll tell Ian where I am, Teddy." Lana shook from fear, but she did not cry. She was done crying over her old life.

His grip tightened enough that Lana wasn't constricted, but it also stopped her from shaking so much. He kissed her on the top of her head, and Lana could feel his hot breath on her hair. "Don't worry, Lana. I will protect you. And what I can't do, God can. Have faith. Be obedient, like we talked about."

Lana only nodded into his chest, the one place that made her feel truly safe in this world. She wasn't sure how this was being obedient, but she knew she would need all the help she could get.

Sure enough, that evening, after Lana and Teddy had

finished their meager supper, a knock came on the back door. A gruff voice followed. "Reverend, you better open up! I know she's in there. I just want to talk."

Strong green eyes bore into her own dark ones as Teddy nodded to her. Lana nodded back. They were prepared. The afternoon had been spent in anxious anticipation and prayer. Teddy has assured her she could handle Ian when he showed up on their doorstep, as surely Lou would blow the whistle on her hiding place.

Teddy calmly took Lana's hand and kissed it gently. Lana's heart felt like it could soar from such a romantic act, but this was not the time for such frivolities. Teddy stood up and went to the back door, opening it for Ian Davidson.

Lana was surprised to hear calm yet demanding words. "I have a right to see her," was all he said.

Teddy invited him in and led him to the kitchen where Lana sat waiting. She tried not to shake, but she could not help the heat that rose on her neck and the uneasiness that roiled in her stomach.

The men walked in, and Lana remained in her seat. Teddy took up a position of sentry just to the side of the door. If anything happened, Ian would not get out unscathed, Lana knew that for sure.

Ian wore a green overcoat and twill pants. His blond hair was longer than she remembered it but was pushed back out of his eyes. He looked very dashing, and Lana was reminded of why she had been attracted to him so many months before. But it had not been love that attracted her. Because the sight of Ian Davidson in that moment made Lana want to retch from disgust.

He smiled at her, but Lana kept her face void of emotion. "I have been looking for you," Ian said. "I had no idea the good reverend was hiding you."

Ian turned and shot a wayward glance at Teddy. Teddy, for his part, merely said, "Not hiding, just safe."

Ian's eyes narrowed at the comment, and he turned back to Lana. "I came to beg your forgiveness, Bell," he said, kneeling at her side. "I acted rashly, and I am very sorry. Please forgive me, and let's forget this whole thing."

Lana turned her body away from him but kept her eyes affixed to his. "You want to forget that you threw me out for telling you I was in a family way? With your child?"

Ian nodded. Lana risked a glance at Teddy, who stood tall and gave her silent confidence.

"We can get that taken care of, my pet, and go back to the way things were before," Ian said with a smile. He was almost begging, Lana realized.

"Get it taken care of?"

"We can see old Doctor Redgood for some remedies for such a ... malady," Ian offered, his expression hopeful.

Lana stood, knocking Ian over in the movement. "My child is not a malady! Your child is not a malady," she fumed, while Ian stayed on the floor. "This is a human life that should have been created by loving parents who were committed to each other and their family. Instead, this will be the bastard child of a former district girl and a vagabond playboy! But regardless of this child's origins, I will love him or her to the utmost of my ability." She took a deep breath and looked down at Ian and finished by adding, "Without you."

In that moment, she realized just how much God loved her. God wanted her and accepted her despite her faults. Her anger at Ian transformed into something different. Bell's heart broke as she towered over his body, and she saw just how dirty Ian really was. But truthfully, they were all filthy sinners, some were just trying harder than others. The revelation filled her with warmth. Turning to face Teddy, Lana saw her future while her past was still sprawled on the floor.

Ian scrambled to his feet. "Fine, just fine, Bluebell," he said, color rising on his face. "I could take care of you for the rest of your life, but instead, you're choosing to have a child I'm not even sure is mine."

Lana raised her chin and pushed her shoulders back but still did not face him. "That's fine, Ian. We won't need you. This child and I have the Lord with us."

Ian snorted. "Oh, Bell," he said, "no matter what you say, you will always be a whore. Now you're just a whore in a church." He turned to Teddy, whose face, while a little red, remained calm. "Don't send her back when you tire of her, Reverend. I don't want her anymore."

He pushed past Teddy and went to the door, never looking back as it closed behind him.

CHAPTER 18

A week later, as Lana and Teddy were reading the paper and sipping cups of coffee, Teddy was unable to concentrate on the paper in front of him. He was trying to come up with a way to ask Lana to marry him right away. He didn't want to wait any longer. He was ready to marry her and become a father to her child.

But the words could never come to fruition as Lana dropped her teacup, shattering on the ground. When Teddy looked up to her, he saw Lana's face drawn and pale.

"What's wrong?" he asked, alarm filling him.

Lana stammered, "I don't – I don't know. Something's not right. My stomach—" She let out a groan of agonizing pain and doubled over. When she finally stood, red liquid began pooling at her bare feet. "Teddy!"

Teddy jumped to his feet but was completely unsure what to do. Where was the blood coming from? Then it hit him. The baby. The baby was in trouble.

Lana began to weep as she stood motionless. "Teddy, please, do something!"

He took her hands into his and silently prayed, *Lord,*

please help her and the baby! He carefully moved her toward their bedroom. He picked up his pallet and laid it on the bed so the blood would soak that and not the mattress. He helped Lana lay down and knelt by her side.

"Should I get the doctor?"

Lana barely nodded. Her face matched the white sheet she laid on, and her body became stiff.

Teddy wasted no time and ran to the doctor's house, praying the whole way he was home. It took him nearly ten minutes to get there, ten minutes without knowing how his precious Lana was doing, how the baby he had grown to love was doing.

"Doctor Smith," he said, out of breath. "Hurry," he heaved, "the baby. Blood everywhere."

The doctor grabbed his bag, and they jumped into a coach. Teddy was thankful that Doctor Smith's coach had not been unhitched from the last call he had made. As they bounded toward Forgiven Grace Church, Teddy prayed for God to protect his little family. Lana had suffered enough; she didn't need to lose the child she cherished already.

Teddy leapt from the coach before it came to a complete stop and ran inside, leaving the aging doctor scurrying to keep up.

"Lana, I have Doctor Smith. Don't worry, it will be okay." He smoothed her sweat-covered brow.

He made room for the doctor and immediately noticed that Lana's nightgown was soaked in blood. She was no longer pale, but instead bright red herself and drenched in sweat. Suddenly, she moaned in pain, calling out for him. Teddy moved toward her, but the doctor held out his hand to stop him.

Doctor Smith stood and turned to Teddy. "The lady, as I recall, should be a little more than three months gone in her pregnancy by now, but it is not good," he said. "She's losing the baby. If we're not careful, we may lose her, too. Right now, we have to just wait and see."

"Wait and see? What do you mean, 'wait and see,' Doctor?" Teddy ran his hand through his hair, then took off his glasses. He wiped his eyes furiously and replaced the specs so he could better see his wife. How could he help her?

"Get a rag and wet it with hot water and wring it out," the doctor instructed as if reading Teddy's thoughts. "Then come sit by her side. I'll stay here until it comes."

"'It?'"

Doctor Smith looked away from him. "The baby, Reverend."

It didn't take long for Lana's perfect and tiny baby to be born. Teddy requested to keep his body so they could give him a proper burial. The doctor had only shaken his head as he left.

Teddy put a chair next to the bed and sat, holding Lana's limp hand. "I am sorry, my love," he said. "I had no idea. I hurried as much as I could. But the baby is gone, Lana. We will bury him when you feel up to it. But please get yourself well. Lord, please heal her body."

With no response, Teddy quickly undressed her and got her into clean nightclothes. He also managed to remove the red-stained sheets from the pallet. He was glad he thought to put that on top of the mattress. He placed two towels under Lana to catch any more blood and took the soiled items outside. He placed them in a steel barrel and lit them on fire. He never wanted to see those things again and was sure Lana would feel the same way. There would be other nightgowns. But her baby was gone forever.

~

*J*t was four days before Lana woke up completely. The doctor had kept her knocked out with laudanum until he was sure most of the physical pain had subsided. But when she woke, she felt drugged and had a hard time focusing.

"Teddy?" she called weakly. Her throat hurt, and her entire body ached. What had happened?

Teddy appeared in the doorway, his eyes wide with surprise. "You're awake!"

"What's going on? What happened?" Lana tried to sit up but found that her body did not cooperate with her. She felt dizzy and achy.

"Shh," Teddy said, sitting next to her. "Hang on, don't move. The doctor said it would be a while before you could really get up and move again."

"Why?" Lana did not understand. She wanted Teddy to start explaining things right away, but the pain was almost too much.

"Lana, do you remember the other day? When you began to bleed? The baby is gone, my love," Teddy said as he kissed her hand. "I'm terribly sorry, Lana. The doctor and I were too late. There was nothing we could do."

Lost the baby? What did he mean? Lana's hand went to her mid-section, where a week prior, it had been beginning to round ever so slightly. Now the area dipped, empty of its precious parcel.

"No, Teddy," she whispered. Tears spilled over her cheeks. "What happened?"

"I'm not entirely sure," Teddy said honestly. Lana watched him wipe his eye under his glasses.

Lana stared at him. The man she loved. She had hoped perhaps they could marry and raise the child together. He was obviously as upset at the news as she was. How could her baby be gone? She closed her eyes as more tears welled up. How could God allow this to happen to her? Now that she had turned from her previous life, things were supposed to go right for her, weren't they? Why did this happen?

"Do you need anything?" Teddy asked.

Yes, she thought, she needed her baby back. She needed to go back in time four days and undo whatever had caused her to lose her child. Tears began to flow, and uncontrollable sobs wracked her body.

"I want my baby back," she wailed.

In that moment, Teddy gingerly laid his head on her shoulder and held her as she cried until nothing was left. As the sobs abated, he sat up and smoothed her hair from her face. His own cheeks were wet with shed tears.

"I have prayed nonstop for you, and I have every faith that your child is in heaven cradled in the arms of the Lord," Teddy said as he ran his thumb over her knuckles.

"Really?" She gulped as she tried to catch her breath. "The child of a district girl and a playboy will be in heaven?"

With a gulp of breath, she had to ask. "Teddy, was—was my baby a boy or a girl?"

Tears swam in his eyes again as he hesitated. After a moment, he smiled as he told her, "He was a little boy. Perfectly formed."

"A boy?" Her heart shattered all over again as tears came anew. "And he's in heaven?"

Teddy only nodded. It was almost more than she could hope for. Even if her child wasn't in her arms, at least he would be waiting for her.

Feeling nearly sick from the crying, Lana was parched. "Can I get some water, please?"

Teddy patted Lana's hand and slipped from the room, giving her a moment alone.

She again tried to sit up and managed to get semi-upright. Her entire body throbbed, worse than when she had been beaten by Nigel Harding. This pain came from the inside out. And it wasn't just physical pain, though that was bad enough. Intense emotions began to flow inside her. Lana felt bitter, angry, and deceived by the God she had grown to love.

When Teddy returned, she asked, "Why would God allow this?"

With a shake of his head, Teddy responded, "I don't know. I wish I did. I've seen many families who have lost a wee one either being born too early or passing shortly after a healthy birth. I have never understood it," he admitted. "And I understand it even less now."

He gave Lana the water, and she drank greedily. Her stomach turned, and she struggled to put the water down on the table beside her without spilling.

"I only know this. 'Weeping may come for a night, but joy cometh in the morning.'"

"I don't think I will be happy when the sun comes up in the morning, Teddy," she said with a scowl across her face. How could he think she would return to normal the following day?

"Not necessarily tomorrow, Lana," Teddy explained. "That passage is from the Psalms. Psalm thirty, verse five. It means that you are crying and sad and angry now, and that's okay. But it won't last forever. One day, you will rejoice again."

"It doesn't feel like it," Lana said with a sniff. "Oh, Teddy, my baby is gone!" She buried her face in her hands and wept again. Teddy came close to her, but she shooed him away, wishing to be alone for a while longer. Lana was sure nobody understood the agony she was in, and she was doubly sure she would never rise out of it again.

A month passed, and Lana was still feeling depressed. She

went through the motions of each day, and nothing more. They ran together as if a blur. Lana could not eat, and the world appeared bleak and gray. Her hands had not gotten the message that the child was gone, and they continually sought the slight rounding that had happened in her mid-section. Each time they found a void instead, Lana was heartbroken all over again.

Teddy had forced her to drink broth and sit by the window. At first, she refused, but with his incessant nagging, she had given in. A week later, he had added chicken and vegetables to the broth and had moved a rocking chair just outside the back door. Lana took in the birds singing and the flowers blooming. And most of all, she soaked up the care Teddy was giving her.

Lana had to admit, with time, she felt a little better. And after a few weeks, she found her smile returning as the world began to show vibrant colors and sounds once more.

Trying her best not to pout over the circumstances she found herself in, she sat down with a pencil and paper and decided to write Ginny a letter. She had not written to her at all since Teddy had taken her friend to Virginia, and Lana felt it was well past due.

Dear Ginny,

I hope this letter finds you well. I wish I had known what was transpiring with you and Teddy. It would have saved me so much heartache. Where shall I begin? I suppose the beginning is the best.

After you and Teddy left New Orleans, a man named Ian Davidson began to come to the spa. I couldn't stand being there without you or Zinnia, and he offered to take me away. He put me up in an apartment of my own. At the time, my heart was so broken I did not think it would ever mend, and he gave me the attention I was craving. But when I came up with child, he turned me out and accused me of things I never did. I had nowhere to go, so I went to Teddy.

I didn't think Teddy would take me in for more than a night, but he did. He showered me with love, and I think he looked forward to the baby as much as I did. But last month, I lost the baby that should not have been born until October. Teddy and I buried him – the first burial of the Forgiven Grace Church. Watching Teddy grieve was just as hard as my own grieving. You would have thought he had fathered the babe, and how I wish he had.

I call my baby Angel since I know he's in heaven with the Good Shepherd. I believe in God, but I don't understand how this could happen. I straightened my ways, I fell in love with a preacher, shouldn't that make up for my past mistakes?

I'm sorry to carry on so. I do miss you, Ginny. Please write back.

Yours Fondly,
Lana (Or Bluebell)

Lana thought a walk to the post office might make her feel a little better. She rarely left the church property as she was sure the outside world would condemn her as a harlot. That, and she just plain did not feel like wandering about. But her spirit told her to move, so she decided to see if Teddy would walk with her to post her letter.

She poked her head into his office. "Teddy? I wrote Ginny a letter," she told him as if it were nothing out of the ordinary.

Teddy took off his eyeglasses and looked at her, one eyebrow raised. "Oh?"

"I would really like to take it to the post office. Would you come with me?" she requested, feeling a little embarrassed to be asking for an escort.

Teddy only smiled. "Of course, Lana. I would be happy to." He stood and grabbed a stack of letters sitting on the edge of his desk. "I'm so glad you're feeling better."

"My heart is broken, Teddy, but I'm trying. You were right."

He cocked his head and looked at her. "About what?"

She sighed. "About the sun coming up in the morning. The fog is lifting, and I want to keep living. And I want to keep living with you. I love you."

Lana saw Teddy's face transform into one that radiated love and light. "I love you, too."

❧

*T*eddy wondered if he should tell Lana that he had been corresponding with Ginny since he left her in Virginia with her brother. They were not private letters, Lana could read any of them, but Teddy did not want to force them onto her. He would tell her another time. For now, this was her move.

"What did you say in your letter?"

"I pretty much just wrote what's happened to me since she left," Lana said with a shrug, looking down at the ground. "I guess it's a pretty sad letter. Maybe I shouldn't send it." She stopped in her tracks about twenty feet from the front door of the church.

Teddy coaxed her along. "I'm sure she's just aching to hear from her best friend," he promised. He knew it was true – Ginny had asked of her many times in each letter she had sent.

Teddy always wrote back with what was happening, even telling Ginny about the loss of Lana's pregnancy. He had just gotten a letter back full of condolences. Ginny had written of good news of her own, but Teddy would wait for Ginny to write back to Lana herself before sharing.

Lana walked slowly, as if every step were a hurdle to overcome, but she held his hand tight. Teddy missed the bold and impetuous girl he had met a year ago. He loved her but wasn't too fond of her newly passive mind-set. The spunk she used to carry with her was hiding. He prayed for God to reveal a way to give Lana that spark she had possessed before losing her child.

Selfishly, Teddy wanted Lana to be his. He wanted to be secure in knowing she would be waiting for him every day when he got home. The thought of a family overjoyed him. And past or no past, Lana made his heart beat wildly out of control. He wanted to marry her and grow old with her.

But first, they needed to get married. And Teddy knew just how to ask his beloved.

≈

That night, Lana was sweeping their dwelling space in an effort to keep the area tidy. She knew she wasn't the best at keeping house, but she was determined to learn. She opened the door, sighing as the heat from outside rushed to meet her, and swept all the dust and dirt back outside, where it belonged.

With the door firmly shut, Lana heard Teddy call her name from the sanctuary space. She replaced the broom in a small closet and removed her apron, hanging it beside the broom. She huffed, blowing curls from her forehead. She slowly walked toward the sound of Teddy's voice.

"Did you need something?" She called as she meandered down the hallway to him.

As she opened the door into the main room of the church,

Lana was immediately dumbstruck. Teddy stood in the center of the room, surrounded by white petals strewn all across the room. Lit candles were also interspersed throughout the petals, casting an ethereal glow. He held a handful of white blooms in his hands. A grin stretched from ear to ear as he caught sight of her.

"Teddy? What—?" She slowly went to him, meeting him in the center of the room. She spun in a slow circle, looking at everything again. Her mind reeled as she contemplated just what Teddy was doing.

As she completed the circle to face him again, she found him bent down on one knee. The air in Lana's lungs seemed to have disappeared, and she gasped. Was he going to ask her to marry him? Was Teddy ready for that? Was she?

He licked his lips, took a deep breath, and placed his hands around hers. "Lana, from the moment I first saw you, I felt that God brought us into each other's lives for a reason. Over time, I grew to love you, and I cannot imagine my life without you in it. We've made mistakes, but nobody can claim perfection. However, my life would be closer to perfect if you would agree to be my wife."

Salty tears began to fall down her cheeks as Lana fell to the floor in front of Teddy. She took Teddy's face into her hands and searched his eyes with her own. Slowly, she brought her face towards his and kissed him.

Immense joy overtook her in that moment. He loved her, he wanted her regardless of her past. Lana pushed all the love she felt into that kiss and wrapped her arms around him. She could feel Teddy's arms envelop her, and Lana never wanted to leave them for the rest of her life.

When their lips broke apart, Teddy smirked. "Is that a yes?"

"Yes, a hundred times, yes," Lana said with giddy laughter.

"I am the happiest woman in New Orleans. No, in Louisiana!"

They stood together, and Lana nestled again into Teddy's arms. He held her silently for a few moments, and Lana savored the feeling. She didn't think any moment could be as perfect at this one.

CHAPTER 19

hey were married the next Tuesday. It was as good a day as any, and it was when Teddy's minister friend, Joseph Becker, could perform the ceremony.

Teddy had offered to purchase Lana a new dress for the occasion, but she insisted on wearing the cornflower blue dress he had gotten her before. She had said it was the most beautiful dress she could imagine. Teddy had worn his plain brown suit, not thinking of anything more formal for himself.

The ceremony was attended by nobody save themselves and Reverend Becker's wife, Marie. But it had been a wonderfully sunny day, perfect for a wedding. Mrs. Becker was a pleasant woman, and she had baked a cake for the occasion, and Lana had thanked her profusely.

Teddy and Lana stood before the reverend, hands clasped, as the man had them speak their vows. Lana recited them slowly, allowing the full weight of them to carry. A tear slipped down her cheek as she placed the simple gold band on his finger. Teddy longed to wipe the tear away, but he could only smile at his bride. The love he felt for her made his heart feel like it would burst from his chest.

When they were pronounced husband and wife, Teddy swept Lana off the ground and spun her in a circle before kissing her soundly. Reverend and Mrs. Becker congratulated them with a laugh, and Mrs. Becker offered to cut the cake.

As a wedding gift, he bought her a complete Bible, and upon giving it to her, said, "All ministers' wives need a Bible of their own. So, this is for you."

Lana hadn't batted an eyelash. She took the volume, wrapped her arms around Teddy's neck, and wept with joy. Finally, Lana had embraced not just the love Teddy felt, but also the God who loved and adored her as well.

Lana threw herself into the mission of the church, reaching the unreachable. They talked all hours of the night about parishioners who came through the doors and how they could help the young women of Storyville change their lives around.

A few weeks after their wedding, Teddy was preparing his sermon while Lana wrote another letter to Ginny. He thought it was finally time to show her the surprise he had been preparing since their wedding day.

As if she could read his mind, Lana looked up at his goofy smile. "What?" She smiled in return.

"I love you, Mrs. Sullivan," he said.

Her pink cheeks deepened, and she almost shied her eyes away, but she didn't. Her eyes remained focused on him. "I love you, too, Reverend," she said with a giggle. She often called him that as a tease, but Teddy knew she meant what she said.

His heart skipped a beat as she batted her eyelashes at him. "Let's take a walk," he suggested.

"A walk?" She furrowed her brow. "Why?"

Standing, he reached his hand out for hers. Without hesitation, she took it and smiled. Her trust in him was complete, and for that, he was eternally grateful. "It's a surprise," he told her.

They strolled outside; the humidity was almost oppressive, but Teddy felt light on his feet. He kept glancing to Lana, who held a shy smile on her lips the whole time.

They paused in front of the Magnolia Apartments right next to Tulane University. Teddy felt as giddy as a schoolboy; he pulled on Lana's hand to get her to move up the walk.

"Oh, Teddy, I don't feel like calling on any of your parishioners right now," she said as she pulled her hand back.

Shaking his head, Teddy assured her they were not on a church call. "No, Lana. We're not here to see anybody. Just trust me."

She looked suspicious but took a step toward him. Teddy grinned at her. She did trust him. It made his heart soar.

Inside, Teddy led Lana up to the second floor and down the hallway. He pulled a key from his pocket and unlocked the door, pulling her inside. The key almost slipped from his sweaty palms, and he took a steadying breath as he stepped back to watch her. A dry mouth kept him from speaking for a moment, but he swallowed and prepared to answer his wife's question.

"Teddy? Why are we here?"

"We're home," he said, almost laughing. "How would you like to live here instead of in the church?"

"Here?" Lana looked at him, her chocolate eyes wide. A smile crept across her face.

She looked from the walls to the windows, taking everything in again. They stood in a modest living room with a small kitchen off to the left. To the right were two bedrooms – small, but suitable. The apartment even had its own powder room behind the kitchen. Teddy had not given up the search for an apartment, but it had taken longer than he thought to find something he thought would suit his wife.

Eyes sparkling and curls bobbing, Lana jumped into Teddy's arms. "Oh, Teddy, I love it! When can we move in?"

"There's the spit-fire girl I fell in love with," Teddy said as he looked longingly at his bride. "We can move in right away. Why don't we go back to the church and pack up our things?"

~

That night, Lana had gotten three grubby little boys, each about ten years old, to cart their belongings from the church to the new apartment. She had given each a nickel, plus an apple in each hand when the boxes were deposited just inside the door. The kids held tight to their treasures as they ran off into the night. Lana sighed as she watched them disappear from the building door.

"How can I help them?" she asked herself aloud. She leaned against the door frame.

As she peered into the night sky and prayed for God to show her a way, Lana felt something calling her to reach out to those children. The girls especially, she felt, who needed saving before their lives were turned upside down like hers was and their innocence stolen before they ever knew what it was to begin with.

Teddy appeared behind her and put his stubbled chin against her shoulder. Lana breathed in his scent and closed her eyes. She leaned her head against his, and she felt butterflies when he wrapped his arms around her.

"What are you looking at out here?" His voice was low and hot in her ear.

"Watching those boys scamper off," she sighed, "I wish I

could help them. Preserve their innocence a while longer before the lure of Storyville drags them under."

Teddy turned her around and searched her eyes. His hands pressed into her back as he asked, "Do you? Do you want to help them?"

Lana nodded; of course, she did.

He smiled. "Then we will help them. I have a wonderful idea about how to assist the unseen children of the city."

Lana beamed. "All I've ever wanted to do is get the girls out. You know that," she said. "It was my driving force when I was there – get the girls out. I still want to do that, especially the younger girls."

"Then let's do it," Teddy said, beaming. But then his voice and face turned serious. "But I have to warn you. We will not be popular here in New Orleans. It will not be easy. God calls us to sacrifice, and we will have to do that in order to save them."

Lana looked down at her fingers intertwined with Teddy's. She thought a moment. A comfortable life would be nice – it was what she longed for. But saving young girls destined for the cribs was more important than her own comfort. She looked up at her husband.

"I have never lived an easy life, Teddy. Those children deserve a shot at living a secure existence."

As the soulful sounds of jazz music wafted to their ears, they stood together and peered out into the darkness.

Then an idea struck him – the district girls. Lana's driving force before had been getting Ginny, Zinnia, and the other girls out of Storyville. And, of course, Teddy dreamed of getting all the crib and bordello girls out of New Orleans. Together they could do that. Lana could get into the places he could not and minister to the girls who needed it most. Who else but a former prostitute turned preacher's wife could get through to these girls?

Teddy was near giddy with his idea. How had he not thought of this before? He had been too focused on what Lana needed; he had not even thought to what God had in store for them. This was it.

The desire to begin their mission blossomed in his heart, and Teddy knew just how they could do it, but he knew he needed to plant the seed in his wife's mind first.

CHAPTER 20

*L*ife became a comfortable routine for Lana and Teddy. The comfort was never mundane, though. Each new day exhilarated her as she woke up, still reveling in being Mrs. Reverend Sullivan. She worked hard to keep the apartment and the church neat as a pin, and she read her Bible daily. She even dabbled in cooking meals, though sandwiches were more her speed.

There was one area, however, where Lana felt like she was at a complete loss. Despite Teddy's affection and declarations of love, he had never shown her in the one way she knew how. She wasn't sure how to broach the subject, either, as it filled her with shame.

Perhaps, she thought, he still saw her as a belle of the night, as she did. Was Teddy ashamed of her, despite his claim to have forgiven and forgotten her past?

A few weeks after their wedding, as Teddy made notes for his upcoming sermon, Lana confronted him. "Teddy, you love me, right?"

He peered up at her and removed his glasses. "You know I

do, my love. What makes you question me?" A crease etched between his eyebrows.

Lana ran her fingers along the opening of her apron pockets, the fabric scratching against her skin. She kept her gaze down. "You don't – you don't show me your affections."

Realization dawned on Teddy's face, and Lana was startled when he stood abruptly and crossed the room to her. He lifted her chin with his thumb and stared into her eyes. Lana looked into the green pools that showed both love and hurt.

"My sweet Lana, I wanted to give you time to be ready and prove that I have never been solely purposed on physical intimacy," he explained. "But believe me, I am willing when you are ready."

A blush crept up Lana's cheeks, and she tried to look away from her husband. However, Teddy's finger remained under her chin, not allowing her to avert her gaze. The look in his eyes turned to one of longing and hunger, and Lana could feel the need rise up in her. She could only nod as Teddy captured her lips with his.

~

*T*eddy had waited for this moment his entire life; he had waited for Lana for the past year. Sure, he had kissed a few girls in his younger years, but he had saved himself for marriage. Oh, how he wished Lana could have said the same. But then, he realized that Lana had never made love before, she had sold herself unwillingly. So it was like the first time for her as well. He smiled as he watched his wife sleeping at his side.

Her hair fell into soft, mussed curls around her face. Her dark eyelashes skimmed the top of her rosy cheeks, and a faint smile lay upon her resting and rounded lips. Teddy could stare at her forever. He closed his eyes and willed himself to sleep, but all he saw was the curve of Lana's thigh, the valley of her pale neck. He needed to think of something else, or he would never sleep.

So, he prayed, thanking God for the blessing of his wife. He admonished himself for looking at Lana as a woman with experience when he should have seen his born-again bride instead. He prayed that they could learn the art of love together and finally drifted off to sleep.

The next morning, Teddy woke to Lana burying her head into his chest, snuggling closer in the cool morning air. He breathed her in and ran his fingers through her dark hair. He would get to wake up like this every morning for the rest of his life. What could be better?

As they readied for the day, Teddy finally told Lana he had a plan, a mission, for them to carry out. She seemed to only half-heartedly listen as she made a simple meal for them to share.

With breakfast on the table, Lana stared intently at Teddy. She batted her eyelashes at him and smiled wide. It almost made him feel bashful until she assertively said, "So, tell me the plan of yours, Reverend."

"Plan?"

"To help the girls," she reminded him.

Teddy chuckled at her boldness and shook his head. Lana was passionate, if nothing else. "Well, I'm sure you know all about the Underground Railroad that was in place some fifty years ago during the war. How people helped to get Southern slaves to free Northern states?"

Lana nodded. "I remember hearing something about it when I was little. What about it?"

"I think we can set something up like that. I'll find people across the country who are willing to help move them from place to place until they can stop. We will help try to get the younger children adopted, the others can hopefully find jobs."

Teddy was waiting to hear Lana's excitement burst forth, but instead, she scrunched up her nose. "Jobs doing what, exactly? Teddy, what would stop them from returning to this life in another town? What woman would employ a former prostitute in her home under the same roof as her husband and growing children? And how would these girls know a man wouldn't take advantage of them?"

He stammered. "I – I don't know. I hadn't thought that far," he admitted. He thought a moment, and with nothing else coming to mind, he asked, "Do you have any ideas?"

Lana's dark eyes lit up. "I do, actually. What about teaching them how to do something first? We can offer them lessons on cooking, sewing, caring for children ... They need a skill that's valuable so they can earn their way."

Together they came up with a plan to have local trades-people teach the girls a set of skills and get them off the street and out of the brothels. Once training was complete, the girls would board a train for a new life away from Storyville.

CHAPTER 21

Six months had gone by, and the Forgiven Grace Church had transformed from weekend place of worship to week-long sanctuary for those looking for a way out.

A bank owner who's own cousin had fallen into a hard life had loved Teddy and Lana's idea about training the girls in a career before moving them and had donated a year's worth of rent on four apartments in the same building Teddy and Lana had moved into. They put two girls in each bedroom, so they could accommodate eight girls at a time. No men – even Teddy – were allowed inside those four apartments. They were for ladies only.

The milliner, two local cooks, and a handful of nuns came to the church throughout the week to teach the girls in whatever they wanted to learn. The day always began with prayer and a Bible lesson from Teddy. Each girl was taught to read and write if she did not know how. Each had to learn how to cook for themselves as well as basic mending skills. Then they could choose a profession – cook, maid, milliner, or governess.

Lana counseled each girl. She helped them overcome their personal demons and put their past behind them. Trust issues and competition between the women was rampant. Most of them were crib girls, only eighteen or nineteen years old. But all of them wanted a way out of Storyville and jumped at the chance to get into the "school," as they called it.

Each girl stayed about three months until she had a handle on what she was doing before boarding a train toward independence. Many went back to their hometowns, some set out for places they had never been. Very few stayed in New Orleans. Lana kept a log of each girl who came through their doors.

Within a few months, more than three dozen women had left the cribs and New Orleans for a new life. Each had worked to earn her train fare and traveled to places like Birmingham, Charleston, and even Roanoke, thanks to help from Ginny and her family.

As the temperatures dropped, unrest filled the city. There was talk of shutting Storyville down for good, and while Lana and Teddy were all for that idea, they wondered what would become of the women who were left with no place to go.

It was on one of these cold days that a familiar face came into the doorway of the apartment building. A dirty, flea-infested girl with yellow hair, dressed in nothing but rags, knocked and asked for Mrs. Sullivan. When Lana made her way to the door, she was shocked to see none other than Madam Knight's favorite girl standing before her.

"Poppy? What in heaven's name? Come in, please," Lana urged, her brow creased with worry.

With a gentle hug, Lana felt something lumpy under Poppy's coats and was shown a half-starved infant of mixed race.

"Oh, Poppy," she exclaimed. "Tell me everything."

Lana led them to her own room and sat Poppy in a high-backed chair. Studying her old nemesis, Lana saw a young woman who had been used and abused. Her eyes were sunken, her cheeks hollow. Her once shiny golden curls were wasted away to strings that hung limply.

Without emotion, Poppy told Lana what the past year had entailed for her.

"I came up pregnant, which was a shock to me," Poppy said with a shrug. "I thought good old Victoria gave us stuff to prevent that, but it happened anyway, and she threw me out. But Jack … Jack promised to marry me. I secretly moved into his room and stayed with him."

A faraway look came over Poppy's face, and she stopped mid-story.

Lana was waiting with bated breath. "What happened then? Where is Jack?"

Poppy's voice sounded distant, like she was still hiding in her beau's room. "A few weeks later, he had gone out and didn't come back. I was too afraid to come out, he worked on the docks, and those men are rougher than johns. But then someone came into his room to clean it out, and they found me. Said he had been killed by Tom Anderson's thugs. I never did find out why. Of course, I had to leave."

Pregnant, homeless, and penniless, Poppy returned to the only thing she knew and rented a crib for a nickel a day.

Once her son had been born, Poppy hid him in under a blanket in the cribs while she worked, but she had finally become desperate. With nowhere to turn, she had sought out the one person she knew wouldn't turn her back.

"What do you call him?" Lana asked as she peered at the baby.

"I don't. I don't call him nothing."

Unsure how to respond, Lana had a bath drawn up for

Poppy and a filling meal brought to her. Lana sent one of the girls off for milk and a bottle to feed the baby.

Lana and Teddy promised to help Poppy get back on her feet. They offered to house her and the baby, but after Lana had bathed the tiny boy, she discovered Poppy had disappeared, leaving the baby and a note behind.

Bell,

Forgive me, please. I need to find a way out, and there is no way out with this child. You're the closest thing I have to family. So, I am leaving him with you. Thanks for the bath and food. I won't be a burden to anyone anymore. I won't be back.

Poppy

A few hours searching found her, drowned at the docks. Nobody had tried to save her.

The Sullivans were quick to tell the police about the baby and the note, and they were told that since the mother had left him to their care, they were now in charge of him. They were free to keep him or turn him over to the nuns at the orphanage.

"We can't turn him out, Teddy. He's Poppy's baby," Lana argued, ready to fight to keep the emaciated child. "Poppy and I may not have been close, but we were sisters together in that horrible place. I knew her. I can't turn her child out."

"I agree," Teddy said, his voice low and calm.

"But, Teddy, I really—" Lana stopped short. "What?"

"I agree with you. We can't turn him out. I saw the pain in Poppy's face at Victoria Knight's and now. She was broken. But we can prevent that for her child. So, we keep him. I'll find out what we need to do to adopt him."

Lana went to the sleeping baby's side. He laid in a dresser drawer until they could get a cradle for him. His eyelids fluttered as he dreamed, and Lana carefully stroked his light caramel skin. Tears welled up in her eyes as he sighed in his sleep.

Teddy came up behind her and put his hands on her shoulders. She turned her face to him and kissed his cheek, the love she felt shattering anything she had felt before.

"He's so beautiful, Teddy. She never named him. We'll have to come up with something," Lana whispered.

"How about Samuel?" Teddy suggested.

"Samuel?" Lana repeated, tasting the name on her tongue. She looked to the baby.

Teddy rested his head on her shoulder and peered at the child as well. "In the Bible, Samuel was the child of Hannah and a prophet. Samuel means, 'God heard.'"

"Oh, that's beautiful. God has heard. This child's plight for a family, and our plight for a child," Lana noted, her voice soft but thick with emotion.

*A*s history will tell us, Storyville was no more after 1917 when branches of the military demanded it be shut down. But shutting down the legal center of prostitution didn't end the trade. Along with speakeasies, gambling centers, and dance halls, prostitution rings were still rampant in the New Orleans underground. Teddy and Lana Sullivan had plenty of girls waiting to attend their school of reformation for many years after the district was closed for business.

Ginny (Astrid) had married a Mr. John Higgs, and together, they raised three beautiful children in Williamsburg, Virginia. She never returned to New Orleans, but she and Lana kept up correspondence throughout their lifetime. Her past did become public, but ever the picture of poise and grace, Ginny overcame that obstacle. She made a point of helping the Sullivans' ministry by sending money and helping girls as they passed through her area on to better lives.

Frances (Clover) and Martha (Jasmine) remained

employed by Ginny's brother until Frances married. She took Martha with her when she moved in with her husband.

Zinnia and Jake Ames disappeared into the Tennessee Mountains, never to be heard from again. Lana always assumed they led a quiet little life with children and family surrounding them.

Madam Victoria Knight was forced out when the district disappeared. She retired and bought a house by the water and lived out her days with every luxury she could afford. When she died, she left everything to the Forgiven Grace Church and its outreach program.

Ian Davidson moved on from New Orleans a year after he last saw Lana and Teddy. His cabaret theater, Maggie's, burned to the ground, and he had burned through all the money he made. He returned to Charleston to seek refuge in his parents' opulent home, where rumor had it he met and married a nice girl with dark, curly hair and dark eyes.

As for Lana and Teddy … they spent more than ten years helping former prostitutes find new ways in life. Over 300 girls came through their door and went through their program. Many of them made a profession of faith. Teddy continued pastoring and loved to teach people about the love and forgiveness of Jesus. Lana relished her role as mother to her children – first, their son, Samuel, and then Charlotte, Evelyn, Paul, Silas, and Anna. She also "mothered" numerous others who came to her seeking help. She and Teddy lived in New Orleans for the rest of their lives, ministering to those who were lost, both living well into their eighties. Lana never forgot her past, and she thanked the Lord for giving her a solid future.

The End

AUTHOR'S NOTE

It was the spring of 2011 when I somehow stumbled across the photos of New Orleans photographer E. J. Bellocq (1873-1949). While the subjects were mainly nude prostitutes (not something I would normally be looking at), I was drawn into the strange juxtaposition of backdrops, furniture, and stiffly posed women.

Then I saw a photo of a young woman with nearly black flowing hair, wearing a beautiful dress, and holding an array of large flowers. She looked down at the blooms and not at the camera, almost as if she was hiding something. Was she shy? Ashamed? I became so enamored with this girl, and I knew I had to tell her story.

She became Bluebell, a young woman thrust into the nightmare of Storyville's brothels, who had almost given up but still possessed a spark of desire to escape.

And who better to play the hero than a soft-spoken pastor who wears glasses? Don't get me wrong, Teddy is quite masculine, but he lacks what we would call 'toxic masculinity' in today's world. He reminds Bell that God loves her regardless of the path her life has taken. And he loves her when she feels completely unlovable.

There are times in all our lives when we feel completely unlovable for so many reasons. It might be physical or mental health, it might be a wrong – real or perceived – we feel we committed, or any number of things. But no matter what life throws in our path, nothing will ever make someone unlovable.

It took me a long time to finish the story, then I guarded it with everything I had. It's scary to let something you love so much out into the world – like a child. Much like Bell feeling unworthy of love, I felt her story might also be deemed unworthy.

Bell of the Night is a story of redemption and about the love of God, but most people I asked to look at it told me it was either too gritty for a Christian audience or too much God for a general audience. Following Christ does not mean life is tied up in a pretty package with a perfect bow on top. Life is not a Hallmark movie. Life is gritty and dirty and unfair and I wanted my writing to reflect that. Redemption doesn't only come for those with unmarred paths. It can belong to anyone and everyone who accepts it.

I hope the story of Bell and Teddy reminds you that you are precious, and that no matter how unpretty life can get, you are worthy of love.

ACKNOWLEDGMENTS

I need to thank Mary, Cammie, Lydia, and the amazing crew at Monster Ivy. Your attention to detail, your encouragement, and your line edits have made this a stunning book. Mary, thank you for taking a chance on me and believing in these characters. Cammie, your edit notes gave me all the feels.

Thank you to E.J. Bellocq for creating the photos that inspired this story. Just be warned if you look them up, many are nudes. There is some fascinating information about Bellocq and his photos out there.

I want to give a shoutout to Michelle F., Sarah, Marissa, Bethany, and Sallie for their love and encouragement. Your friendship means more than I can ever express, and I am so thankful to have you all in my life.

Special thanks to Kim and Michelle L. for being my reader guinea pigs and reading all the random scraps of stories I've sent you over the years.

My thanks to the good Lord for allowing me to tell this story. It's been close to my heart for so long, and I am amazed He allowed me the chance to write it.

And finally love, hugs, and kisses to my mother, Laura, my husband, Marshall, and my four children – SB, Mac, Jay, & Cal. You believing in me is the biggest gift I could ever receive. Thank you.

ABOUT THE AUTHOR

Allison Wells is an avid reader, writer, and author. She grad-
uated from Clemson University with a degree in Communi-
cations and she spent several years as a newspaper reporter
who quickly grew tired of always writing bad news. She
began writing novels with happy endings. Bell of the Night is
her newest release and the one she is most proud of. She lives
in the foothills of South Carolina with her husband and four
children. Allison's motto is "Life is short, eat the Oreos."

Made in the USA
Columbia, SC
27 September 2021